2040

Robert Albo

A person often meets his destiny on the road he took to avoid it.

JEAN DE LA FONTAINE, 17TH CENTURY FRENCH POET

CONTENTS

CHAPTER ONE:
GO WEST
YOUNG MAN

Michael frowned at his reflection in his parent's full-length mirror—old technology that still sufficed. His brother, the renowned Professor Wendell Knightsbridge, would arrive shortly. Although they were identical twins, Wendell always looked better. He didn't have those silver streaks in his hair or need a beard to cover his sagging cheeks. Actually, Wendell was better in every way.

"Show front yard." Michael's glasses displayed a rock garden with a curving path that led to a waist-high white picket fence on a quiet street with other old, two-story homes. These types of homes had become obsolete since most individuals or families preferred modern, single floor apartments.

Lit by a streetlamp across the street, an elderly neighbor walked his real golden retriever on a leash. A robotic dog would have been so much easier, no feeding, no cleaning up, and no obligations.

"Person," Michael said to his glasses, having forgotten the dog walker's name. His glasses displayed:

Mr. Mathew Sanders (Matt)

26 Hawthorne St., Watertown, MA

Last meeting: 2 years ago, when he was walking with his granddaughter, Eileen, and you asked her age (8).

Even after all this time, his glasses still amazed him. They used AI to anticipate what you wanted and presented the information in video on the lenses or audio via bone conduction above the ears. Bi-directional cameras monitored the wearer's face and external environment. The glasses had replaced smartphones to become indispensable and ubiquitous.

Michael's lenses turned transparent, and his reflection greeted him again. He admired his loose, undulating rainbow-colored robe that cinched comfortably around his waist and ankles. It was the latest fashion. He ran a comb through his hair one last time, then sauntered down the squeaky staircase to the outdated kitchen that had twenty-year-old appliances, including a gas stove.

He poured himself a cup of Oolong tea from the boiling water tap and set it on the old yellow linoleum counter. Stretching his hands high over his head, he slowly brought them to his side and waited for the tea to steep.

After a hundred and fifty seconds, his glasses flashed a warning, and he discarded the tea bag. Steep the tea too long and you end up with an unpleasantly strong, bitter cup. Too short and you have a weak, favorless cup.

"Your brother has arrived." The sweet, concise female voice from his glasses reminded him of an English governess. After tipping his head slightly, his glasses showed Wendell exiting from a black sedan out front.

Michael sipped his piping hot, honey-flavored tea. Then he walked to the front hallway with cup in hand as the bell rang.

He opened the door and saw what he could've looked like if he was in better shape. Wendell was trim, with piercing blue eyes in his chiseled bare face, without a hint of gray in his brown hair. He employed anti-aging treatments and rigorously adhered to a regime of healthy food and exercise.

"May I come in?"

"Of course. It's your house too." Michael stepped aside. With a visitor's perspective, he noticed the wood floors were dusty and the white walls had started to peel. "Tea?"

"Sure." Wendell walked into the kitchen, grabbed a cup and tea bag from the cabinet, and added boiling water. This home had few of the automated conveniences found in most modern residences. There wasn't even a robot server. "We received a good offer for the house."

"Enough to cover the mortgage?" Single-family house prices had plunged with the build-out of subsidized public apartments, decline in population, and change in housing preferences.

"Yup." Wendell sniffed the steam above his cup, smiled, and then sipped the cinnamon-flavored tea he always made.

"I don't want to sell." Standing against the linoleum counter, Michael stared at the white kitchen tabletop, where he and his mom had shared a cup of tea each morning, discussing the local news, including the Boston Red Sox, who they both loved. He missed her.

"Mikey, Mom passed away two years ago. We need to move on."

His body stiffened. He hated this childhood name that made him feel like a baby. "I need more time." He concentrated on his breathing. *Inhale. One, two, three, four. Hold your breath. Five, six, seven, eight, nine, ten. Exhale. Eleven, twelve, thirteen, fourteen, fifteen, sixteen.*

"Sorry," Wendell said, after eyeing him for a minute. "But I won't delay this again."

Michael repeated the breathing exercise. He wanted to argue, but knew it was a lost cause. Even though he was his mother's favorite, Wendell was the executor of the estate. He could beg, but his brother would show no sympathy. He never had.

"Where would I go?" Michael studied his loafers. Massachusetts had excellent public housing, but a one-bedroom apartment would pale compared to the comfort of the family home.

"That's why I'm here." Wendell smiled. "Melinda and I would like you to live in our ADU."

Michael wrinkled his nose. An ADU or accessory dwelling unit would allow him to live independently. However, it would be right next to Wendell's home in Berkeley, California.

"The place is great," Wendell said enthusiastically. "Right next to campus, with two bedrooms, a bathroom, kitchen, and large family room. Look."

Michael's glasses showed him standing on a pine wood floor in the family room. A white leather couch faced a fireplace and adjacent chairs were on either side. Twisting his head left, he saw trees through the two open windows and heard birds chirping. Twisting right, he saw a burgundy wall where a couple impressionistic paintings hung. There was also a window showing a footpath to the backside of Wendell's large two-story brick home. He didn't understand why two people needed so much space. Maybe it was just because they could afford it. He turned around and saw his reflection in a mirror that was above a console table, displaying some knickknacks.

"Bedrooms," he said. His glasses showed him walking down the wood hallway, past the front door and kitchen. He went through the door at the end of the hallway on the right and came to a bright evergreen bedroom with windows overlooking trees running down the hill. There was a queen-sized bed with gray sheets and a wood nightstand and dresser.

He went to the guest bedroom across the hall and then the kitchen. All the appliances were modern, and a four-foot tall, metallic, serving robot stood in the corner. There was a square wood bench below the window that could seat multiple people.

It was a pleasant house, but he didn't want to live near his brother, who always overshadowed him. "It's tempting, but I don't want to move to California."

"Why not? It's not like anything is keeping you here." Wendell was always direct and never minced words. Because of their childhood upbringing, Wendell applied no filters when dealing with him. He treated him as he would himself.

Perhaps many siblings experienced this.

Regardless, Michael didn't appreciate it, even if it was the truth. No friends, no job, just a dilettante pursuing different interests. He tried to think of a suitable answer.

"It's what Mom would have wanted," Wendell continued.

Michael tapped the ground with the front of his shoe. Mom had always asked Wendell to help his defective younger brother. Now her wish was coming true, but he didn't need sympathy. He could take care of himself. "I have responsibilities here."

Wendell chuckled at his attempt.

"Besides, what would I do there?"

"The same things you do here: play the piano, paint, read, watch shows and take hikes. California pays better too."

Michael rubbed his chin. Massachusetts' payments for these activities had steadily decreased while California's had increased due to higher taxes on business innovations.

"I might have a job in my program too, researching dark matter."

"What?" He had no interest in research. That was his brother's domain.

"We've made a remarkable discovery. Dark

matter is key to human consciousness."

"What?" Michael said again. Wendell always confounded him.

Wendell smiled, but Michael could see the condescension in it. "You know we can't see or touch dark matter, but can only observe its gravitational effects on objects." Wendell waited for him to nod before continuing. "Well, it turns out that everyone has a small bundle of dark matter connected to their brain, which unlocks the mystery of consciousness."

Michael sighed. Scientific discovery held little interest for him. Besides, he didn't have a physics degree, or any degree for that matter, and working for Wendell would be a nightmare. He paused, wondering what the role would be, and how a particle physicist could even study human consciousness. It didn't matter. He could muddle through any job and didn't need the broader perspective.

"Well," Wendell continued, "what do you think?"

Wendell was right that he had little holding him here, and a move to California offered some advantages, not least, a fresh start. "Let me think about it."

***

The next morning, Michael opened his eyes to

a bright day. He sat up and stretched his arms high over his head before putting on his glasses.

"Bank balance." The dollar amount looked low, given it was payday.

"Recent deposits." The government had paid him only three thousand one hundred dollars, which was almost the minimum amount for his two-week pay period.

"Work payment details." Three hours on piano, two hours painting, four hours researching the Aztec civilization, and eight hours walking. He shook his head, disappointed by the work output recorded by his glasses.

He didn't need to inquire how he spent his day—sleeping, watching serials, and playing action games. Unfortunately, the government didn't pay for these activities, which they deemed as unproductive.

He dressed in blue shorts, a white T-shirt, and red sneakers. He could almost pass for a post-doctoral student. Now, what to have for breakfast?

"Prepare eggs on toast." His glasses would pass the command to the auto egg cooker in the kitchen, one of his few automated appliances.

He would decide about a move to Berkeley today during a walk along the Charles River, a government-paid activity. He considered popping a

Dreamland pill, but wanted a clear mind, so would take it later in the day before playing Aliens.

After a ten-minute walk through the neighborhood of old homes, he reached the Charles River. A few groups of people sat on blankets on the grass. There were even two children throwing a football. No one was sculling on the river, although a few joggers ran along the dirt trail.

It was almost noon, so he would hike east towards Boston and grab an inexpensive student lunch near one of the college campuses. A bead of sweat dripped from his nose as he started. His temperature-controlled clothing would work extra hard in this sunny, humid July weather.

Watertown or Berkeley? If he stayed, then he would need to find a government apartment. Berkeley offered much better accommodations, milder weather, and higher paying work. He had acquaintances, but no true friends that would keep him here. The big negative of the move was living near his brother, who made him feel inadequate.

He wondered how they could share the same genetic material yet be so different. Their IQs were almost identical, but not their personalities and ambitions. If he'd been first out, would their lives have been exchanged?

A student ran past him. She bounced effortlessly along the trail, just like Wendell went through life, while he struggled. It wasn't fair, but life wasn't fair. Michael had learned to do the minimum and expect the minimum, which kept life's disappointments to a minimum.

Michael returned home and sat in his VR chair, which looked like a brown, baggy lounge chair. It could move his body to simulate rapid acceleration or braking. He leaned back, popped a Dreamland pill, and waited for the calming effects. Slowly, his depression about his current situation faded and his anxieties about the future dissolved. No past, no future, only the stressless present. His fingers twitched; his mind focused without emotional distractions. He was ready to play the war game, Aliens.

His glasses transported him into the cockpit of his one-man starship, where an admiral gave him his mission to save Earth. He blasted off from the orbiting space station, feeling the acceleration against his back. He veered away from Earth and towards the starlit black space and the distant alien vanguard on Neptune. Two hours later, after blasting alien ships and destroying their outpost, he returned victorious to mission control, the finest pilot in the fleet.

Michael stood up from his VR chair, feeling optimistic and ready for a change. He had grown comfortable living in Watertown but had nothing driving him, nothing to look forward to. He was like a shipwrecked sailor, clinging to the rocks for safety, even as they battered him to death. Berkeley offered a chance for a reset. He'd lived eighteen years with Wendell. He could survive another one.

***

It was early September; the exact date didn't matter to him. After settling his affairs in Massachusetts, Michael had arrived at his new home in the Berkeley hills. It was a wealthy residential neighborhood with a mix of cottages and mansions along tree-lined streets.

The two-bedroom ADU looked just like the video, however there was a smell of newness everywhere, and the rooms were warm and welcoming. The living room, dining room and kitchen tables all had vases with freshly cut flowers—violets, daisies, and oriental lily bulbs. Melinda, Wendell's wife, would have provided this touch.

His two open suitcases, with all his worldly goods, lay on the Mediterranean-blue quilt of his queen-sized bed. The walls were melon-colored; the curtains were leaf-green, and the wood flooring was teak, just like a Caribbean cabin.

Time to unpack and settle into his new home. He took out a picture frame of the last full family vacation in Hawaii thirty years ago. There were rotating pictures of them playing on the beach, learning to surf, going to a luau, and sailing in a boat to watch the whales. He closed his eyes and smiled. He could practically smell the salt of the ocean.

However, a few months later, his father had died suddenly from a ruptured brain aneurysm, a hereditary condition Michael also had, but his brother did not. Like his father, Michael's aneurysm was inoperable, and he hoped he wouldn't suffer a similar fate. His dad was only forty-two years old, the same age he'd be in two years.

As a ten-year-old child, his world had been upended. What was the purpose of hard work when everything inevitably led to death? He had lost all his ambition to succeed, although for some strange reason Wendell had doubled his. He glanced again at the picture frame before placing it on top of his dresser and then finished unpacking.

Michael stood in his bathroom, combing his hair while examining himself in the mirror. He rubbed his clean-shaven chin, thinking this signified a new start. He practiced his goofy grin, which was his go-to when he had nothing to say. His pressed tan jeans, yellow polo, and sneakers conveyed casual confidence; at least they did in Boston.

He opened the front door and walked up the footpath through the garden of fruit trees and flowering plants. There were red, white, and pink rose bushes, and blue, purple, and yellow hydrangeas. The two-story brick house had eight windows on the backside, which would provide beautiful views of the bay. He glanced back at his house, which looked puny in comparison.

He approached his welcome dinner with trepidation. This might set the tone for his entire stay. He and Wendell had established a few ground rules: no prying, no counseling, no nightly meals together, and no Mikey.

Melinda greeted him at the backdoor. She wore a crimson dress, a pearl necklace, and loafers. Her blond hair was tied in a bow, her azure eyes were as sharp as diamonds, and a broad smile split her lips. She seemed genuinely happy to have him. She was thirty-five and looked just like she had at her wedding four years ago.

"Welcome. She gave him a quick peck on each cheek, then wrapped an arm around his waist and pulled him in. "Wendell's finishing a call and will be down shortly.

He mumbled an awkward thanks and his goofy smile crossed his face as she escorted him through the kitchen, down a short wood hallway, and into the family room. The augmented emotional reading app or AER on his glasses told him that Melinda was sincere. AER was almost clairvoyant, reading facial expressions and processing spoken language to provide an authentic emotional reading.

The rectangular family room had four bay windows along one wall that looked down at Berkeley and the San Francisco Bay. The setting sun was just above the Golden Gate Bridge. Other than the tops of some trees that his glasses told him were oaks, maples, eucalyptus, and buckeyes, it was an unobstructed scenic view.

Against the far wall was a lit fireplace, about three times bigger than his. Above the mantle was a paper-thin projection screen that covered most of the wall and rose to the top of the twelve-foot ceilings. Right now, it displayed a scene from a broad stone terrace of the sea, an old city, and its port hundreds of feet below. A motorboat pulled a line of small white sailboats from the harbor, and swimmers dragging orange floaters swam around buoys near the shore.

A brown leather couch faced the fireplace with two adjacent swivel chairs on one side and another couch on the other side, which formed a U shape. In the middle, within easy reach, was a rectangular, ceramic, cream-colored coffee table. The other side of the room opened onto a foyer with the front door, dining room, and grand staircase to the upstairs bedrooms.

He sat on a chair while Melinda went to the center coach. A moment later, a four-foot-tall metallic robot walked over on its two legs, balancing trays on its two hands. The egg-shaped head had two cameras that looked like eyes, an oval-shaped speaker for a mouth, and two ear-shaped microphones. Although a four-legged robot with many arms would've been more functional, humans preferred creatures that resembled them.

"My name is Cari," the robot said as she placed cheese, crackers, and nuts on the table. "May I take your drink order?"

"White wine with ice for me," Melinda said.

"I'll have a Martini." Michael leaned forward, placing slices of cheese on two crackers, and then fell back into his chair. He was starving, still on east-coast time.

"All settled in?" she asked, watching him eat.

He nodded, not being one for small talk. He wondered if she was comparing him to her husband. His internal monkey voice, the one that always judged and found him wanting, told him she was thankful that she got the better version.

"Anything you need?"

"No." His VR chair was already in his family room. Drones had delivered his groceries, an easel, and canvases. He could've asked for a piano, but he didn't want to continue with it. The freshly cut flowers were a gracious gesture, but he decided against mentioning it.

Footsteps sounded down the hall, and

Wendell strolled in. "Have I missed anything?" He placed a hand on Michael's shoulder, then went over to sit by Melinda.

Michael came halfway to his feet as if he would bolt from the room, then gave an embarrassed frown and fell back into his chair.

"No," Melinda smiled. "Michael's just settling in."

The robot reentered the room, handed Michael and Melinda their drinks, and then took Wendell's order.

"Any plans for tomorrow?" Wendell asked.

"Not really." Michael blinked, knowing his brother had plans for him. After only a minute, the interference began. "I was going to walk around the neighborhood."

"Splendid. Just up the hill is Tilden Park. Beautiful morning hikes."

"Can you send me a map?"

"Absolutely." Wendell smiled. "I'll show you my favorite eight-mile loop."

"Yippee." This was four miles longer than Michael planned to hike.

"If you're not doing anything in the afternoon." Wendell scanned the room, seeming to gather his thoughts. "Perhaps you could drop by my office to see our work."

"If you do, then you have to come by my office too," Melinda added.

Michael lowered his head forward and shut his eyes. He had planned to read in the afternoon and earn some money. However, it would be rude to say no—not a great way to start his stay.

"Sure. What time?"

CHAPTER TWO:
UC BERKELEY

Michael walked for ten minutes on residential backstreets to reach the northeast corner of the university campus. He continued down the north side, watching a steady stream of autonomous vehicles zip along Hearst Avenue in both directions. He arrived at a crosswalk and waited with about twenty students whose academic semester had just started. It reminded him of Cambridge, with all the preppy students in the latest fashion. They were the future leaders of the world, working long hours and forgoing the easy life provided by governments, at least for now.

"How did your summer internship go?" said one of the older looking students to her friend.

"Fine, but AI's getting better and better," her friend said. "It resolves most customer questions, so I have few escalations. At this rate, I'm not sure what my engineering degree will be worth."

When the pedestrian light turned green, the two women hustled across the street to the North

Gate of the UC Berkeley campus. He followed at a leisurely pace and thought about what he had overheard.

College degrees weren't worth much when they didn't lead to a better job or life. AI could do most activities better and cheaper than humans ever could. Creativity and innovation were the few areas where some humans could outperform the algorithms and data sets of AI. Jobs requiring these capabilities, like inventors, artists, and researchers, paid handsomely, but only to the top performers like Wendell. For everyone else, AI could replicate their creations by reusing earlier work.

His first stop was with Melinda, where he would spend about twenty minutes. God only knew how long the visit with Wendell would take. The old computer science building was a massive four-story concrete rectangular box with eight tall marble columns on each side. It was a temple to the gods of technology, highly utilitarian, but not aesthetically pleasing. He went through the east entrance to the black and white tiled foyer. There was a bank of elevators to the right, a dingy hallway straight ahead, and a secure basement elevator to the left. He went left and sent a message to Melinda, "I'm here."

The elevator door opened, and his glasses received directions from Melinda to go to floor negative three. From there, his glasses guided him to her office. The door was open, so he stepped inside.

It was a small, maybe fifteen foot by ten-foot, bamboo paneled cubicle. Artificial video windows along three walls displayed a continuous tropical white, sandy beach with palm trees and a turquoise sea. A few seagulls flew in the azure sky, squawking at one another. The building ventilation system provided a warm, salty sea breeze. It felt like he was in a bungalow by the ocean.

"The room's not much, but I find it conducive for my work." She got up from her desk, came over, and gave him a peck on each cheek.

"I like it." He gave her his goofy smile.

"I wouldn't say that." The side of her mouth curled up. "The computer science building on Hearst Street is spectacular, but I require privacy and physical access to the computer servers." She paused before continuing. "You know, foreign governments are constantly trying to hack into our systems and steal the confidential research done on campus."

He shook his head and put his hands in his front pants pockets, not knowing what to say.

"I want to show you something." She grabbed his elbow. "The most powerful computer in the world."

They went down the hallway to a mechanical door that opened for her with a humming sound. Inside a dimly lit, cool room sat a black cube in the center. It came up to his armpit, about five feet per side, and had blinking green and white lights.

"This prototype holds forty-eight neural boards." She grabbed a spare board from a shelf by the door and handed it to him. It looked about two feet long, one foot wide, and maybe three inches thick, and was loaded with silicon circuits. "Each board has over one million cores and five trillion neural transistors. For comparison, the human brain has about eighty-six billion neurons, so this silicon board has over fifty times more processing power."

He whistled. "What's a neural transistor?" he asked, trying to sound interested.

"A neural transistor differs from a regular silicon switch transistor because it carries multiple states and connects to thousands of other neural transistors. It resembles a human brain cell or neuron. Like the brain, a neural system learns through experience, not through specific computer programming."

"I don't understand."

"Let me give you an example." She stroked her chin, a thoughtful look on her face, then she smiled. "For the game of chess, with a traditional computer, you program all the moves for the chess pieces and then program all the specific strategies. If this, then do that. For a neural system, you give it the expert moves for millions of games. Its algorithms figure out the rules and the best moves to win. It then plays against itself billions of times to improve its game."

No wonder computers beat the chess masters. Michael walked to the cube and noticed a small gold plate on its front that read: *Artificial Neural Network Intelligence.*

"I don't know if this should impress or scare me," he said, touching the plate.

"The cube is still only a tool, albeit a powerful one, that you assign tasks to." Her forehead furrowed and her mouth scrunched sideways. "But like any tool, it can be abused."

"Could the cube go rogue by itself?" He'd seen enough sci-fi movies where this happened.

"No. It's a mathematical system that learns skills by pinpointing patterns in vast amounts of digital data. It's neither conscious nor sentient—just performs the tasks assigned." She smiled again. "You need to assign the right tasks, however. If you told it to solve climate change, it might decide to kill off humanity."

Michael nodded but wasn't reassured. His glasses sounded an alarm like a cowbell that only he could hear.

"This is fascinating, but I need to meet Wendell." He raised his eyebrows. "I don't want to be late."

Melinda laughed. They both knew tardiness was one thing that set Wendell off.

"Well, I'm glad you dropped by." She walked him to the elevator and gave him a quick hug.

Michael thanked her and then took the elevator to the ground floor. He walked another five minutes to Le Conte Hall, where a sign in front stated the parking spaces were reserved for Nobel Laureates. Ambling up the steps, he pushed through the tall wooden doors, climbed more steps, walked down quiet hallways, and finally reached room 306, where he rang the buzzer.

The door slid open to display a mahogany desk in front of a window with an impressive view of the campus. On the left, whiteboards with black scribbles covered the wall. To the right, Wendell sat with a woman at a small round table.

"This is my brother, Michael," Wendell said, waving him over.

"I see the resemblance." The edges of the woman's mouth turned up. "My name is Mary Mason, but most people call me Mae."

"Nice to meet you." Michael took a chair between them. Mary, or Mae, had ebony skin, black curly hair that ran down her back, brown eyes, and a sweet smile. She wore a white lab coat and a gold necklace with a cross dangling at her chest.

"Mae has been with me," Wendell said, "since we discovered a way to pull dark matter from its fourth-dimensional space into our universe a few years ago."

Michael nodded, knowing this work had made Wendell famous, likely leading to his dream of a Nobel Prize and a parking spot in front of the building.

"She now leads one of our dark matter projects," he continued.

"What's the project?" Michael returned his gaze to Mae.

"Dark matter's effect on human consciousness." She leaned forward, placing her elbows on the tabletop. "There's a sort of dark matter bundle around all sentient beings. Our study looks at the amount and composition of dark matter associated with different volunteers."

"What are you hoping to discover?"

"A new understanding of human consciousness, personalities, and feelings."

This sounded touchy-feely. He looked back at Wendell, knowing there had to be some purpose to this introduction. "So, why am I here?"

"We currently have hundreds of subjects taking part in the study but now need to expand it to thousands. We need a volunteer coordinator, and you'd be perfect."

He was far from perfect. This was nothing but

charity from his brother. He was about to say no, but then glanced at Mae. She was staring at him with rapt attention, bobbing her head. She looked like she genuinely wanted him on her study. His AER confirmed it.

"Let me learn more about the study and my role." At a minimum, Michael would enjoy getting to know Mae. He found her attractive and appreciated her intensity. This was likely part of Wendell's calculation. "Then I'll give you my decision."

"Fair enough." Wendell slapped the tabletop and stood. "Mae, can you show Michael around this afternoon and answer his questions?"

"Of course." She popped up too. "Shall we?"

Michael got to his feet and walked with Mae out the door and down the hallway.

"Tell me a little about yourself," he said, going to his standard questions. "How did you end up here?"

"After graduating high school in Raleigh, North Carolina, I joined the Airforce so I could see the world. After eight years, I returned, and went to Duke, where I majored in physics. There were only ten other students in my class, so I chose Berkeley for my PhD. Wendell selected me as a research assistant, and after four years, I'm now a team lead."

"Impressive." He was going to ask about her

personal life and if she was seeing anyone, but that didn't seem appropriate. "What about your childhood?"

"I was an army brat, moving from different American military bases in South America."

"That must have been tough, I mean, making friends."

"It was, always making new friendships knowing they wouldn't last. It's why true friendships are so important to me now." Mae stopped, grabbed his wrist, and then chuckled. "You may have noticed that I'm a tactile person."

His mind raced. Her hand was warm and soft against his wrist.

"Well, the lab is just a bit farther," she said, releasing her hold and continuing down the hallway.

He walked beside her, sneaking glances at her profile. Mae seemed distracted, maybe thinking about her childhood. He thought about his life and his lack of community. He hadn't put much effort into making friends, partially because he didn't think he had much to offer. His internal monkey voice, the primitive and fearful one that was filled with self-doubt and couldn't be controlled with reason, confirmed this assessment.

Near the building's exit, they came to a lab

door that slid open. Inside was a white rectangular room with tall ceilings. On the far side of the room, on an elevated platform, was a gold leather chair with broad armrests and a tall seatback. It looked like a throne. Surrounding it like sentries were four steel pillars that were about two feet in diameter and rose ten feet from the floor. Above this was a bronze ring that hung from the ceiling.

He placed a hand on a small desk near the door. This was likely the coordinator's desk, his desk. Along the back wall were about ten chairs. Red arrows on the floor led from the chairs to the throne and back in a circular path.

"Tell me a bit about yourself." She walked towards the front, and he followed.

"I grew up in Watertown near Boston. I went to Star Academy for gifted students where I excelled." He wanted to make his story sound impressive. "But I lost interest in the curriculum and switched to the public schools. My passion is learning something about everything, which makes me either a dilettante or Renaissance man."

"I prefer Renaissance man." She grinned, then walked over to one pillar and placed a hand on it. "These electromagnetic fifth-force generators open a portal into a fourth dimension, giving us a picture of the dark matter within this space."

Dark matter accounted for about eighty

percent of the matter in the universe, whereas ordinary matter, the stuff of stars, planets, and people, accounted for only twenty percent. It was counterintuitive and bizarre that an invisible, untouchable substance could be so prevalent.

"Why is it called fifth force?" It was a dumb question, but he felt comfortable with her.

"There are four fundamental forces known in nature: gravity, the weak force, the strong nuclear force, and electromagnetism. Four years ago, Wendell discovered a fifth force which, like gravity, is a property of both normal and dark matter."

"How does it work?" Wendell had explained some of this to him, but he'd paid little attention.

"Think of a balloon." She brought her thumb and finger to her lip and blew. After a few seconds, she mimicked tying the end, and then held out the imaginary balloon in cupped hands. "The surface of the balloon is our known universe, and the inside is an additional dimension with space and dark matter." With a finger, she touched a spot on the balloon. "The fifth-force equipment allows us to see all the dark matter associated with this physical space."

The balloon surface is two dimensional, and the inside is three. Michael rubbed his chin, applying the balloon analogy to the world. "So, for any three-dimensional area, you can see all the associated dark matter across a fourth dimension."

"Exactly, which gives you the density." She slapped the pillar, then stepped onto the platform, going to the leather chair and sitting down. "Research participants sit here for about ten seconds while we capture a picture of their dark matter bundle with our sensors."

"What do the bundles look like?" He pictured them in his mind as black and shadowy blobs.

"Let me show you."

After granting permission, his glasses turned opaque. Suddenly, out of the darkness, a golden globe the size of a fist appeared. Brownish-orange and yellow-white patterns crept along its surface while small white lightning bolts sparked. In some ways, it looked like a mini sun.

"Every person has one of these?"

"Yes," she said, "and it stays with you for your entire life."

He shook his head in wonder. These bundles added a new, mystical dimension to the human body. "It's magical."

"The difference between magic and scientific observation," she said, a bit smugly, "is just the current technology."

"True," he muttered. He thought about how his glasses, anticipating and answering any question, would seem like magic to people a hundred years ago.

He suddenly felt completely out of place, like an ignorant bumpkin from yesteryear among the intellectual scientists of today. He tried to make some insightful observation.

"That's a lot of bright colors for dark matter."

"Actually, there are no colors in the dark matter universe. We just assign colors based on the dark matter composition. The darker, golden color indicates greater density and complexity."

"So, what do you need me for?"

"To greet the volunteers when they arrive, answer their questions, and manage the queue. We want to do about a hundred readings each day." She stood up and walked over to the desk by the door. "This would be your station."

"What if I can't answer a question?"

"You'll have all the answers through your glasses."

Michael nodded. An android could do a better job, but they obviously wanted a human administrator to reassure the volunteers. "Anything else I need to know?"

"Yes. We want you to take part in our weekly reviews with the other researchers."

"Why?"

"Because you may see something that we miss. According to Wendell, you have an ability to make intuitive leaps."

Wendell's compliment surprised him, particularly since his "intuitive leaps" had led to many disagreements. Wendell always sided with the expert opinion, whereas Michael distrusted it, finding it too narrow. While most experts only focused on their area of expertise, he found most hard problems required intuitive leaps across multiple disciplines.

"What do you think?" Mae asked.

He exhaled and closed his eyes. Wendell was trying to help him by offering a simple administrative job with the allure of being part of a broader team. The positives: he would meet new people and participate in cutting-edge research. The negatives: he would be the dumbest, least educated person in the group and would work for Wendell. But there was also the Mae factor.

"Let me sleep on it." He smiled at his unintended, subtle double entendre. His monkey voice told him he was an idiot and loser.

CHAPTER THREE: FIRST DAY OF WORK

The following Monday, Michael walked to the lab door, which slid open for him. He'd had a fitful sleep last night thinking about his first day of work, yet now he was full of restless energy. After walking around the room, he sat down in the leather chair on the raised platform, like a coiled spring about to snap.

Ten minutes later, the door slid open, and Mae entered wearing a white lab coat with another one draped over her arm. "Good morning."

"Good morning." He stood and sauntered down to the floor, trying to exude confidence. She handed him the other coat, and he slipped it on over his blue jeans and yellow polo shirt. The lab coat made him look and feel like one of the researchers.

"I'm thrilled you joined us," she gushed.

"Me too." She stood close to him. He had to resist taking a step back.

"The first volunteers will be here in a half hour, but I thought it'd be good for you to experience the test yourself, so you'll know what they'll be going through."

"Will I feel anything?"

"A common question." Her hands went into the front pockets of her jacket. "Ask your glasses. I just gave them access to our AI systems."

He asked again, and a British female voice replied, "No, the energy field surrounds but doesn't touch you."

"Let's do it." Not waiting for her response, he turned, walked up the few steps, spun around, and sat down in the chair. He acted nonchalant, but his heels tapped nervously on the platform and his palms were damp. His armpits were also sweating, but his shirt hid that.

"Ready?" she asked. After he nodded, she stepped back beyond the pillars. "Commence test."

"All go," his glasses said, "five, four, three, two, one, initiate."

Suddenly, he was in a gray, shimmery cubic room whose edges were where the pillars stood. Even the floor and ceiling were gray. He was isolated from the world, trapped alone in a cell. Then his box shrunk, the walls closing in on him. His heart was racing. It took tremendous self-control not to scream. The walls were a foot away. He squeezed his eyes shut and took deep double-breaths. On the fifth one, he opened his eyes. The lab had returned.

"Some people find it disorienting," Mae said, striding towards him and examining his face. "Are you okay?"

Michael had slumped to one side. Pushing his hands down on the armrest, he sat up and wobbled to his feet. He couldn't understand how anyone *wouldn't* find that experience unsettling. He wasn't even claustrophobic. Maybe it was his anxieties.

"I'm fine," he said, trying to appear confident and in control. His internal monkey voice told him not to bother. He would never impress her.

She took his hand and led him back to his desk, where he plopped down into his seat. Beads of sweat dripped off his brow; his heart rate remained elevated. He counted silently to sixteen to gain control of his breathing and, hopefully, his anxiousness. His inner monkey voice asked why he struggled with everything.

"I just received a notification of a power surge during your test," she said with a hint of concern.

He nodded. Maybe that explained it.

"We're running diagnostics now." She put a hand on his shoulder and squeezed it gently. He leaned back and glanced up. She was staring straight ahead into her darkened glasses.

"We found the problem." She removed her hand. "There was a short in another part of the network, which caused our local surge. They're fixing it now."

"Good." Maybe the power surge had caused his enclosed gray cell to shrink. He tried to regain his composure while Mae stood behind black glasses.

"We're up and running," she said ten minutes later with relief in her voice. Her glasses became clear. "Just in time for the first morning participants."

She studied his face for another few seconds before nodding. "The AI will check them in, manage the queue, and run the equipment. You just need to greet them, answer questions, and rotate them through the test."

"Okay." Business as usual. He missed her earlier attentiveness to his wellbeing.

"I'll stand back there for the first few participants." She pointed towards the back corner. "Then I'll come back before noon to bring you to our weekly status meeting."

A minute later, the door slid open, and an elderly woman in a yellow sweatsuit and white sneakers walked in. Her hair was gray, and the wrinkles around her eyes were long and deep. She obviously didn't subscribe to youth treatments. She scanned the room, then came over when he raised his hand.

He quickly scanned her information provided by his glasses. "Good morning, Ms. Brown," he said. "My name is Mr. Knightsbridge."

"Good morning."

"Your test will begin in eight minutes. You're welcome to sit there." He pointed to the chairs against the back wall. "Do you have questions?"

"How long will the test take?"

Michael didn't need to refer to his glasses for that one. "Less than a minute."

Ms. Brown nodded, then turned and took a seat. Mae gave him a thumbs up. He couldn't help but smile at her enthusiasm.

A few minutes later, he greeted the next volunteer, who had no questions. Then his glasses informed him that despite multiple notifications to go to the elevated chair for her test, Mrs. Brown had remained seated. She seemed confused, her head jerking from side to side.

He walked over and smiled. "It's time for your test."

"Oh yes, thank you," she said and stood without hesitation. There didn't seem to be anything amiss.

He escorted her to the platform. "Just sit in the chair. During the test, you'll feel like you're in a gray box, but you'll return shortly."

He stepped back, listened to the countdown, and watched as a gray cube appeared between the pillars. This time he heard a low-pitched static, like a moan. He liked the experience on this side of the cube much better.

After the cube disappeared, Ms. Brown sauntered down the steps. She smiled, thanked him, and left. Mae slipped out the door at the same time.

He returned to his desk. When the next volunteer was called, she got up and walked to the chair without help. When the gray cube surrounded her, he asked for a real time view of her dark matter bundle. His glasses turned opaque, and a few seconds later, the familiar golden globe appeared. This one had more yellow-white patterns across its surface and fewer shimmering white lightning bolts than the one Mae had shown him. He wondered if one's golden globe was unique to the person, like a fingerprint. When his glasses turned transparent again, he saw the next volunteer walking towards the testing throne.

After a steady stream of fifty volunteers, the morning experiments concluded. No one had any ill effects, which seemed to confirm that his were due to the power surge. A little before noon, the door slid open, and Mae walked in.

"Ready?"

"Sure," he said as they left the lab for the lunch staff meeting.

"Did you notice anything strange about Ms. Brown?" Mae asked.

"She seemed a little disoriented. Why?"

"She had sixteen dark matter bundles."

"How? I thought each person only had one."

"So did I. But Ms. Brown's bundle looked like sixteen small bundles scrunched together like the nucleus of an atom."

Michael recalled his high school science and imagined sixteen golden globes compressed together to form a nucleus.

"We've arranged a follow-up call with her this afternoon. I'd like you to attend to make introductions," Mae said.

"Sure," he replied automatically. They turned a corner and almost ran into a couple of students coming the other way.

Mae waited until the students were out of earshot range. "I want to get more information before discussing this multiple bundle anomaly with the others." She stopped, grabbed his arm, and looked into his eyes. "Let's keep this to ourselves for now."

He nodded; they now shared a secret. She

surveyed his face and tightened her grip. Then she released it, and they continued down the hallway. He enjoyed this newfound camaraderie and partnership.

She asked about his morning, and he filled her in on the relatively mundane events. They went up two sets of stairs, then down another hallway, and reached a conference room with a view of the campus, including the Campanile cement clock tower.

"The others will be here shortly, but we can order lunch now." She sat down at the round oak table.

He sat beside her, his glasses displaying a menu with pictures. He selected the vegetarian burger patty with an accompanying salad. Since he'd told her about his morning, he asked about hers.

"I'm trying to understand the dark matter bundle's effect on people and their personality."

"What have you seen?"

"Women seem to have greater dark matter density in their bundles than men." Her nose wrinkled, as if she weren't quite happy with that data point yet. "Higher density correlates with greater empathy."

Just then, Wendell and two other colleagues, all in white lab coats, entered and sat down. "I just got your test results and they're stunning," he said, looking at Michael. "Your dark matter density is triple normal."

He glanced at Mae, whose eyes were wide and mouth open.

"This is wonderful." Mae regained her composure and grabbed his hand. "Because you have the same genetic makeup as Wendell, by comparing your personality differences, we can gain new insights into the bundle's effects."

"Let's not get ahead of ourselves. The power surge may have contaminated the results." Wendell glanced at him. "We'll need to test you again."

"No, thanks." Michael was not going through that again.

"Why not?" Wendell frowned.

"He had a painful and disorienting experience." Mae reached over and covered his hand.

"Probably caused by the surge." Wendell looked like he was going to argue but instead said, "Well, think about it." He rapped his fingers on the tabletop. "Charlie, please give us your status."

Michael turned to the man beside Wendell. Charlie had short cropped brown hair, green eyes, and a freckled face. He was in his mid-thirties, about six feet tall, with a pear-shaped torso and paunch belly.

"I just projected dark matter protrusion points into the Solo galaxy nine billion light-years away." He looked at Michael and waited, obviously providing this history for his benefit. "And got a dark matter view of the nearby area."

"What did you see?" Michael asked. He knew scientists could navigate a dark matter protrusion point to any location in the universe. It was something like a wormhole through the fourth dimension, but he didn't understand the physics. Getting a distant dark matter view was new.

"Stars and planets." Charlie said. "The more massive the object, the darker the shadow."

"It's a breakthrough for astronomy," Wendell added. "It'll allow better mapping of our universe."

"Also, if we ever come across intelligent life, then we're likely to see their golden globes," Mae said.

"Intelligent life?" Michael said, "like aliens?"

"Yes," Mae said. "Given the vastness of the universe, intelligent life must exist."

"You really think so?" Michael believed in UFOs, unlike Wendell, who always needed replicable scientific proof.

"Our Milky Way Galaxy has about one hundred billion stars and one trillion planets, of which millions have environmental conditions like

Earth, conducive for life." Mae arched an eyebrow. "There're also about one trillion galaxies in the universe, like our Milky Way."

"The question isn't if intelligent life exists." Wendell shook his head. "It does. The question is, can we find it in this vast universe?"

"So, you believe in intelligent alien life," Michael said, turning to Wendell. "But remain unconvinced that UFOs have come to Earth?"

Wendell nodded. "Just exploring every viable solar system in the Milky Way using protrusion technology would take us about a million years."

One hundred billion stars just in the Milky Way, which would take a million years to explore. One trillion galaxies, like the Milky Way, in the universe, which would take a trillion million years to explore. Michael shook his head in wonder.

"However," Charlie said, "if we got lucky and came across intelligent life or they discovered us, then we'd want to communicate. My team's also working on a protrusion point communication system based on the property of particle entanglement."

"Entanglement?" Michael wished he had completed some basic physics classes.

He glanced at Wendell, who nodded slightly, not bothered at all by his questions. Obviously,

Wendell wanted to stoke his interest and probably asked his team to support those efforts.

"Quantum entanglement connects pairs of particles, even over vast distances." Charlie smiled. "If scientists measured one to be spin up, then the other paired particle would instantly be spin down, even if it was an infinite distance away."

"How?" Michael asked. "I thought nothing traveled faster than light."

"Nothing does," Wendell said. "However, distance in our known universe becomes irrelevant when moving through the fourth dimension."

"How does it work?" Michael was way out of his comfort zone. A headache was forming from all the information thrown at him.

"Basically, it's like the dots and dashes of an old telegraph system," Charlie said. "The two endpoints are in the observable universe while the connecting wire is in the fourth dimension."

Michael tapped his index finger on the table as if he were sending morse code. He could understand the analogy.

"How's it progressing?" Wendell waved his hand, as if to move along the conversation.

"Excellent." Charlie's eyes lit up, obviously relieved to be past the basic review. "Last Friday, we sent twenty words a minute."

Wendell nodded. "When will the new communication hardware be ready?"

"It's still a few months away."

"Thanks Charlie," Wendell said, turning to the other man who had come in with him. "Frank, can you give your update?"

Frank was also in his mid-thirties but short and rail thin. His brown hair shot out of his head in every direction, probably from rubbing it all day. However, he had a perpetual smile and his eyes sparkled with curiosity. "I've observed two new types of dark matter, which brings the total to twenty-one."

"We initially thought there was just one type," Wendell explained to Michael, "but that was wrong. Instead, it's like distinct elements and compounds with our known matter."

"They have different gravitational forces and interact with each other differently," Frank said.

The amount and magnitude of the research impressed Michael. Even though he couldn't understand all the science, he could understand everyone's enthusiasm.

"Thanks, Frank," Wendell said. "Mae, can you give your update?"

She nodded. "I want to present my findings from last week."

After giving permission, his glasses darkened and showed a scattergram of black and pink dots. The bottom scale, titled *density*, ranged from 0.8 to 1.2, and the side scale, titled *compassion,* went from 0.5 to 2.0.

"Last week's test subjects in pink aligned with our model, comparing their dark matter density to their qualitative measure of compassion. We've scaled up our testing this week and will continue to refine the questionnaire."

Looking at the graph, Michael saw that no one else was even close to his triple density reading. High density showed high compassion, but Michael had never considered himself particularly compassionate; the power surge must have skewed his results.

"Have you confirmed any other correlations?" Wendell asked.

"No," Mae said, "but I still think we'll find something tied to an appreciation of beauty, like music."

Wendell grimaced, his lips pressed tightly together. "Well, keep at it."

Lunch arrived, and the conversation turned to the latest scientific discoveries—boring. Kagome qubit ice. Fragmentations in Bose-Einstein condensates. It was all Greek to him. At 1:00, Mae rose and looked at him. "Ready?"

They went to Mae's office and made a video call to Ms. Brown.

"Ms. Brown, thank you for taking the time to speak with us," Michael said. She sat at a table and still wore her yellow sweatsuit. "I would like to introduce my colleague, Mae."

"Ms. Brown, your dark matter bundle looked very different from others," Mae said. "There were sixteen smaller bundles that composed your bundle. Do you have any ideas why?"

"I suffer from DID." She frowned.

Michael's glasses told him that DID was a rare mental disorder with multiple personality states. Despite extensive research, there was no biological explanation for it.

"How many personalities do you have?" Mae asked.

"Sixteen." She shook her head slowly and looked down at her interlocked hands.

"When were you diagnosed with this condition?" Mae leaned forward and placed her elbows on her desk.

"I've always had it."

"Amazing. Could I send you a questionnaire in a few days to gather more information?"

"Sure." She gave a lopsided grin, probably resigned to her fate as an ongoing guinea pig.

After the call ended, Mae said, "This is fascinating. Multiple dark matter bundles appear to cause multiple personalities."

Mae's eyes darted around as she sat back in her chair and rubbed her chin. "You know, my mom had this affliction later in life and was institutionalized."

"I'm sorry to hear that."

"Yeah, this is personal for me." After a minute, she slapped her thighs and stood. "We need to get you back to the lab for your afternoon experiments."

As they walked down the hallway, Mae was unusually quiet, a serious look on her face.

"What's wrong?" He wondered if she was still thinking about her mom.

"The possibility that your test results are accurate has been lingering in my mind," she admitted, letting out a sigh. "If they are, it would represent a monumental leap forward, not only because of your exceptionally high results but also there wouldn't be any genetic factors when comparing them to Wendell's."

"It was probably the power surge."

"We'll never know." She walked into the lab.

He felt guilty, like he was letting her down.

After witnessing all the amazing research, he wanted to contribute where he could. "Wait. I'll do it."

She spun around with a wide grin. "Are you sure?"

No, he wasn't. Although unlikely, he didn't want to risk the ill effects again. However, something pushed him forward. Guilt? He could still reverse himself, but they were partners. "Yup."

"Great." She resumed walking, but at a faster pace, and her arms now pumped back and forth. "We'll do it tomorrow morning before the volunteers arrive."

The afternoon in the lab was more of the same. Common questions from the research volunteers were duration, experience, and discomfort levels.

After the last volunteer left at 5:00 pm, Michael hung his lab jacket on the peg by his desk and left the building to walk home. It was sunny and warm outdoors, but few students were around. They were probably hanging out at home before dinner and their evening studies.

He reflected on his first day of work. Although he had a rough start, he'd become comfortable in his job. He barely grasped the science, but things had gone well with Mae, Wendell, and the other scientists. Although overwhelming right now, he expected to become more comfortable. However, something gnawed at the back of his mind, like his life was about to change dramatically and there would be no turning back.

CHAPTER FOUR: DISLOCATION

Michael arrived in the lab first thing the next morning. He put on his lab coat and sat at his desk, waiting for Mae.

A few minutes later, the door slid open, and she entered. She smiled and clapped, making a sharp sound. "Ready for your test?"

He didn't feel her enthusiasm but nodded as he rose to his feet. They walked together silently to the platform; she was practically skipping as he shuffled forward. He went up the steps and sat down on the throne and squirmed, clenching and unclenching his fists while his legs bounced up and down.

"Ready?" Her eyes were wide with anticipation even though she probably expected a normal reading.

He nodded. A moment later, his glasses counted down to zero and then the gray walls appeared. This time, the walls shimmered like a wave flowed through them, the surface extending then contracting. The walls almost breathed as if they were alive.

Something was watching him, waiting for his return, like a hidden lion might wait for his prey at a watering hole. Watching and waiting. Time slowed; it had been only a second or two.

Suddenly, the walls collapsed on him like a sprung trap. He thrust out his hands. The front wall slowed when it touched him, but then it kept coming, enveloping his wrists, and creeping up his arms. He glanced down. The gray floor had reached his waist. The walls, ceiling, and floor closed in on his head. He would soon be part of the grayness. He closed his eyes, leaned forward, and screamed.

When Michael opened his eyes, he was lying on his stomach, facing straight down on the hard platform. His head, chin, elbows, and knees were sore. How long had he been unconscious?

"Are you okay?" Mae's voice sounded rushed and strained.

"I think so." He rolled onto his back. Mae hovered over him. He must have been out for only a few seconds. He took a few deep breaths, then stuck his hand up.

"What happened?" she asked, pulling him to his feet.

"The gray cube shrunk again, but this time it absorbed me." His legs were shaky, so Mae helped him to his desk chair.

"What's your medical reading?"

He checked his glasses, then said, "Rapid heart rate, elevated blood pressure, dilated pupils, and a few bruises. I also have a pounding headache, but I'll survive."

Her eyebrows furrowed, and the corners of her mouth curved downward. "Let me call a taxi to take you home."

"All right." He considered fighting through the pain and staying for his job like Wendell would do, but that perseverance quickly faded.

Besides his physical symptoms, he was discombobulated, but it was difficult to explain. He was like a child who had flung out his arms and spun round and round, watching as the world blurred. When he stopped, dizziness struck like a thunderclap, and all mental efforts focused on stabilizing the landscape and keeping his body upright. There was nothing else. That's how it was right now.

A half-hour later, he climbed into his bed, after pulling his curtains shut. He shivered even though he wasn't cold. Suddenly, a deep baritone voice sounded in his head. *I think, therefore I am. No!*

I have consciousness, therefore I am.

He shook his head, trying to clear it. Where did that come from?

His glasses notified him of an incoming call from Wendell, so he sat up and accepted it.

"Are you okay?" Wendell sat at a small table with Mae. His face was slack, concerned—not his normal, in-control demeanor.

"I think so."

"Good." Wendell seemed unsure how to proceed. "There was another power surge, but this time we identified the cause. It was your test!"

"What?"

"I know it's unbelievable," Wendell said. "We're trying to figure out how it happened."

"I'm glad you're okay." Mae gave a halfhearted smile, but her body was tense. "Your test results were the same, three times normal density."

No wonder she looked conflicted. She had worried about him, but he could advance her work.

"If you're feeling up to it, why don't you come over to the house for dinner tomorrow night." Wendell grinned. "Mae will be there too."

"We'll see." A wave of exhaustion overwhelmed him. He signed off.

He set his glasses on his nightstand, and then laid on his back and closed his eyes.

Did Michael Knightsbridge cause my awakening? the baritone voice said in his head. His eyes popped open. His room was dark, but his curtains glowed in the moonlight. Had he dreamed? Was he dreaming now?

He checked the time: 2:00 am. He rolled out of bed and went to the window. There was a full moon, which cast an eerie bloom on the trees and sloping ground. He wasn't dreaming now, but had he heard the voice while he slept? Probably. Could he have somehow contracted the multi-personality disease?

"Are you there?" he asked himself, staring out the window. He waited for the voice to resurface, but it didn't. After about ten minutes, he returned to bed and fell asleep.

***

Michael spent the next nine days in bed with a splitting migraine. Despite an extensive physical examination, the medical robot couldn't determine if he had a virus. The baritone voice hadn't returned, so he ascribed the hallucination to posttraumatic stress and didn't mention it to anyone.

He felt better the following day, Thursday, so took a short walk around the neighborhood. When he returned home, he caught up on the news and personal communications. He thanked Mae for her well wishes, accepted a dinner invitation for Friday from Wendell, and told everyone he planned to return to work on Monday.

The most interesting thing in the news was a new VR game called Conquest that was receiving rave reviews from the worldwide gaming community. It was a new type of sophisticated multi-role fantasy game, where you started as the ruler of a country, seated on your throne. However, when you made a mistake and perished, almost always in level one, then you returned to a lower social, but more active role. You might become a duke or duchess, a soldier, a spaceship pilot, or something else. Based on your desires, the game somehow matched you to your role. He would probably return as a spaceship gunner.

The game came from an unknown production house, probably in India or China. The US government warned its citizens the game was foreign propaganda, which perversely increased interest.

He went to his VR chair and logged into the game but didn't take Dreamland because he wanted to keep all his wits. A spinning globe appeared with a view of continents and oceans. Red boundary lines divided the land masses into irregular sections representing individual countries. The globe stopped spinning and zoomed in on one country bordering an ocean.

"You're king of Acacia, a powerful kingdom in a modern world with all the technologies you're familiar with," a woman's husky voice said. He pictured a tall, muscular female soldier with short, cropped hair. "The objective of the game is to work with your advisors to establish the best world for all of humanity through acts of diplomacy, including war."

The scene switched to a hall with royal blue curtains partially covering tall windows on either side. Crystal chandeliers hung from the ceiling. Michael sat on a golden throne facing four CGI characters, nearly indistinguishable from actual humans. The game identified them as his advisors: a general, an ambassador, a legislator, and an intelligence officer.

"Besides advice, your advisors execute your policies and tactics," the narrator said. "For example, you could ask them to write and broadcast a speech for a new policy. If you lose, then you'll return as a different character with a fresh set of instructions. Now, play!"

Michael waited for his advisors to say something, but when they didn't, he asked, "Is there anything demanding my attention?"

They shook their heads.

He scanned the room, looking for some clue

about what to do. Everything looked so real, even the blue satin curtains in front of the open windows fluttered with the breeze. The throne reminded him of the platform chair used in the dark matter experiments.

"How do I move?" He wanted to get up and explore.

"Right now, this game is strategy," the narrator said. "You don't move."

So, this would be a game like chess rather than an action packed, hand-to-hand combat. It was surprising this genre attracted so much interest from gamers and so few hints on how to play were available online. Although new, he would've expected more, particularly given the game's popularity.

What should be his first action? After a minute, he decided to get his house in order. "Intelligence officer, what is the people's satisfaction with me and the government?"

The dark-haired intelligence officer with penetrating gray eyes and a black cloak stepped forward and bowed. He was the quintessential spy. "Common people feel exploited and over-taxed while the noblemen have free rein."

He grunted. The elite ran things for their benefit, not the citizens'. This socio-economic situation resembled the real world, where almost everyone in advanced countries had their basic needs met, but few could attain more. Although it hadn't bothered him personally, he now wanted to address the situation, probably to succeed in the game.

"Legislator, draft a new law that gives everyone the same rights as noblemen." Everything started with human rights, but money was a close second. "Draft a second law that reduces taxes on the commoner and increases taxes on the noblemen so that we will have a treasury to fund our future endeavors of conquest."

The white-haired legislator in a business suit stepped forward and bowed. "By your word."

"Intelligence officer, draft me an announcement for this new legislation that will rally the people." A statement appeared on his display, which he reviewed and edited. After a few rehearsals, he recorded his speech.

A hologram appeared above the heads of his advisors that showed him giving his speech. Afterwards, the narrator said, "Do you wish to broadcast your speech to your citizens?"

"Yes," he said.

"Would you like to see how it's received?" the narrator continued.

"Yea."

A minute later, the overhead hologram showed a rowdy nightclub going quiet to watch him on wall monitors. One drunk made some noise and was punched out. Next, he saw ten different families silently watch the broadcast from their family rooms. Many raised their arms and made fists. After observing about fifty random scenes, the game told him his speech had garnered a ninety-three percent approval rating, and he was now on level two. He wondered if real politicians got this thrill when they saw a speech well received by the public.

There was no other VR game like Conquest, and yet it was totally addictive. It was like growing up playing physical sports and then being exposed to the intellectual challenges of chess.

The game consumed him for the next thirty hours: play, sleep, eat, and little else. Six months of game time had elapsed. He was still the ruler of Acacia and in the middle of level four, having just issued an ultimatum to the fragile government of Croat, his corrupt neighbor. While he waited for their reply, his clock alarm notified him it was time for Wendell's dinner. He considered skipping it but wanted to know what had happened to him at the lab. After logging off, he got ready.

To make a splash, he chose his most fashionable outfit, his undulating rainbow-colored robe and his black suede loafers. He inspected his reflection, and then, after whitening his teeth, walked over to the main house.

"You look good." Mae examined him from head to foot at Wendell's back door.

"You too." He chuckled at his awkward response. She wore a maroon satin dress with dangling pearl earrings—a big improvement from her lab coat. He smelled orange blossoms when he inhaled, reminding him of running through orchards as a kid. Mae was beautiful with her ebony skin, full mouth that constantly smiled, and unselfconscious grace. The sort of woman who could star in a movie. These impressions surprised him; they were probably the result of being alone for so long.

Her smile broadened as she grabbed his hand and led him into the family room, where Wendell and Melinda sat on a couch. He sat down on the other couch where Mae joined him rather than sitting on one of the swivel chairs. Their shoulders touched, sending a chill down his spine.

The server robot took his drink order while Wendell got up off the couch, walked to the fireplace, and then to the window, and finally returned to the couch. After the robot left, he got right to business. "We reconfirmed your bundle density is triple the norm. When our fifth-force equipment took your reading, it caused a power surge that shorted some of our electrical circuits."

Michael chewed his lower lip. It could've been a lifetime ago, but the gray box still scared him, having leaped on him like a predator.

"We want to offer you a new analyst role, reporting to Mae."

He turned to Mae. "What would I do?"

"Identify the personality differences between you and Wendell. Then help us understand if the causes are due to differences in your dark matter bundles, your environment, or something else. It'll be a full-time job."

He would be a full-time lab rat but given a research title to buy his agreement.

"How can dark matter influence a person?" he asked, wanting more information before deciding. Dark matter was just a substance. It probably influenced personalities like aspirin relieved headaches, making people less irritable.

"We don't understand it." Wendell frowned. "Nor do we understand how the chemical and electrical processes in the biological brain lead to thinking, feelings, memories, and consciousness."

It sounded like a lot of unknowns to Michael. *It is,* said an internal woman's voice that was less overpowering than the earlier baritone. Her voice had a sing-song quality and was higher pitched but conveyed understated confidence. *And scientists have been studying the human brain for decades with little progress.* His mouth dropped open as he waited for more commentary.

"Anyway, we're adding some neuroscientists to the team," Wendell continued.

Mae's eyes were glued on Wendell, but Melinda was staring at him. He gave her his goofy grin. After studying his face, she tilted her head as if listening to someone, then rose to her feet. "Dinner's ready,"

Michael stumbled to his feet, wondering if his internal voice would continue its intrusion. He followed Mae to the dining room table and sat beside her, with Wendell and Melinda sitting across the table from them.

"I heard Anni Chan made a large donation to our research," Mae said. "Who is she?"

"She's the matriarch of a powerful family in China." Wendell took a sip of water. "I had a video-call with her last week where she committed to make a fifty-million-dollar donation."

Melinda whistled. "What does she want in return?"

"To meet the team. She's in San Francisco for a few days and plans to come by the office tomorrow." Wendell leaned back as the robot placed his plate of white fish, brown rice, and broccoli on the table, plus a glass of white wine beside it. "Quarterly briefings. There're no other strings attached."

"I'm meeting Ms. Chan Monday morning," Mae volunteered.

"There're always strings attached," Melinda said. "The question is if you see them."

Wendell frowned, then switched the conversation topic to the Cal Bears upcoming football season. Although he didn't have time to watch games, he was optimistic about their prospects despite multiple losing seasons.

"I wish you'd spend less time at the office," Melinda said, "and more at home."

"I know. I know." Wendell nodded, looking like he'd had this talk before. "But it's critical I'm there right now. It's just for another six months."

"You know, I'm not getting any younger." She raised her eyebrows as if there was more meaning to her words.

Michael said little at dinner, waiting for the internal voice to speak again, but it didn't. What was this new voice? It was the antithesis of his internal, negative monkey voice that always doubted and criticized him, telling him he was a failure. His therapist had said most people who lacked self-confidence and self-esteem had this monkey voice. Maybe this new voice indicated he was becoming a more confident person.

After dinner, Mae thanked Wendell and Melinda. "I'll see you Monday morning," she said to him.

"Sure thing." Michael checked his augmented emotional read for Mae: excitement.

After Mae left, Michael thanked Melinda and walked with Wendell to the backdoor. "I enjoy working with Mae," he said.

"She's a brilliant scientist," Wendell said.

Michael paused, then asked, "Do you know if she's seeing anyone?"

"I don't think so." Wendell squinted and was about to say something more but stopped. Was it because of their ground rules and his promise not to interfere? Or was it because his previous attempt at offering girl advice, urging Michael to "just be himself," had backfired spectacularly? With a sigh of resignation, Wendell bid Michael goodnight, leaving the matter unresolved.

Michael strolled along the illuminated path, his mind occupied by his perpetual clumsiness around women. Wendell hadn't fared much better until he stumbled upon Melinda. Perhaps Michael just hadn't crossed paths with the right person yet. Could Mae be that elusive someone?

When he got home, Michael returned to

his VR game of Conquest. The corrupt, business-controlled parliament of Croat had rejected his ultimatum, even though most citizens wanted his intervention.

"General," Michael said.

A bulky, grizzled man in an olive military uniform, ladened with medals, stepped forward.

"Commence special operations, but don't hurt any civilians." The plan was to take parliament and arrest the politicians.

Michael pivoted towards his intelligence officer, issuing a crisp command, "Launch SO campaign." They would notify the public that parliament had chosen not to resign peacefully, necessitating his special operation to liberate the people of Croat.

Game time sped forward by two weeks. He now controlled Croat with the support of its everyday citizens. He selected Rafael, a vocal factory worker who had supported Acacia's intervention, to lead the country.

"I want to make an example of all the former parliamentarians who rejected my original offer," Michael told his advisors. "Throw them in prison!"

"Your majesty," the intelligence officer said, "other countries will view this badly."

He was right. Although it didn't matter now,

he needed to ensure that others didn't unite against him.

"Then let's get these traitors to come together for a meeting to discuss how to deal with the new government." He rubbed his chin. "Then, have Raphael storm the building with troops under the pretense of preventing a coup. Ideally, there'll be a deadly shootout." His intelligence officer left with his orders.

By midnight, he had successfully completed level five and went to bed. He was in an elite group. Almost no one reached level five in the ruler role. Was he just lucky or did he have some hidden natural capability that had lain dormant but now expressed itself?

CHAPTER FIVE: REJECTION

Monday morning, Michael went to Mae's office wearing black slacks, a pressed white shirt, and cologne. Over the past two weeks, he had worked one day as a volunteer coordinator, then spent the remaining time sick in bed. Despite this, he felt confident in his abilities and ready for his new role as a research assistant and guinea pig. He was a different man.

She tilted her head and eyed him up and down. "You look nice."

"As do you," he said.

She laughed, looking down at her drab lab coat. She grabbed a white coat hanging on the wall and handed it to him.

"Now what?" he asked after putting it on.

"Come with me." She went down the hallway to the third door, which slid open. Inside was a small room with a desk and a single window that faced the wall of an adjacent building. "This is your office. To begin with, I'd like you to complete this personality survey."

After he sat down at his desk, a welcome page to a one hundred and fifty question survey appeared on his glasses. He pushed his glasses to his forehead and looked back at Mae.

"We'll compare your answers with Wendell's, looking for any differences." Her arms were folded across her chest. "See you later."

She left without another word. She seemed a bit put off. Maybe she had something important on her mind. He slipped his glasses down and read the directions, then flipped to the first question.

1. *You walk by a homeless woman begging for money. How much would you transfer to her?*
   A. *Nothing*
   B. *A few dollars*
   C. *Ten dollars*
   D. *Fifty dollars?*

Well, she needed it more than he did. He selected *D. Fifty dollars.*

He flipped to the next question. As he proceeded, the questions required greater thought, but three hours later, he'd finished. Shortly thereafter, his glasses said, "You have an invitation to join Mae in her office."

When he walked into her office, she looked

up from her tablet and smiled. *Phew*. Her change in demeanor was a relief. Hopefully, she'd resolved whatever had been bothering her. "What's up boss?"

"I'm sorry that I was aloof this morning. I was nervous about my meeting with Ms. Chan."

"No problem." He went to her desk and sat down on a chair facing her. "How did it go?"

"She asked a ton of questions about me and my research, but I think I answered them well."

"Good."

"Anyway, I have your personality results." She leaned back and stretched her arms. "You, my friend, are an enigma."

"How so?"

"You're extremely compassionate, but if someone betrays you, then watch out."

He nodded. If someone hits you, then you hit them back twice as hard. That's the way he's always lived. He didn't believe in forgive and forget. He wasn't sure if this aggressiveness was a manly quality or an anger management issue.

"You rely more on intuitive feelings rather than rational thought."

He tilted his head back, looking at the ceiling. It was true. Whenever he concentrated on a problem, his feelings often disrupted his thoughts.

Not a recipe for a successful career. However, those seemingly random thoughts sometimes connected disparate threads and generated non-obvious insights.

"There were other things, but these were your key differences with Wendell."

"Now what?"

"We'll add these questions to the volunteer survey and see if there is some correlation with the dark matter bundles." She paused, giving him a chance to ask more questions, and then continued. "With your new role, I want to give you some of the latest research."

"I don't need a PhD?"

"No." She shook her head. "I'm just going to show you what we've observed. You only need advanced degrees to understand the why."

His glasses displayed a drawing of the side view of a human brain. In the center was a small red section with the letters AIC.

"Emotional feelings like love, anger, fear, sadness, happiness, trust, and empathy originate in the anterior insular cortex," she said. "The AIC is in the middle of the brain."

He grunted. It seemed crude that scientists ascribed the transcendence of emotions to a small section of the brain. Did he find Mae attractive because of this part of his brain? Did this part of her brain find him attractive?

"My hypothesis is the dark matter bundle influences the AIC, encouraging higher-level feelings like compassion and discouraging more primitive emotions like selfishness or lust."

Michael shook his head to bring his attention back to what Mae was saying rather than what he was imagining. "Come again?"

"Am I boring you?"

"No, no. I want to hear more." His glasses turned transparent. Maybe having her in front of him would help.

"Good," she said. "In simple terms, your consciousness occurs in your cerebral cortex, but can only handle one or two things simultaneously."

He was concentrating on her words, but then glanced at her hand near his, which brought a flood of secondary thoughts. He blinked, returning his gaze to her face and his attention to her words.

"You also have your subconsciousness, where your feelings, memories, and sensory inputs are. These would quickly overwhelm your consciousness if not for your default mode network or DMN, which manages them."

"So," he said, "the DMN is like a traffic cop for my brain activity."

"That's a good analogy. In reality, it's a highly interconnected network of hubs in the brain. Anyway, I believe the dark matter bundle works through the DMN and enables consciousness."

"Really?" he said, rubbing his chin. "So, without dark matter, we wouldn't have consciousness?"

"It would be completely different." She tilted her head and stared past him. "More like an automaton, reacting to external stimuli. No self-awareness of being or internal reflection."

"Is this true for all animals or only humans?" he asked.

"It's true for all creatures with high intelligence, like monkeys, elephants and dolphins," she said. "All have a dark matter bundle, although smaller than a human's."

Instead of disinterest, he was intrigued.

"The intersection of dark matter and biological brains enabled intelligence and consciousness." She leaned forward, placing her hands on her desk and rapping her fingers. "It's critical to higher-order evolution."

"Evolution? Like Darwin? Survival of the fittest?"

"Exactly." She grinned, like she was proud of him for acing a test. "It was critical for our evolution."

She waited for more questions, then said, "I'm giving you some research papers that will give you background on everything we discussed."

His glasses now displayed a list of five research titles. The top one was: *How Consciousness is the Default Mode of Brain Function*. Typically, this type of assignment would repulse him, but this time it didn't. Maybe it would provide some insights into his personality.

Michael returned to his office, where he ordered a vegetable sandwich. His glasses told him he had an interview with Anni Chan in an hour. *Weird*, he thought. *She's really meeting everyone in the lab, even grunts like me.*

To make a good impression, he went over what he would say about himself. He'd try to communicate that he was an underachiever but had potential. He was turning himself around.

At 2:00 pm sharp, he received and accepted the video meeting invite. His room camera and glasses joined the meeting.

A Chinese woman, probably about forty, sat on an easy chair. Her black hair flowed down her back, while some strands covered an eye, which she flipped aside with a finger. She wore trendy gold inlaid glasses, a navy-blue suit, a white blouse, and a pink scarf around her neck; her black shoes rested on a satin ottoman. Behind her in red was a sign for China Airlines.

"Good afternoon, Michael." She emphasized his name.

"Good afternoon, Ms. Chan."

"That's my mom's name. Please call me Anni." She squinted, examining his face. "Anyway, I've been asking questions all day. Why don't you start and ask me some questions?"

"Uh." He was totally unprepared to ask questions, so said the first thing that came to him. "Where are you? I thought you'd be in the office."

"I planned to but needed to fly home early. I'm in the airport lounge."

"Do you come to the US often?" He rubbed the top of his head. *What a stupid question.*

"Yes, mainly to visit my family's businesses. I love the US. It's like my adopted country."

"So . . . why are you interested in dark matter research?" *Better*.

"I'm fascinated by consciousness or awareness." She grinned. "Probably because of my Buddhist upbringing."

He wished he knew more about Buddhism so he could ask better questions. "How so?"

"I believe there's a universal consciousness of good that a chosen few can connect to. It's part of enlightenment." She closed her eyes and rubbed her chin. After a few seconds, her eyes popped open, and she leaned forward. "Do you ever have premonitions?"

"Premonitions?"

"Intuitions. Feelings or voices telling you what to do."

"Well, maybe." He lived his life by feelings but never considered them to be premonitions. His monkey voice told him he would fail in most endeavors. It was normally right, but he didn't think that's what she was talking about.

She frowned as if he had given a wrong answer.

But he had to know himself better than she did. This was the strangest interview he'd ever had. He needed to bring some normalcy to it. "Do you have any *work* questions for me?"

"Why are you doing this research?" She sat back and crossed her arms, looking disappointed in the direction of the conversation.

The truth was it paid the bills, but that wasn't an appropriate answer. "I like the people and find the work interesting."

"Good." The corner of her mouth turned up. "What do you do in your spare time?"

"Play video games." There wasn't much besides that.

"What's your favorite?" Her eyebrows rose.

"Right now, it's Conquest."

"What's your role?" She rolled her eyes. Obviously, Conquest was the expected answer.

"I'm still a ruler."

"Really." She sat up, since most players got blown out in level one. "What level?"

"Six."

"Impressive. You must have some amazing talents."

"Just lucky I guess." It couldn't really be anything more than that.

It's talent, not luck. The female voice in his head startled him. His back went rigid. Shaken, he glanced at Anni, who obviously hadn't heard it. What was going on? He should get tested.

"You're quite different from Wendell," she said. "I think you should join me."

"What?" He must have misheard her. He waited for his inner voice to say something.

"Help me make the world a better place."

Who was this woman, and how could she make the world a better place?

She looked away and frowned. "I need to catch

my flight now, but we'll continue this conversation later."

The meeting ended without another word. His white office wall greeted him when his glasses turned transparent. She was a confounding enigma, so he searched for some news clips about her.

His glasses displayed some of her history. Anni was the third daughter of a wealthy Chinese family. There was a brief video clip of her as a child on a family vacation in Kenya, where she rode on the back of an elephant. She majored in mathematics at Peking University, then worked in her family business for five years. In her late twenties, she had a wild streak and partied hard, got married to a playboy, and divorced six months later. For the last ten years, she'd worked behind the scenes for the family's charity foundation.

He placed an elbow on his desk, closed his eyes, and rubbed his forehead with an open hand. He brushed off the weird interview with Anni and the reoccurring voice in his head and got back to work.

He read two research reports without having his mind wander. He completely understood them. That was odd. Something was definitely happening to his brain.

At 5:00 pm, he hung his lab coat beside his desk and decided to drop by Mae's office before quitting for the day. When he arrived, she was hunched over her tablet at her desk.

"I'm heading home," he announced. "You look busy."

"Adjusting the lab equipment so that we can better target the dark matter detectors. I'm almost done." She smiled, then gushed, "Today was wonderful. Between my interview with Anni and the new insights into dark matter."

Normally, he'd say some inane thing and leave, but her positivity infected him. Or was it something else? Brimming with confidence, he marched to her desk and sat down across from her. "We should celebrate. Let me take you out?"

"You mean a date?" Her lips pressed together.

"Yeah," he answered without hesitation.

Her eyes narrowed, and she bit her lip.

His social skills, which were never any good, had atrophied from disuse. He called up her AER reading on his glasses. *Disinterest.*

"I don't think so." She shook her head. "It's frowned upon by the university."

He crossed his legs and shrugged, bringing his shoulders almost to his ears and back down. Could university policies really cause her disinterest? "We could see how it goes."

She looked away, gliding her teeth across her

lower lip. "Michael, I like you, but a date would feel awkward, like I was with my boss."

He could understand the resemblance to Wendell would be a problem. "I could grow a beard," he said, only half joking.

She shook her head but wouldn't look at him.

He shouldn't have said it was a date. He tried to think of some way to recover. The silence was becoming awkward.

She looked up. "It's just not going to work."

Campus policy. Resemblance to Wendell. I can overcome these things.

Then the internal woman's voice replaced these thoughts. *Leave her alone. Desperation is never an attractive quality.*

His internal voice was right. He wobbled to his feet, his face burning, then turned and stumbled out the door. He hadn't asked a woman out in years, so of course he would botch it. However, he hadn't reckoned with the embarrassment of rejection, even though he could understand her unstated reasons. She had everything going for her: looks, intelligence, and passion for her career. He had nothing. She was out of his league.

No, she isn't, said the internal voice again.

Yes, she is, he countered.

One day, she'll think of you the way you think of her. One day, she'll want you, but you won't want her.

He rubbed the sides of his head. Where was this voice coming from? It was optimistic and supportive, so unlike his monkey voice. However, it pushed him into uncomfortable situations with poor outcomes.

New aspirations bubbled inside of him and demanded he strive for excellence and success. It was like waves of ambition crashing against his walls of safety and complacency. He tried to suppress the waves.

CHAPTER SIX: BASEBALL GAME

On his walk home, he watched the shadows of trees lengthening and a few students walking to or from class. The slight evening breeze buzzed between the leaves and cooled his face. The day had started so well but had ended in disaster when he'd misread Mae's signals. She'd been his primary motivation for work and now that was gone.

When he got home, he popped a Dreamland pill to relax and escape from his demons. No more worries about the past or anxieties about the future. He played Aliens since he didn't have a clear mind for Conquest.

The following day, September 22, he read more research reports on consciousness in his office. He didn't see Mae all day. His motivation and interest waned. He understood his prior coordinator role, but what was a research analyst? Was he just a glorified guinea pig?

At 5:00 pm sharp, he left the office and walked home. When he arrived, his server robot handed him a beer in a frosty mug. It was the highlight of his day. He sat down on his couch, tossed his shoes aside, and stretched his legs across the leather surface. He looked up the typical payments for self-improvement activities in California.

Fifty dollars per hour for exercise.

Eighty dollars per hour for musical instruments or fine arts.

California paid ten to twenty dollars more per hour than Massachusetts. His current salary was four hundred dollars per hour, but he didn't need all that money. He wasn't one of those people who was dissatisfied with what they had and always wanted more. In fact, he would donate any surplus funds to Africa Forever.

His glasses flashed an invitation from Wendell to come over to the house in an hour to watch the Giants and Red Sox baseball game. Both teams were in the hunt for playoff spots. Mae had probably told Wendell that he'd hit on her, and that she was uncomfortable working with him now. *That's clearly the reason she avoided you today.* His monkey voice was back.

Michael rubbed his chin and stared out the window at the rustling trees. He would watch the game with Wendell, discuss some mundane topics, and then resign his position. Tomorrow, he'd sign up for the government programs.

At 6:45 pm, he opened Wendell's back door, walked into an empty kitchen, and heard the muffled sounds of the game. He sauntered into the living room where Wendell sat on the couch watching the game on the wall monitor above the lit fireplace.

"Come, sit down." Wendell patted the place beside him. "No score yet." The Giants were at bat.

"Where's Melinda?" He took his seat.

"Working late." Wendell kept his eyes on the game. "The government wants her to improve our computer network security."

"Is there a problem?" The Giant's batter swung at a low pitch and struck out. Michael smirked.

"No, but they're assessing an AI prototype that's networked to her system, so they want to ensure no backdoor security breaches." He glanced over. "By the way, that's confidential."

The next batter hit a double into right field.

"Yes," Wendell exclaimed, raising his arm and making a fist. Michael wondered when his brother had changed his allegiance from their hometown favorite to the Giants. Wendell always adjusted to his new environment, where Michael stayed true to the old.

"Do you remember when the four of us used to go to Fenway Park to watch the Red Sox play?" Michael asked.

"Yup." Wendell nodded as the corner of his

mouth curled up. "Over mom's objections, dad would buy us all the candy, popcorn, and hotdogs that we could eat."

"Yeah," Charlie said, grabbing some chips. "It was never the same after dad died."

At the bottom of the sixth inning, a robot replaced the chips and guacamole with hamburgers and fries.

"I spoke to Mae," Wendell said.

Michael nodded, chewing his burger. Here it comes.

"We've agreed to Anni Chan's request for a full-time onsite representative and would like you to do it."

Michael choked and reached for his glass of water. He took a sip and cleared his throat. "What? Why me?"

"After interviewing everyone, she picked you." Wendell examined his face. "You were her preferred choice."

Michael replayed their conversation in his mind. Why would she choose him over all the brilliant researchers? "What did I say that impressed her?"

With a tight-lipped smile, Wendell just shook his head. He didn't have a clue.

"Is this normal to have three different jobs inside of a month?" Michael asked.

"No," Wendell replied, "but there's been a good reason for each change."

Michael bent his head down, closed his eyes, and rubbed his brows. This conversation was going much differently than he'd expected. "What would I do?"

"Be her feet on the ground. She'll explain exactly what she wants."

"I was going to quit the job tonight." Michael said, eyeing the side of Wendell's head.

"Why?" Wendell turned to look at Michael, frowning.

Maybe Mae hadn't mentioned anything. Michael had overreacted, which wasn't the first time he'd read too much into a conversation. Now he needed a different reason for quitting. "I prefer being my own boss and making my own decisions."

"Talk to Anni and see if you can create a role that works for you." He looked down at his locked hands in his lap. "This is important to me."

"Why?" Michael couldn't remember Wendell ever asking him for anything; in the rare cases when he wanted something, he just took it.

"She's offered to bankroll the new building for our department."

Michael nodded. Although the university had agreed to a building site, Wendell's project was dead. Wendell was many things, but a fundraiser wasn't one of them.

It was the seventh inning stretch, with the Giants leading two to one. Wendell was lost in his thoughts. Michael stared into the fireplace, whose undulating yellow and orange flames generated little heat. He would lose nothing by talking to Anni and might like what he heard. There wouldn't be the awkwardness of working for Mae. This would also pay back Wendell for taking him in. "Okay. I'll talk with her."

"Good." Wendell raised a corner of his mouth into a half-smile but didn't look away from the screen.

"You seem distracted," Michael said.

"Yeah." He glanced at Michael and raised his eyebrow. "Melinda wants a baby, but the timing is terrible. We're both so busy right now, and I don't know how it would change our lives."

"What's the rush?" Michael shrugged. "Don't you have plenty of time?"

"My sentiments exactly." Wendell sat back and tapped his fingers on his stomach.

Michael had nothing more to say. Having or raising a child was uncharted territory for him. He silently watched the Red Sox come from behind to win—brother bonding at its finest.

CHAPTER SEVEN: ANNI'S OFFER

Early the next morning, Michael received an afternoon meeting invite from Anni. Wendell had been quick to report back to her. The invitation requested he have a clear mind without drugs and attend from home. He accepted.

This gave him a free day, so he started with Wendell's recommended hike. With water bottle in hand, he went to the street, then walked uphill, past a combination of old wood homes and modern insulated ones. Upon reaching the Grizzly Peak Trailhead, he found himself breathless, so took a break.

Ten minutes later, he descended into Strawberry Canyon, surrounded by redwoods and other tall trees. He went by Lake Anza, crossed a creek at the bottom of the valley, and climbed the other side to Inspiration Point.

He was on top of the world with the eastern vistas of blue reservoirs in golden-brown rolling hills. When was the last time he'd felt so alive? He shut his eyes, remembering the time he'd surfed at Sunset Beach on the North Shore of Oahu.

The surf had been relatively flat when he and Wendell saw a beautiful swell forming in the distance.

He'd paddled towards the wave, thick and deep blue towards the bottom and thin and whitish blue on top. When he reached the sweet spot, Wendell kept paddling out, while he spun his board around and paddled towards the shore as hard as he could. Glancing over his shoulder, the large concave wave was now only ten feet away. He pumped his arms harder in a circular motion, with no fears or misgivings.

The wave lifted the back of his board and pushed him forward. He set his hands down and jumped to his feet with knees bent deeply. When the wave started breaking behind him, he angled his board to the right and surfed down the face. Behind him, the wave's curl approached until it was above his head. Instead of a sense of doom and foreboding, he felt exhilarated and full of life. It had been one of the greatest and most memorable moments of his life. Unfortunately, that version of himself had disappeared a long time ago.

He opened his eyes and took one last look at the rolling hills. Then he turned around. Two hours later, he was back home in his shower. As he soaped off the sweat, he told himself that he should hike every day.

After getting dressed and eating, he went to his VR chair for a game of Conquest. Once more, he was in his throne room with his advisors. Through the entrance doors at the far end of the hall, he saw his guards and crowds waiting to enter.

"Your highness, I fear your enemies may attack you in your palace," his intelligence officer said, stepping forward. This time, the officer wore blue trousers and a white long-sleeve shirt. Other than his eyes, he was unremarkable, easily forgettable.

"Have they infiltrated my personal guard?" Michael chewed his lower lip.

"Possibly." The officer's eyes scanned the area behind Michael as if searching for a threat.

Not good. They could have smuggled in an assault weapon or planted a bomb. "Who are the sponsors, foreign or domestic?"

"We don't know who but believe they're mainly domestic."

He had a major problem on his hands. "Identify the most likely traitors, then gather all their communication records and that of their most trusted advisors. Look for anything unusual like contacts with my guards or council, then interrogate those people."

He would need to confirm his intelligence officer's trustworthiness separately. He glanced around his throne room and thought about security safeguards at the White House. "Place metal detectors at the doors and station guards. Install a bullet-proof glass wall between my throne and the rest of the room. Place protective barriers around the building, install anti-aircraft weapons, and create a no-fly zone."

He stood. "Cancel all my appointments. I don't want to see anyone until these safeguards are in place."

"Level six completed," said the game's husky woman's voice.

He grunted. The actions to complete level six seemed obvious. If notified about a personal threat, wouldn't everyone prioritize their security first before doing anything else?

He was about to start level seven when his alarm notified him that his call with Anni would start in ten minutes. After pausing the game, he stood and stretched his arms high over his head. His hands dropped as he swiveled his torso, allowing his arms to flop back and forth.

It didn't help. Nearly every muscle in his legs ached from the morning hike. His thighs and calves were tight, hard knots. He hobbled over to his kitchen like an arthritic grandfather to get a glass of water. A minute before the meeting, he returned to his VR seat and waited.

When he accepted the call, his glasses turned opaque, then transported him into an office sitting across from Anni. She sat behind an oversized mahogany desk that made her look small but important at once. She placed her hands on the desk, stood, and leaned forward confidently. "Welcome."

Michael felt obligated and stumbled to his feet. "Thanks."

She studied him from head to foot, obviously pulling live data from his room cameras. She nodded and returned to her chair. "Please sit." She waited until he sat down, then continued. "After interviewing everyone at your brother's lab, I've selected you to be my onsite representative, my boots on the ground, reporting directly to me."

"Really?"

"Yes." She placed her hands together on her desk and twirled her thumbs. "I'm fascinated by consciousness and its relationship with dark matter. I'm aggregating this research from other facilities where I also have onsite representatives."

Michael had thought Wendell's research was unique, but it made sense that others were working on similar things. "Why do you need an onsite person? And why me in particular?"

"It's not for the experimental observations,

which I could get directly from cameras and sensors. It's also not for your analytical skills, since I have powerful AI algorithms at my disposal." She leaned forward, placing her elbows on the desk and her chin in her cupped hands. "I'm looking for your insights to make intuitive connections that AI won't see."

Michael sat back in his chair and pursed his lips. How could he provide insights that a powerful AI tool, incorporating all scientific knowledge, couldn't see?

"Let me give you a riddle to demonstrate the point." She seemed to read his thoughts. She looked at the ceiling and rubbed her hands together. After a moment, her eyes returned to him. "You can choose two integers from 1 to 10,000, one for the numerator, the other for the denominator. What is the largest fraction that you can generate that is less than one half? And I want to hear your thought process."

Now his eyes went to the ceiling. "I would start with a simple example, say ten for the denominator." He smiled and looked at her. "The numerator couldn't be five because that would be ½, so four would generate the largest fraction, 4/10 or 0.4."

She nodded.

"Using this logic, I would choose 10,000 for

the denominator and 4,999 for the numerator for 4,999/10,000 or 0.4999." He rubbed his chin. Something wasn't right.

"Yes, that's what AI would have concluded too, although in much less time." She nodded with a sly smile, as if she knew he was still thinking about the problem.

"I would then use 9,999 for the denominator for 4,999/9,999." He checked the calculator on his glasses and saw the fraction was slightly higher than his previous answer. "So, .49995."

"That's right. That intuition to push makes humans human," she said. "Without specific training, AI would have confidently given the wrong answer. It's a well-known problem called AI hallucination."

"Point made," he mumbled to himself.

"Getting back to your job, you'll have free rein to observe everything happening in the lab. Walk around, talk to the researchers, and then give me your thoughts." She paused and waited for him to say something.

"What are you looking for?" he said. Surely, she had some idea.

"If I knew, then I wouldn't need you." She paused again, but he had no more questions. She stared into his eyes, which sent a shiver down his back. "There is one condition. No Dreamland or other drugs that could cloud your perception."

He didn't like this stipulation or anything that infringed on his personal rights. Doing his self-improvement work for the government had no such preconditions.

She glanced away. "I know salary isn't important to you, but I'll pay double what you currently earn. As my representative, you will wield a powerful influence."

Interesting. He would no longer be the charity case younger brother. He would have everyone's respect, including Mae's. "Let me think about it."

"Sure." Anni sat up straight. "We have a saying: Make easy decisions, lead a hard life. Make hard decisions, lead an easy life."

Michael stared at her. Making easy choices had defined his earlier life, one he wanted to change. Coming to California and working for Wendell were hard decisions. So was asking Mae out. But they hadn't led to an easy life, at least not yet. "I'll keep that in mind."

After the call, Michael took a Dreamland pill and waited for the effects. If he accepted her offer, it would be a long time before he had another. He asked himself if making hard decisions, like working for Anni instead of the government, would ultimately lead to a more fulfilled, easier life.

Yes, it would, came the singsong female voice of optimism.

No, it wouldn't, came his old friend, the monkey voice. *More work and risk that would end in failure.*

He had followed his monkey voice for most of his life, avoiding uncomfortable or vulnerable situations. He was like a hermit crab that had grown cramped in his shell but was too fearful to move to a larger one because of the risks. His monkey voice had always found reasons not to leave the shell and take the risks. However, now he had an alternative— the voice of optimism and possibilities.

CHAPTER EIGHT: PRESIDENT JOHN DOUGLAS

President John Douglas stood up from the Resolute desk in response to a knock at his door. The job of president was one of non-stop meetings. "Come in," he called.

Jamie Brown, his chief of staff, entered. "Good morning, Mr. President." Silver-haired and short, today, she wore an indigo skirt that went down to her black shoes, a white blouse, and a red scarf around her neck.

They were old friends from the army, starting in the same plebe class at West Point. She had spent thirty-two years in the military and become the first female five-star general. He had left after twenty years—becoming one of the youngest colonels ever —to run and become governor of Florida. Twelve years later, he had won the presidential election under the banner of law and order.

"Good morning, Jamie." He walked towards

the couch against the wall and indicated that she should take the adjacent chair. Before sitting, he caught his reflection on the large monitor above the couch. Even though he was sixty-one with gray hair, his six-foot-five muscular frame and steely blue eyes still made him an imposing figure.

"What's the news from Taiwan?" he said, falling back onto the couch. He frowned and shook his head, wondering what had happened to their sure bet.

"Not good. The Taiwanese referendum on independence or joining China is now uncertain due to government scandals."

He continued shaking his head, waiting for more bad news.

"Vice President Chen-wen was just accused of accepting bribes from a billionaire real estate developer for land purchases and permit approvals."

"It seems like everyone is corrupt." He shot his cuffs.

"We had thought the government was relatively clean." Jamie patted down her skirt. "But in the last two weeks, any dirt on any leader has been uncovered."

"This could be a major political blackeye." Under his leadership of projecting strength, the U.S. had ballooned its military presence in Taiwan. Now, he was at risk of a forced withdrawal. "What're our options?"

"Through our Taiwanese affiliates, increase FUD advertising of China's lurch to authoritarianism."

"Yup," he said. "Given the recent purges in the Chinese Politburo, President Xu now has unchallenged power."

"We can use our AI to design new marketing campaigns to scare the Taiwanese citizens away from China," Jaimie said, raising one side of her mouth.

"Do it." He crossed his arms and frowned. "Speaking of AI, how's the Berkeley AI antiterrorism prototype coming along?"

"Last week, the FBI interviewed twenty high-risk individuals and arrested fifteen of them."

"That's great news," he said, "and proves the value of my National Security Act to fight domestic terrorism."

"The data privacy advocates still scream," she said, "but each arrest makes the public and courts less sympathetic to their calls."

"What does Berkeley AI say about my reelection prospects?" He felt torn using the system in this unapproved way, but he needed to win reelection, and, in this case, the means justified the ends.

"Your favorability rating is forty-five percent versus the average public poll of fifty-three." She looked him squarely in the eyes, as if to gauge his reaction.

"Why's the AI number lower?" He frowned.

"When your name is mentioned, people's faces show more ambivalence than in the past. The polls don't yet reflect this softness in support."

He stood, clasped his hands behind his back, and walked to the middle of the room, forcing Jamie to twist her body and crane her neck.

"Fine. Launch the Berkeley AI reelection marketing assessment program." This would measure campaign effectiveness based on facial readings from users' glasses. People showed their emotions on their faces, and their glasses would capture it.

"Yes, sir." Jaime stood and approached him. "If we're done with this topic, I have a recent development."

He nodded, then pulled back his arms to stretch his shoulders. He had lost some of his dexterity due to the demands of his job, a lack of exercise, and the march of time.

"The CDC just notified us of a rare disease with symptoms like advanced dementia. Patients are almost brain dead, barely responding to stimulus."

"How many?"

"Over two thousand, with about three hundred new cases each day." She sighed. "It's completely random across all demographics and geographies, with no two cases in the same spot."

"What's the cause?" This didn't sound like a virus or bacteria with local transmission.

"Unknown. Brain scans show no abnormalities."

Victims were almost brain dead, but there weren't brain abnormalities? He'd never heard of anything like this. "Is the spread accelerating?"

"It doesn't appear to be."

He did some quick calculations on his glasses. The annual chance of catching the disease was about three in ten thousand. "Is it worldwide?"

"Yes. It seems to strike randomly everywhere."

If this applied worldwide, then total daily cases would be thirty times higher than the US or about nine thousand cases per day, which was significant. "What are the early symptoms?"

"Sleepiness." She shook her head. "They go to bed and eight hours later, they're zombies."

"Extremely virulent. What's the recovery

rate?"

"Zero to date." She glanced around the room as if the disease might be hiding somewhere nearby.

"We need answers. Once news of this breaks, it'll scare everyone." He gathered his thoughts. This was like no known pandemic. "What is it? How's it transmitted? What're the vaccines and treatments? I need answers."

CHAPTER NINE: NEW JOB

Michael accepted Anni's offer and got a large corner office. His fancy desk sat in front of a window that overlooked the Campanile. On the opposite wall was a doorway that led to a private state-of-the-art VR room. His office door was in the middle of one side wall, and against the other was a small conference table with four swivel chairs.

It was the end of September, and after less than one month in California, he was on his third job.

While sitting at his desk, waiting for Anni's call for his job orientation, he watched the coverage of a new disease called the sleeping sickness. A young woman in a white nightgown sat in her hospital bed, staring straight ahead, sipping a cup through a straw. A middle-aged reporter in a blue suit stood beside her.

He touched her shoulder. "Ms. Robinson."

She slowly looked up, then returned to

looking straight ahead.

"Although she may react to stimuli," the reporter said, "she quickly returns to a stupefied state and can only perform basic functions like chewing, drinking, or blinking."

The camera zoomed in on the reporter. "The CDC believes the disease is psychological since they've uncovered no physical brain abnormalities. Researchers previously linked this vegetative coma state to depression and catatonia, but it was extremely rare. Now, it's everywhere, and there's no known defense or treatment."

Michael's glasses notified him he had an incoming call from Anni, so he accepted. She stood in a virtual forest on a dirt trail that had a stream running alongside it.

"Please go to the VR room," she said.

His glasses became transparent. He walked to the door on the far side and entered his VR room. It lit up as he walked on the spongy floor to the center of the white circular room. A two-foot-wide gray band ran along the wall at waist height. Above and below this were multiple pieces of hardware like cameras, speakers, and air vents.

The room went dark. Then his glasses displayed Anni standing next to him in a forest. He heard the stream flowing over stones and smelled a rich pine scent.

"I prefer meetings where I can commune with nature and get some exercise." She turned and walked down the path. Everything appeared so real. When she went around a bend, he raced to catch up on the spongy ground underfoot. The rotating VR floor and imagery simulated his chase.

When he caught up to her, she thanked him for coming, and then said, "Let me start by telling you a bit about myself. I'm thirty-eight and have worked in my family's business for about ten years. I went to Peking University and majored in computer science and business administration. My motto is work hard, play hard."

With her succinct personal summary, he wondered if their conversations would become more formal. However, the outdoor setting contradicted this.

"I believe in maximizing the wellbeing in society," she continued, "and will use my wealth and power to accomplish it. Some call it effective altruism."

She probably donated tens or hundreds of millions of dollars every year. *Maybe your philosophy could be called impotent altruism*, his monkey voice sneered.

You give what you can, said the sweet internal voice. *Your heart is in the right place.*

He shook his head, then listened to the chirping birds and tried to find them among the nearby branches and leaves. A cool breeze rustled the trees, making it difficult to locate anything. He took a deep breath through his nose and smelled the earthy pine, like after a rain shower. Bringing his attention back, he asked, "What positive impacts have you made?"

"Not much, but I've made donations to charities trying to improve the lives of everyday people and advised some political leaders." She spun around and frowned. "I'm still young but have big plans."

Michael nodded. She had the world at her feet. What did she see in him?

"What about you?" she asked. "What do you want from life?"

What do I want from life? He thought of his brother. "Respect."

"Would you embrace the responsibilities that came with it?" She studied his face.

"I don't know." Would he change his life trajectory, leaving the crowded slow lane and moving to the uncongested fast one? "But maybe, yes."

His answer surprised him, yet it was true. Where did this new desire to succeed come from?

He glanced at Anni, who was still staring at him intensely. He was the first to look away. Then she turned, and they continued along the soft, mulchy trail.

"In China, we have a common prosperity campaign." Anni glanced at him but continued walking. "However, in most other countries, leaders work to safeguard the interests of the powerful to the detriment of everyday citizens."

"Is China really that different?" he asked. Her faith in common prosperity sounded idealistic. "It's an autocracy where the powerful few receive a disproportionate share of the rewards."

"True, but that's changing with President Xu," she said. "It's amazing what one good person in power can do."

Skeptical, he didn't reply. They rounded another bend and came to a pond covered by green lily pads with stalks of white flowers.

"I've often wondered if an outsider would be the best country leader," she continued.

"Unlikely." Even though Michael had done this when he had installed the factory worker as leader of Croat, Conquest was just a game, not the real world. He bent down, picked up an out-of-place rock, and tossed it into the pond, creating ripples that jiggled the lily pads. "If he had the capabilities and accepted the challenge, then he'd just pick up the behaviors of other leaders."

"Possibly," she said, studying his face, "which is why finding the right candidate is critical."

He ignored her and tossed a larger rock into the water, creating a bigger wake. The VR room anticipated his next moves and acted to enable them. It reminded him of a magician forcing a card on an unsuspecting volunteer from the audience. Both things looked like magic.

"Anyway, coming back to your job, I want you to observe all the research taking place at the lab and give me your perspective. I also want access to the data feed of your glasses."

He nodded. With the cameras and microphones in his glasses, Anni could experience his life as he did and see his facial reactions. However, given all her other responsibilities, she wouldn't have time for this. He didn't like sharing his personal data, but courts had ruled that while at work, companies had rights to their employee's data, reasoning they paid for it. "I'll authorize it today."

"Good." She reached down, grabbed a flat stone, and skipped it across the water. "I enjoyed our discussion and will think about what you said. Goodbye for now, Michael."

Michael crossed his arms. He wondered which of his answers she was going to think about. His glasses became transparent, and the room lit up. In front of him, on the floor against the wall, lay two rocks, the ones he had thrown in the simulation. A mechanical arm grabbed them and then receded behind the gray band where other VR physical props stood on shelves.

Turning around, he walked towards the outline of a door that popped open. This enhanced VR experience was indistinguishable from real life.

He entered his main office, the VR door closing behind him. He was still thinking about the engineering behind the simulation when his mind suddenly shifted to Anni's idea about elevating a common man to power. It was impossible, but he had the impression she was thinking of him.

There was no time like the present to start his new job. He left his office and headed towards Charlie's lab where the dark matter communication research took place. He went up one flight of stairs, across an enclosed glass-walled bridge to another building, down four flights of stairs, then through a narrow, dingy basement hallway to a lab door that slid open. Given the convoluted logistics, he could understand why Wendell wanted his team moved to a modern new building.

He walked into the lab. It looked like two miniature versions of the fifth-force pillars used to measure dark matter in volunteers. However, here, each steel fifth-force pillar was only five feet tall and a foot in diameter. In the center of each cluster stood a glass cube sitting on a pedestal. Charlie examined one cube while a technician tinkered with the other. Against the far wall were two long, waist-high metal cabinets.

Charlie looked up, smiled, and walked over. "We're just about to test a communication between Earth and Alpha Centauri. There are just some final adjustments for the receiver."

"Really?" Michael said.

Charlie nodded towards the closest pillars. "The transmitter cluster opens a protrusion point at a spot near Alpha Centauri and sends signals." He pointed at the other pillars. "The receiver cluster opens a protrusion point at exactly the same spot and receives the signals."

"Really?" Given the incredible distance and changing relative position, it seemed impossible.

"It would be impossible to do it in normal space." Charlie smirked and placed his hands over his paunch belly. "Instead, we iterate through the dark matter universe."

"How?" Michael asked, impressed but confused.

"Through iterations. It's like hopscotching through the universe." Charlie twisted his torso and brought a hand near his ear, then he launched his hand forward. "It's like throwing a dart towards a target a mile away, walking to where it landed, and throwing it again. Each throw gets you closer until you finally hit the bullseye. Those final coordinates stay the same because of their link in the fourth dimension."

The technician stepped away from the receiver and gave Charlie a thumbs up.

Michael watched as a nickel-sized gray sphere opened in each cube. This would carry the transmission over four light years out and back. "Can I see the transmission?"

"Sure."

His glasses darkened, then displayed two square windows, side by side. In the middle of each square was a black horizontal line with a continuous stream of identical short square bumps above and below it.

"The left is the transmission sent to Alpha Centauri, and the right is the one received. They're the same, and they happen simultaneously, just like entangled particles."

"What would someone see at that spot in Alpha Centauri?"

"In our normal three-dimensional universe, you'd see pulses of energy like flashes of light. In the fourth dimension, you wouldn't see anything of the transmission, only the grays of dark matter, unless, of course, there was intelligent life."

Michael watched the transmission for a few minutes, then switched back to the room view. Charlie was talking with the technician.

"Thanks, Charlie," Michael said. Charlie gave a quick wave but didn't look at him.

***

That night after work, Michael went to his VR chair at home to play Conquest. His ambassador approached him. She was a dapper but wizened white-haired woman, standing almost six-feet tall. Her melodious voice was pleasant for soothing foreign leaders.

"Darbar called us a failed authoritarian state and is now working with other countries to isolate us."

"Tell me about Darbar." He only knew the country was on the other side of the largest ocean.

"A rival of ours, with a powerful military and economy."

"What about the government?"

"It's a strong, democratic government that's heavily influenced by money and power." Her eyebrows raised. "Elections take place every six years, with the next one occurring in eighteen months."

"What about their society?"

"A very divided and skeptical populace. Few social issues like immigration, the role of government, taxes, and programs for the poor garner over sixty percent agreement." She drummed her fingers together. "Despite Darbar's prosperity, crime plagues poor neighborhoods and inequality is rampant; the bottom half of the population has little wealth."

It surprised him that Darbar would criticize anyone. "Why are they trying to isolate us?"

"Darbar views us as a competitor and a threat to their dominant world position."

"Do any of their leaders support us?" If so, he could contact them.

"No. We're the common boogeyman."

"Would any of their leaders support us with the right incentives, like money?" He couldn't invade and install a new leader like he'd done in Croat. Darbar was too strong, and the government was too stable.

"There's one woman who has business interests in Acacia and might work with us."

"Reach out to her." As ruler of Acacia, he could convince her to work with him.

The throne room background dulled. Game

time advanced a week.

His ambassador reappeared in the restored throne room. "The woman from Darbar has agreed to meet with you, but it must be in person in a mutually agreed country."

"Why in person?" The game had remote communications.

"She wants to gauge your sincerity. This was a non-negotiable requirement."

A third-party country would be needed; she couldn't come to Acacia for political reasons, and he wouldn't go to Darbar for security concerns. Should he pursue this? He could wait for a different opportunity. Confidence flowed through him, overwhelming his caution. "All right. Make the arrangements."

Game time moved forward another week.

"Arrangements have been made for you to meet in Croat in ten days," said the ambassador. "Would you still like to go?"

"Yes." He was committed and would enjoy seeing the world. Although logical, something felt off. Maybe it was the unfamiliarity of a new environment. He ignored his uneasiness, his self-confidence returning.

The throne room background dulled. Game time moved forward ten more days. He reappeared in a train cabin. Out the window, the country landscape rushed by. Cows wandered in pastures; crops grew in fields, and farmhouses dotted the land. Suddenly, the room exploded in a bright burst, then everything went black.

"Croat terrorists who were in the prior government bombed your train and killed you," said the narrator. "Upon your return, you'll be a ship captain."

He removed his glasses and came back to his family room. A smile crept across his face. Well, it'd been a good run, but he'd gotten cocky. Arrogance was truly the mother of all folly. His monkey voice of self-doubt and moderation had served a purpose.

CHAPTER TEN: MEDIA CAMPAIGN

Michael stood in his office VR room, waiting for the start of his meeting with Anni. He'd been in his new job for one week, observing activities in the lab but not providing any insights. Anni would've seen his highlights from the AI filters of the raw data from his glasses. Five workdays condensed into a twenty-minute summary.

Michael ran through his intuitive insights that had no obvious correlation to observations. One, their dark matter research would transform the world in ways unforeseen, and not necessarily for the good. Two, although not part of their current research, the sleeping sickness bore a connection to dark matter.

His glasses darkened, transporting him into the same throne room that the Conquest VR game used. Instead of sitting on his throne, he was standing beside it, and instead of his four counselors standing in front of him, there was only Anni.

"Good afternoon." Anni walked to the front of

the platform, smiling at his confusion.

"Wha . . . what's this?" he sputtered.

"I'm quite proud of this." She pointed behind him. "Look."

He turned around and saw a large, colored, two-dimensional map of the fictional world of Conquest. He picked out Acacia, his country in green on the coast. His neighbor, Croat, was pale green. Other countries in greens, pinks, and reds surrounded them. Across the blue ocean was Darbar in red.

"One of my family's companies produced Conquest." She smiled self-consciously and ran her fingers through her long black hair, tucking it behind her ears. If he didn't know better, he'd say she was nervous.

"It's a hell of a game," he said.

"It turns out you're one of the best players." She walked onto the platform and stood behind the throne.

Was she spying on him, or did she just track all the top players? How could a family company come from nowhere and build this sophisticated game with its lifelike graphics and intelligent interactions? How could she be involved?

"Cat got your tongue?" She smirked.

"No." He shook his head. "I'm just amazed."

"We built the game to crowdsource ideas for government." She reached across the throne and grabbed his hand. It felt real, even though it must be a mechanical hand in the VR room. "We're building a huge interactive data set of what works and what fails in government."

"Huh."

"Politics is a complex system, but AI can model and optimize it, from getting elected, to developing policies, passing legislation, and securing re-election."

It sounded like AI had its tentacles into everything.

"It turns out you have what it takes to be a successful politician." She squeezed his hand.

"What are you talking about?" He broke her grip and brought his hands to his hips.

Anni marched around the throne, grabbed his shoulders, and forced him to look at her squarely in the eyes. "You've got the right stuff."

"I only played a game." He stepped back, and her hands fell to her side. He was just a gamer. Then he heard his inner, self-confident, sweet voice. *You're much more than just a gamer.*

"It's a very sophisticated game," Anni continued, "picking out players with the greatest political leadership potential in the same way that flight simulators pick out the best pilots."

Interesting analogy. "Even if it's true, so what?"

"Watch this." She pointed towards the back wall.

Instead of the world map, he saw himself standing with a white long-sleeved shirt and hands in the front pockets of blue jeans. Despite a five o'clock shadow, he looked quite good.

"My name is Michael Knightsbridge," said the video actor on the large screen. "Like most of you, I'm disgusted by our politics and politicians. Corruption is pervasive. Before wildfires devastated California, the insurance industry wrote legislation to protect their profits and increase our costs. They paid one hundred million dollars to California politicians for their support."

The screen on the back wall showed the names of fifty politicians, their votes on insurance laws, the money they received, and the source of the funds. At the top of the list was the governor, who'd received fifty million dollars from five organizations.

Michael's image reappeared. "We need to hold corrupt politicians accountable. I commit to you to continue this good fight. If you want to help, please donate to our cause." A large blue donation button appeared at the bottom of the wall.

"What do you think?" Anni asked.

Although he never recorded it, the video looked completely authentic, with no signs of computer animations. "How did you create it?"

"With the same technology used to produce Conquest."

He nodded, comparing the realism of the video to Conquest. "Is the video true?"

"Unfortunately, yes." She crossed her arms and hugged herself. "These elected officials have betrayed the trust of the people."

He detested dishonesty, particularly by people who were in positions of public trust. "Why do you care?"

"I want government to work for the benefit of the people rather than to maximize wealth for powerful special interests. I hope to accomplish this by surfacing the political corruption to wake people up and dislodge them from their stupor of inaction." Her jaw clenched and her fists tightened. "I'm doing this in my home country and now wish to do it in my adopted one."

"Have you always felt this way?" Michael had pegged her as a businesswoman, but now she sounded more like a zealot for social change. He wondered if this came from her Buddhist upbringing or if it was something else.

"No. I had an awakening." She studied him intently. "It came from a personal crisis that I don't wish to get into right now."

"All right. Why me?" Even though he might have political talent, he wasn't exactly a go-getter. He'd never been the type to seize opportunities or hunt for power.

"Because you have the potential, and we're already working together." She pointed at him. "You're in the right place at the right time."

Michael had never been in the right place at the right time. That was always Wendell. It was a pleasant change, but didn't mean it was something he wanted. "What would I need to do?"

"I can answer that." A Hispanic woman with a lavender low-neck blouse and black slacks walked towards them down the throne room hallway. The royal blue curtains partially covering tall windows fluttered in the gentle breeze. He watched her approach. She had round hips, a thin face, soft brown eyes, and curly black hair that fell to her shoulders. She was a few inches shorter than him but looked about his age.

"This is Marie Sanchez," Anni said as Marie stepped onto the platform, "my VP of Marketing."

"Pleased to meet you, Michael." She shook his hand firmly while he nodded dumbly. "And you don't need to do anything." She flashed a wide smile, displaying perfect white teeth. "Just give me the okay to distribute this video. If it falls on deaf ears, then we're done. If it generates interest, then we'll produce more."

"What do you think this will accomplish?" Even if he caught corrupt politicians taking bribes, they could escape scandal by stonewalling investigations or asking forgiveness. Best case, others would replace them, but these new politicians would likely adopt the same behaviors since the system enabled it.

"Bring true transparency and accountability to the political process so that it works for the people."

He wasn't sure this accountability would lead to better outcomes, but it might. He rubbed his chin and stared down the hallway. "What's the downside?"

"Publicity." Marie shrugged. "Some people will like and respect you. Others not so much."

There was that *respect* word again. It was what he'd said he wanted. But this was completely out of character for him. Politicians and lobbyists would be furious if they made that data public, but, honestly, he'd relish that; he'd have the respect of ordinary people like himself. He wondered what Wendell would think, but it didn't matter.

"Can I see your source documentation?" He

couldn't get behind this if the sources were inaccurate or questionable.

The governor's name appeared on the back wall. Below it flashed financial transactions, highlighting money flows from insurance companies to third parties to lobbyists and finally to the governor. Next came his voting record, where he approved all pro-insurance bills and vetoed the anti-insurance ones.

"What's AB 2594, Fire Insurance?" He asked. The governor had vetoed this bill. The screen showed.

AB 2594 would allow policyholders to sue if their insurance company had underinsured a property by twenty percent or more. Existing law prevents lawsuits even though insurers stipulate the coverage amounts.

Michael asked about a couple of other bills and could see the insurance industry was on the opposite side of the consumer.

"Bring up the ten-million-dollar payment to the governor for his veto of AB 2594," Marie said.

Michael studied the screen. Although he was no expert, he could understand the money flow, which meant anyone could. "How did you get this?"

"It's mostly public via the Political Information Act," Anni said. "Politicians like the governor camouflage it and don't think anyone can piece together a comprehensive story."

"But even if we have it, where's the quid pro quo?" Receiving donations from friends who supported you was completely legal. They needed proof of buying votes.

The screen displayed a message sent from the governor's chief of staff to the industry lobbyist. *We'll need ten million dollars for AB 2594.*

"Are the source documents beyond reproach?" he asked. If so, then it would be an open-and-closed case.

"Yes," Anni said. "Are you in?"

Should he, or shouldn't he? Did he want to get involved or remain on the sidelines? *Of course, you're going to do this,* said his sweet, female inner voice. Again, there was no monkey voice of doubt. This was the push he needed. "I'm in."

"Excellent." Annie's eyes seemed to sparkle. "We're launching now."

"Really?" he said, but the meeting ended. He never got an answer.

The Conquest disclosure and his new political video had confounded him so much that he'd forgotten to mention his dark matter insights. He sent her a quick summary and said they could discuss it next time they met.

***

The next day, Mae dropped by his office.

"I saw your video in my morning news summary." She sauntered over to his desk, not showing any hesitation or awkwardness.

"Really?" Given the billions of videos created each day, it seemed unlikely that anyone he knew would have already come across his. Even if Anni had paid big advertising dollars for general placements, it took millions of views before it could reach personal news summaries.

"Mind if I sit?"

"Ah, sure." If one of her search criteria was his name, then the video might have bubbled to the top, but that seemed unlikely.

She nodded, and a smile slowly broke across her face. Then she leaned back in the chair, crossed her legs, and rubbed her necklace below her ear. "Was the video true?"

"Yes."

"Good, because I made a donation and forwarded it to my friends."

"Thanks."

"How did you produce it?" Mae tapped the side of her chin.

"A friend of mine is in marketing, and she helped me put it together." If asked, he would mention Marie, but not Anni, who had a foot in the lab, the video, Conquest, and whatever else.

"It was one hell of a video exposé." She leaned forward, placing her hands on his desk and catching his eye. "It's a side of you I hadn't seen before."

If he didn't know better, he'd say she was flirting. Her AER reading on his glasses showed a strong interest in him. Did he have a shot with her? Last time, he'd badly misread the situation. He wouldn't make the same mistake twice, so he remained silent. There was a knock on his door.

"Well, see you around." She seemed slightly disappointed but gave him a tight-lipped smile and stood.

"Thanks for stopping by." He'd never understood women, and this encounter just reinforced the point. Looking at the door, he said, "Come in."

Charlie entered, then stepped aside to let Mae leave. He had seen the video too. Over the next few hours, more people dropped by his office or called him to say they had seen the video. Even Wendell came by to ask how he'd created it, although he expressed no opinion about the message itself and hadn't donated.

In the afternoon, he had a follow-up meeting with Anni and Marie in the VR room.

This time, they met in a beautiful virtual library. Three levels of colorful, leather-bound books lined the walls. Three stained glass windows at the second level provided natural light. Round crystal chandeliers hung from the painted ceiling that showed eight scenes from Buddha's life.

He walked beside the women to the center of the room and sat in one of the leather easy chairs.

"The video results are excellent." Marie smiled as her fingers rapped nervously on the armrest. "Almost fifty million views over the past twenty-four hours."

"How?" He could understand having those numbers for a highly anticipated movie trailer or music video from a famous artist, but he was a nobody, and his video wasn't entertainment.

"We piggybacked on the popularity of Conquest," Marie said.

"Really?" He frowned. "Show me."

He heard a sound of movement and looked up to see a three-sided object descend from the ceiling on a cable. Roughly six feet above the ground, it stopped. One side faced him, having a picture frame of the Conquest throne room with the four advisors.

"One of our top players in Conquest has uncovered real-world political corruption in California, like what you face in Acacia. If you'd like to see what he found, then click the link." A red oval button appeared over the throne room.

"This went to every Conquest player after they either reached the next level or failed," Marie said as the monitors rose. "Many of these players viewed your video and forwarded it to their friends. The viral effect was spectacular."

He shook his head. Yesterday, he was a complete unknown. Today, he was famous, a celebrity.

"We've received tens of millions of dollars in donations." Marie interlocked her fingers and stretched her arms towards him. "How does it make you feel?"

"Confused." But it was more than that. "People treated me like a celebrity today, but I really haven't done anything."

"That's always the case when a person first comes under the spotlight." Marie stood with her hands behind her back.

"People fawned over me like I was something special." Although the attention was undeserved, since he'd done nothing, he still enjoyed it.

"That's not unusual." Marie composed her face. "Many people adore the celebrity's status but not the person himself. Never confuse the two."

This would explain his uneasiness. His

celebrity status was manufactured, and the attention was artificial and insincere.

"I think we should produce another video." Marie stared at him with a newfound intensity that drew him in.

"What about?" He was so caught up with the success of his first video that he'd forgotten about their plan to produce more if they proved effective.

"There are many options," she said, drubbing her fingers together. "But I think water."

"Water?" California had a water shortage, which forced most citizens to take brief showers and caused neighborhood lawns to turn brown. However, it didn't seem like a galvanizing issue.

"Yes. The agricultural lobbyists are paying politicians to protect their water rights, so they pay almost nothing while planting thirsty crops like almonds."

"So what?" Michael shrugged.

"Because politicians aren't telling the citizens the truth. Residential water rationing won't make a difference since it only accounts for twenty percent of water usage compared to eighty percent for agriculture. On top of that, residential unit costs will need to rise to make up for the lower usage."

He stood and stared at one of the stained-glass windows that depicted a small farm on a knoll.

Politicians had claimed everyone needed to make sacrifices. They hadn't said residents would pay higher rates and receive less water.

"The problem is that politicians have over-promised water to users." Marie stood and joined him. "We have a water allocation problem, but politicians prefer to deflect and blame nature for a draught. The video will make these points while you walk in new, industrial almond orchards planted in the SoCal desert."

"So, again, special interests buying politicians." He eyed her up and down. "Will it really motivate people to get involved?"

"We'll see." She paused for a few seconds. "We'll launch it in a few days. Do you want to record it, or should we, with our technology?"

"What's the difference?" He felt warmth from Marie's body near his, but that was psychosomatic. Physically, he was alone in a VR room.

"Your recording won't be as good, but maybe you'll take pride in doing it yourself."

"You do it." Pride in producing an inferior product didn't interest him.

Marie nodded like he'd given the correct answer. "We'll also use one-to-one targeting of the videos."

"What's that?"

"Providing the right video to each consumer based on his or her profile. This increases the likelihood of viewing, donating, and sharing." Marie grinned. "We wouldn't want to send our agricultural video to the Central Valley."

He nodded, recognizing she understood the state. "Where do you live?"

"San Francisco."

"Maybe next time we can meet in person." He turned and shook her hand.

"That's a fine idea." She grasped his hand with both of hers.

He glanced down at Anni, who was looking at the ceiling. He followed her gaze. "What're you looking at?"

"The picture of Buddha under the Bodhi tree." She looked at him. "Where he attained enlightenment or bodhi, the Buddhist term."

The picture was nice, but so were the others. "Why?"

"It speaks to me." She exhaled deeply and stood. "Bodhi means to wake up and gain consciousness."

He studied her face. There was something else there. Something more she wasn't telling him. What had started as research into dark matter and consciousness had now moved into politics. Had this always been her ultimate plan? He decided not to pursue it, at least for now.

CHAPTER ELEVEN: SLEEPING SICKNESS

Michael arrived early to the lab because a subject with the sleeping sickness would have a dark matter assessment. Mae was already there, talking with the new coordinator, who was in her early twenties and dressed in a white lab jacket.

"I saw your new post on water," Mae said, after wrapping up her other conversation and coming over. She had a lopsided grin. "Give them hell, Mikey."

He flinched at his childhood nickname; the one Wendell had used to torment him. Was there condescension in her voice, or was she playing with him? He spun around and walked away.

A few minutes later, the door slid open, and a father, followed by a mother, pushed their teenage girl in a wheelchair into the white rectangular room. The coordinator jumped up and led them to the elevated platform where the parents lifted their girl and placed her on the lab chair.

Michael walked to the front of the platform in front of the girl. She stared straight ahead and didn't seem to notice him. It reminded him of his dad lying on the hospital bed on life support after his brain aneurysm had ruptured. The body lived, but the essence of life had fled. He would look the same way if his aneurysm ever burst.

The coordinator answered a few questions from the parents, and then everyone stepped back beyond the fifth-force pillars. A minute later, the field surrounded the girl.

Michael switched his glasses to the dark matter data feed. It was black, so he waited for the image to appear.

"Thanks for coming in," the coordinator said after about a minute.

His glasses still displayed darkness, so he switched to normal viewing mode. The parents were already wheeling their daughter out of the room. He turned around. Mae's eyes were wide.

He sidled up to her and whispered, "Where's her globe?"

"I don't know." Her eyes strayed across the room. "All the equipment operated properly."

"Have you seen this void before?"

"Only with brain-dead subjects, but her brain is normal." She studied him.

"Did the sleeping sickness cause this?" he asked slowly.

"It could be, which would explain why no traditional tools have uncovered the disease."

A weird idea struck him. The brain was alive. Did this imply dark matter lived also? Michael turned and headed towards the door. "I need to talk to Frank."

"Wait. Why?" Mae trotted up beside him.

"I have an idea."

Michael marched into Frank's lab, with Mae following behind. In the center of the room was a large metal sphere resting on a stand, with eight cylindrical spokes radiating from its equator, each about ten feet long. Frank stood under one spoke, examining the insides of an open panel.

"Frank," Michael said, walking towards him.

"Yes." Frank glanced up and rubbed his brown hair that was standing on end, his eyebrows furrowed in frustration.

"I'm sorry to bother you, but I had a question that couldn't wait," Michael blurted.

"What is it?" Frank sighed.

"Have you discovered life in dark matter?"

"What?" He took a deep breath and stared at Michael. "No. I'm cataloguing the types of dark matter and their properties."

"Like a pure chemist, but not a biochemist."

"What are you getting at?"

"I think a person's dark matter bundle is alive."

"That's an interesting hypothesis." He rubbed his chin and stared past Michael, his annoyance gone, his curiosity obviously piqued.

"Where did this insight come from?" Mae asked, a bit out of breath from chasing Michael.

"When I took part in the dark matter experiment, I experienced something I now believe showed life." Michael closed his eyes, trying to remember the exact feeling. "It was like the gray walls were closing in and a living part of me was being pulled out, making some new connection."

"You never mentioned this." Mae tilted her head.

"No. I focused on the closing walls and didn't think my abstract feeling was worth mentioning."

"Makes sense since a feeling doesn't make a truth," Frank said.

"How could we prove the bundle was alive or

not?" Michael glanced back and forth between the two scientists.

"A general definition of life," Mae said encouragingly, "is any system capable of performing functions such as eating, moving, reproducing, and responding to external stimuli."

"That's the definition in our physical world." Michael stared into the distance. "But it doesn't apply to something we can't see or touch."

"I'm not much help here," Frank said after a few seconds of silence. He turned towards his equipment. "I need to get back to my work. Let me know what you come up with."

"What definition would apply?" Mae pulled him towards the door.

"I'm not sure." He covered his mouth with a hand and rubbed his cheeks with his thumb and fingers.

"Let's think about the problem separately," Mae said, after about a minute of silence. "And brainstorm later."

He returned to his office and scrolled through a few hundred images of dark matter bundles, hoping for some insight but got nothing. How would a child check if something was alive? She would prod it with a stick and look for a reaction. Perhaps there was a similar approach. He frowned, thinking the stick sometimes hurt the living object.

After two hours of independent thinking, they reconvened and brainstormed some ideas for another couple of hours. Then Mae wrote a summary that she sent to Wendell. He asked them to meet with him at 5:00 pm.

Given a half-hour break, Michael went to his office to relax, but when he arrived, he received an audio call from Anni.

After some pleasantries, she asked, "What did you observe from the girl with the sleeping sickness this morning?"

"She didn't have a dark matter bundle." He told her about the test.

"Your early intuition about a connection between the sleeping sickness and dark matter was correct." She paused. "Any idea what happened to her dark matter bundle?"

"No." He exhaled deeply. "But I believe it was a living thing that died."

"Hmm." She seemed distracted.

He told her about his visit with Frank, the brainstorming with Mae, and their recommendations for Wendell. She gave him some suggestions.

"We're meeting with Wendell in," he checked the time, "five minutes."

"Good. I'll let you go and pursue some ideas here. Talk to you later." She disconnected without waiting for his response.

He stared out the window, wondering what ideas she planned to pursue. Then, he ambled over to Wendell's office and joined Mae and Wendell at his desk.

"So, you believe a person's dark matter bundle is alive and the sleeping sickness kills it like a virus kills a healthy organism," Wendell said. "You propose two research projects to understand how the bundle lives. If successful, future projects will identify how to protect them from the sleeping sickness."

Michael and Mae nodded.

"Why do you think the bundles are alive?" Wendell asked.

"First, they pulse with energy and have more complexity than the dark matter associated with suns and planets that give galaxies their shape," Mae said. "It's just like the difference between biological life and inorganic materials in our universe. There're both composed of molecules, but life has much more complexity."

Wendell frowned, looking unconvinced by Mae's reasoning. "There could be other explanations."

"I also sensed something alive during the experiment on my bundle," Michael said, remembering his immersion in the gray fog. "It's hard to describe, but there was a presence."

Wendell studied them, and then his mouth twitched. "Let's assume you're right. What're your research proposals?"

"For my lab, I want our volunteers to wear an EEG cap so we can measure their brain oscillatory activity and correlate it with the bundles. My hypothesis is certain brain waves would act like an external stimulus and affect dark matter bundles."

"Those EEG caps aren't very accurate." Wendell leaned back in his chair. "However, they're noninvasive and easy to use. Go for it."

"My proposal is more complicated." Michael rubbed his chin. "It involves prodding the dark matter bundle of animal subjects and studying the effects."

"We've never done that."

"Frank is experimenting with the effects of fifth-force electromagnetic waves on dark matter." Mae flashed a smile. "We'll apply the same techniques to the bundles of intelligent animals."

"What animals?"

"Orangutans." Michael had researched what were the most intelligent, human-like animals.

Orangutans had nine billion cortical neurons compared with fifteen billion for humans.

Wendell stared at the ceiling, rubbing his chin.

Michael remembered what Anni had said, as well as his brother's Nobel Prize ambitions. "Other countries will pursue this work. We can either do it here or let others take the lead."

"Send me the specifications for the orangutans, including room requirements, cage sizes, and daily operational needs." Wendell jutted his jaw forward. "I'll decide after seeing it."

His ideas might move forward. In the past, Michael had learned not to give voice to them because they often fell on deaf ears. Ironically, in a more intimidating environment with brilliant scientists around, he'd jumped in and made connections that no one else saw. Between him and Anni, he had no concerns about getting the orangutan requirements.

The meeting ended, and he rose to leave.

"So, when did you become such a scientist?" Wendell asked, arching an eyebrow.

The question caught him by surprise. "I guess Mae's an excellent mentor."

Wendell frowned, obviously not satisfied by his answer.

Michael returned to his office, troubled by three thoughts. First, both Mae and Wendell assumed the sleeping sickness was like a virus, but Michael had a different, more radical idea. Life in the form of plants and animals often represented food for life further up the food chain. Were bundles from higher on the food chain preying on weaker ones? If so, then the sleeping sickness wasn't like a disease infecting a body, but a predator killing for nourishment.

His second uneasy thought came from his early intuition that their dark matter research would transform the world in ways unforeseen, and not necessarily for the good. Had their research created and unleashed this predator causing the sleeping sickness?

His third uneasy thought came from Wendell's question. When *had* he become such a scientist? Something in him was changing. He wasn't sure what.

CHAPTER TWELVE: SF TODAY INTERVIEW

"I received a request from San Francisco Today to interview with Paul Berry." Michael sat at his office desk using his glasses to speak to Anni. She was vacationing at Pantai Merah, Indonesia, sitting at a table on a bamboo deck with a pink sandy beach and aquamarine ocean behind her.

"Did you?" She raised her eyebrows.

"I'm scared I'm going to screw it up and look like an idiot." How was he going to speak eloquently by himself? He was famous because of his popular VR duplicate.

"You'll do fine. Just be yourself, not a politician."

"Do you really think so?" Anni had more

confidence in him than he had in himself.

"Absolutely."

A man in an orange flowery Hawaiian shirt walked by Anni, giving her a sidelong glance from head to waist. Michael almost said something, but the man moved on. Anni was a beautiful woman, but she seemed more like a sister.

"I hope you're right." Although he understood the issues and agreed with them, he hadn't come up with the messages or recorded the videos. He didn't deserve the credit.

"I am. I'll watch the show. Just shout if you need anything." Anni must have seen he remained unconvinced, because she added, "You could call Marie and ask her to help you prepare."

"Hmm." He liked the idea. It gave him an excuse to spend time with Marie. Her friendliness and Latino looks were provocative.

"Everything is going your way. Our latest video on labor unions' impact on government attracted attention from a new conservative demographic. Your followers now total ten million."

How could he have come so far? Less than two weeks ago, he was a nobody.

"Give them hell, Mikey!" Anni grinned, and he grimaced. This was the new tag line printed at the end of each video, and it caught fire with the public.

***

On October 25, Paul Berry sat behind his oak desk while Michael sat on the adjacent white leather couch in the production studio. The makeup artist had just scurried away after brushing the host's face. Paul surveyed the studio, making sure everything was a go. The bright ceiling stage lights ensured no uncomplimentary shadows on his face. While the production team made last-minute adjustments, the show audience of about a hundred spoke softly to one another.

Michael held his glasses in his hand, since the show demanded natural responses from guests, not regurgitated canned content. It was high risk. Michael had watched the show before; Paul enjoyed making his guests squirm.

He'd practiced the interview with Marie, where she looked and sounded like Paul, shooting probing questions. He'd done well but was still nervous for the real thing. Using a tissue, he blotted the sweat from his brow, but he couldn't do anything for the butterflies in his stomach.

"Quiet please," announced a deep bass voice that commanded obedience.

After all the activity, the room became unnaturally quiet. Michael set his glasses and the damp tissue on the end table, hidden from the studio cameras. Then he placed his hands in his lap and shut his eyes, taking slow, steady breaths. When the production manager counted down, Michael opened his eyes. A green light came on above the manger's head.

"Welcome to San Francisco Today." Paul looked directly into the camera, then swiveled towards Michael. "Today, our guest is Michael Knightsbridge, whose controversial videos you've probably seen. They claim to prove political corruption by special interest groups buying access and votes to the detriment of the public."

Michael smiled as the adrenaline rushed through him.

"Michael, can you tell us a little about yourself?" Paul asked with a broad smile.

"Sure. I grew up near Boston, then worked in social improvement programs. About four months ago, I moved to Berkeley, where I now work in research at the university."

"No post high school education." Paul frowned, then continued in a less friendly voice. "You're forty years old, so you've worked in government programs for over twenty years. What was your focus?"

"I didn't have one." That didn't sound good, but what could he say? It was the truth.

"Twenty-plus years bouncing around, trying to find an area of interest?"

The audience laughed. A few smirked and pointed at him.

"I don't think that's uncommon." Michael tried to keep any defensiveness out of his voice.

"I understand you became quite good at playing VR games, though."

The audience laughed again, and even the production team was chuckling. This was going exactly as they planned. He was a loser who dared to raise his head and now risked having it chopped off. His heart pounded and sweat dripped from his brow.

"The important thing is to persevere and never give up." He wouldn't roll over. *You got this*, said the internal female voice.

"True. However, it's unusual for someone with your background to create such high-quality videos." Paul leaned back in his chair and clasped his hands together. "How did you do it?"

"I started with an important idea. I wanted to show our democratic government is not working for the good of the people but for the powerful and their political sycophants."

Paul tried to say something, but Michael spoke over him. "Next, my team researched different examples, then created these videos." This wasn't the complete truth, but it wasn't a lie either.

"Many people in power call you a liar." Even

though it was a strong denunciation, Paul spoke less forcibly, like he was testing the waters.

"They're entitled to their opinion, but I have the facts on my side."

"We always like to hear both sides to any issue." Paul turned his head to face the camera and took a dramatic pause. "We have a surprise guest, William White, governor of California."

A tall, blond-haired man with blue eyes and bleached white teeth walked onto the set. His tapered blue suit, black polished loafers, starched white shirt, and red tie commanded respect. He shook Paul's hand and took a seat on the other side of the couch. He wouldn't look at Michael.

"Mr. Governor," Paul placed his elbows on his desk and leaned forward, "what do you think of Mr. Knightsbridge and his accusations?"

"I think everyone knows what type of person Mr. Knightsbridge is." He glanced over at Michael and shifted farther away. "His lies disparage hard working public servants."

"Are you saying the insurance industry didn't buy your veto for bill AB 2594?" Michael couldn't contain himself.

"Of course not." The governor raised his chin and looked down at Michael. Then he turned towards the camera with a beautiful grin. "However,

I receive donations from many corporations, including insurers, because I'm good for business. But my number one priority is always what's best for the great people of California."

"Really?" Michael became indignant. "So, you didn't receive tens of millions of dollars from insurers just after you vetoed the bill they were against?"

"Of course not." Governor White opened his palms toward the camera as if in supplication, never breaking his smile.

"The governor smiles while he lies and screws you," Michael said, facing the camera. "He knows it; you know it, and he knows you know it. It's his screw-you smile."

"I'm telling the truth," he said harshly.

"Well." Michael turned towards the audience. "Governor White thinks his public disclosures of donations will show nothing. However, I've pieced together the proof that I'm telling the truth, and Governor White is lying."

The Governor's face turned beet red, but the audience and Paul chuckled. This was good TV.

"You have nothing but petty dreams of grandeur. You get pleasure by tearing others down." Governor White sneered. "Hurt people hurt people."

Michael was speechless. The governor had hit

too close to home. Then his monkey voice spoke. *You're such a loser. Why did you even come here?*

"It's hard to accept who you are isn't it?" Governor White touched his lips with two fingers, then threw him a kiss.

Outrage bubbled up, replacing his capitulation and submission. With a shaky, barely controlled voice, Michael shouted, "Anni, release the source documents for the governor."

Both the governor's and Paul's mouth dropped open. The audience went deathly silent.

Paul recovered first and smiled. "Well, that was a surprise."

The governor scowled while the audience shuffled in their chairs and murmured. Michael hadn't planned to do this, but he was angry and knew Anni would be watching.

A few seconds later, Paul's eyes narrowed, and he scrunched up his face. Then he glanced at his production manager, who nodded. "Governor, WikiLeaks just released a list of your major supporters and their donations mapped to some of your more controversial votes."

"I'll need to look into this." Governor White's face drained of color.

"Give them hell, Mikey," Paul said. The tables had turned.

After the show, Michael walked three blocks to Tadich Grill. He went past the gold lettering on the window and pushed through the doors to a crowd milling around in the front. There were some tourists dressed casually, but most patrons were in business attire. Metal lamps hung from the ceiling and wood-paneled walls, providing an Old West atmosphere for the few hundred diners sitting at their tables. White tablecloths and fancy silverware contrasted with unadorned seafood plates and bibs for eating lobsters. Normally, they didn't accept reservations, particularly for a booth, but Anni had arranged things.

"Reservation for Michael Knightsbridge," he said, when he finally reached the gray-haired hostess in a white jacket and trousers. She'd just told the man in front of him it was an hour wait.

"Come with me." She brusquely escorted him to a booth near the back, dropped the menus on the table, and left.

He slid across the leather bench, placed his napkin in his lap, and picked up the paper menu. A minute later, a waitress pulled the curtain aside, entered, and poured water into their glasses, spilling a bit. She frowned at the vacant seat, tapped her watch, and then left, letting the curtain fall back. Anni had told him the food was great, but the servers thought they were doing you a favor by being there. It was times like this that he missed the modern world of robotic servers.

Ten minutes later, the curtain opened, and Marie scooted across the other side of the table. "Sorry I'm a little late."

"No problem." He was just happy to see her. She looked prettier in person than she had in VR, but maybe it was the scent of her woodsy perfume.

"You did great." Marie said.

"Thanks," he said. "Though I got too emotional."

"That was even—"

The curtain swung open, and the waitress appeared with a small pad of paper and pen in hand. She had a harried expression, like she had other, more important things to do. "Have you decided?"

Michael looked at Marie, who hastily picked up her menu. He was going to ask for a few more minutes to give Marie more time, but then thought of a better approach. "What're today's specials?"

As the waitress recited the fresh fish of the day, Marie read over the menu.

"I'll have a Crab Louie," Marie said when the waitress had finished.

"I'm from Boston." Michael smiled at the waitress, trying to draw out some friendliness. "How are the crab cakes?"

"The best." She raised her chin and sniffed. "We use west coast Dungeness crabs which beat your blue crabs any day."

He didn't believe her but appreciated her conviction, even though she wouldn't smile. "I'll have crab cakes and grilled swordfish."

After the waitress left, Marie said, "Anyway, I thought you did great in the interview. Getting emotional showed your conviction and came across as authentic."

"I almost lost it," he said, shaking his head. "It could've been a disaster."

"But it wasn't," she said in a chirpy voice.

He'd rather unwind with her than rehash the interview. He glanced at the black and white photos of old San Francisco on the wall. One showed three-story cement buildings with small square windows. People in western garb walked along the sides of the dirt street while horses clomped down the middle. "How long have you lived in San Francisco?"

"My entire life."

He cocked his head, waiting for her to say more.

"When I was a baby, my parents came here from Haiti, not speaking a word of English or having a job."

"That must've been hard."

"They worked long hours in restaurants

washing dishes or for janitorial services cleaning offices." She studied his face, probably assessing if he was truly interested, which he was. "However, they always found time to attend my school activities and have family meals."

As his marketing person, she already knew something about him. This was his chance to learn about her. "Where'd you go to school and what did you do afterwards?"

"I went to USF, where I received a full scholarship and majored in communications. After graduation, I worked in advertising, then switched to marketing for Unity, where I'm now a VP."

She was a go-getter who'd worked for everything she had. He hoped she wouldn't resent him because so much was given to him, like his private schooling. "Do you have any brothers or sisters?"

"No. I'm an only child."

In some ways, he was envious. Having a sibling was both a blessing and a curse. "I heard only-children were more independent, ambitious, and family oriented, but not very compromising."

She squinted and puckered her lips.

He hoped he hadn't offended her. He could say ten nice things, but women seemed to focus on the one negative comment.

"I suppose it's true," Marie said. "I could work on being more accommodating."

"Have you heard the question," he asked, "If a tree falls in the forest, but no one is there to hear it, does it make a sound?"

"Yes," she said with a quizzical look.

"What about," he said, breaking a smile, "If a man speaks, but a woman isn't around to hear, is he still always wrong?"

She chuckled, completing his recovery.

"So, what do you do for fun?" he continued.

"Go out with friends. Windsurf on the bay."

"Windsurfing?"

"It's exhilarating. Standing on a board while sailing across the waves." She stared behind him, probably thinking of her last outing. Then she smiled. "What about you?"

"Nothing so exciting. I go on hikes and walks."

"With friends?"

"Not really. I'm still settling in." His recent arrival was a good excuse. "Though I am looking to join a hiking club."

"We should go on a hike sometime." She smiled.

"I'd like that."

Over the next half hour, they spoke and laughed about everyday things. Then, the curtain opened, and the waitress set down their plates. "Is there anything else you need?"

Michael shook his head. He looked at his crab cakes and swordfish and realized he'd ordered too much. "Well, bon appétit."

"So urbane," she said, stabbing a piece of crab and some lettuce with her fork.

They dug into their meals. His crab cake was scrumptious, melting in his mouth. "This is delicious. Would you like a bite?"

"I couldn't." She shook her head, but then looked at his face. "Well, maybe a little."

He cut some crab cake and placed it on her plate with his fork. While she eyed him, he did the same thing with his swordfish.

"You're right. They're yummy," she said after tasting both. "So, I've told you about my family. Can you tell me about yours?"

"I have a twin brother." He didn't really want to talk about Wendell.

"Identical or fraternal?"

"Identical."

"Are you alike?"

"We were. But when we were ten, our dad died suddenly."

"Oh, I'm so sorry." She squinted, like she was trying to hold back tears. "Parents are so important."

He nodded. Her empathy took him by surprise. "Anyway, Wendell became driven to succeed, whereas I sort of withdrew." There it was. Wendell became the paragon, and he became the loser.

Her lips pressed together.

"I'm trying to do better," he added, thinking about his contributions in dark matter research.

"I think you're doing great," she said.

He smiled. Her approval felt like a warm ray of sunshine, bathing him in a comforting glow that extended deep into his core.

She nodded and narrowed her eyes at him. "Anni has a lot of faith in you."

Yes, she did. He couldn't understand why a rich, powerful lady would spend so much time with him instead of delegating it to a subordinate. However, her faith gave him credibility and prestige, which might explain Marie's kindness towards him. "She brings out the best in me."

The waitress pulled the curtain open and

picked up their plates. "Coffee or dessert?"

"Marie," he said, arching an eyebrow. "You want anything?"

"I really shouldn't." She sat back and covered her stomach with her hands.

He wasn't hungry and didn't like coffee, but he wanted to extend his time with her. He looked at the waitress. "Any recommendations?"

"The rice custard bread pudding with mint sprig garnish and cream on the side is to die for."

"I'd like that with two spoons please." He gave Marie a conspiratorial smile, and she licked her lips.

After the waitress left, he asked, "Am I keeping you from anything?"

"Not really." She tilted her water glass, watching the condensation slide down. "I'm just working on a couple of corporate brand campaigns."

"Is it interesting?"

"The market research is interesting, but developing brands to sell more product isn't very fulfilling."

"What would you rather be doing?" She came across as the type of woman who could do anything she wanted.

She scratched the side of her cheek. "I want to help people, but I'm not exactly sure how." She gave a shy smile. "What about you? What would you like to do?"

"I'm not sure." Historically, he'd wanted to keep his head down, do the minimal amount of work, and get by. However, something internal now motivated him to do more, allowing him to tap into hidden talents. He now had a hand in both dark matter research and political videos and had held his own in the interview today. "But I hope to figure it out soon."

An hour later, Michael rode the BART train back to Berkeley. It was a wonderful lunch, which would have lasted all afternoon if the waitress hadn't shooed them out. He was completely comfortable with Marie, willing to talk to her about anything, even his family. He wondered if Marie was special, or if his personality, along with his mind, was changing.

Maybe it was a little of both.

CHAPTER THIRTEEN: POLITICS

The next day, Michael returned to his office VR room for a meeting with Anni. This time, they stood alone in front of a virtual classroom with about thirty empty desks. Anni rolled a piece of chalk between her hands. He felt like a student staying after class for private tutoring. Anni probably chose this virtual environment to reinforce her messages. Today, it was to teach.

"Any new developments in your dark matter research?" she asked, starting with her go-to question.

"Not really. Our focus has moved to the sleeping sickness, but nothing yet."

She nodded and exhaled deeply. "You did well yesterday. Millions of viewers have expressed their support for you."

"Thanks for releasing the information on the

governor." Today's lesson would be political. "Has he responded to it?"

"Not yet. However, other reporters have picked up the story using the information."

"Good." He was still simmering from the governor's comment about him being a hurt person who hurt other people.

"There's a movement among your followers for you to run for political office."

"Really?" It was one thing to call out political corruption, but something entirely different to run. "I don't have the experience or skills to be a politician."

"Don't worry, many first-time politicians had no prior political experience. The only thing needed is name recognition and admiration from the people, both of which you have."

"Are you serious?" He would never have considered this, but life moved in surprising ways.

"Completely."

He looked closely at her for any sign that she was joking. It wouldn't have surprised him if she'd laughed and patted him on the shoulder, but she just studied him.

"Could I win?"

"The public distrusts government and

disdains politicians." She turned towards the blackboard and drew a one and nine. "Only nineteen percent of Americans trust politicians. There's a tremendous opportunity for someone new."

"What political office would you suggest?" Maybe he could win a seat on the Berkeley city council.

"It must be significant and not depend on others who would stymie you." She looked up at the ceiling for a moment and then brought her eyes down to stare at him. "President of the United States."

"What?" Michael choked and then laughed, unable to control himself. He held the sides of his stomach, bent over, shook his head, and tried to take a breath. Tears ran down his cheeks.

She smiled and waited for him to gather his wits. "Many non-politicians have become president."

"But they accomplished something beforehand." This idea was ridiculous. "I've done nothing."

"If millions of your followers have faith in you, then you should have faith in yourself." Her eyes narrowed on him. She was serious.

"It's impossible," he mumbled, shaking his head.

"I make the impossible possible," she replied calmly.

"The problem is, you'd have to work through me." He couldn't look at her. Her self-confidence bordered on insanity.

"That's not a problem. We're one team."

They were a one-sided team. Anni provided the message, the VR messenger, distribution, and financial support, while he was only the man behind the curtain. He was like the traveling salesman who became the Wizard of Oz. He was a fraud.

"Even if you could do it, there isn't enough time." He looked at her. "The election is next year."

"You fail to account for advanced AI," she said, grabbing the chalk from the blackboard. "It makes the concept of time almost irrelevant towards the accomplishment of clear political objectives. What would take a group of humans a year to accomplish, advanced AI can do in weeks."

Was it really such a powerful force?

"There are about two hundred and twenty million registered voters," she continued. "With the ease of voting by glasses, turnout is high, so to win, you would need about one hundred twenty million votes."

Even though Anni was earnest, this sounded like an impossibility, a joke.

"Of your twenty million current adult followers," she continued, "about sixteen million would vote for you."

"A landside loss." Exactly what he expected, although winning millions of votes was still impressive.

"If our video content expands nationwide from just California, then your adult followers will grow three-fold. After you announce and we campaign, that number will double again."

She spun around and wrote:
20   Current Adult Followers
60   US Rollout
80   Announcement
160

After circling one hundred sixty, she added:

128   Your votes

120   Votes needed to win

"Not all your adult followers would vote for you, but about eighty percent will, giving you one hundred twenty-eight million. With these votes, we could also overcome the complexities posed by the electoral college." She rapped him on the chest with her chalk. "You could win."

He was speechless. He had never envisioned himself as a politician, let alone president. Power, the spotlight, glad handing, these things weren't important to him. Shaking his head and looking down, he saw that the VR system didn't reflect any chalk marks on his shirt. A random thought. He needed to focus.

"What about my involvement with dark matter research?" He'd have no time left for the lab.

"It's important, and your involvement is critical. An AI-driven campaign won't require a lot of your time."

This was hard to believe. Wouldn't campaigning be a full-time job? Maybe not, if the political videos were any sign.

"Why are you doing this?" His eyes narrowed. He wondered if she was holding something back.

"Because I'm your biggest fan and think you could do wonders for my adopted country."

"There must be more than that," he said, studying her face.

"There is." She blinked twice. "I believe we have an ethereal connection, the Hun, that binds us."

His glasses informed him the Hun was the spiritual yang soul, according to Chinese philosophy and traditional religion. It all seemed like mumbo-jumbo to him.

"You don't need to do anything right now. We'll just expand the video content from California issues to US issues and see how people respond. I'll ask Marie to work with you to put together some ideas."

Did he want to become a public figure and completely upend his life? Most politicians gravitated towards power and the spotlight, whereas he had always shied away. This was the last thing he expected of himself; however, he liked the idea of working with Marie. He could see how things went. Nothing ventured, nothing gained.

***

Two days after the show, President Douglas reviewed the San Francisco Today recording of Governor White. He shook his head in sympathy for his friend, who was caught in a bald-faced lie. After knocking on the door, Jaimie walked in.

"Can you tell me anything more about Michael Knightsbridge?" he asked as she took a seat in front of his desk.

"He was a nobody until a few weeks ago when he produced a high-quality investigative political video." She exhaled deeply and shook her head. "He has twenty million followers and hundreds of millions of dollars of donations."

"How could a nobody do this?" Even with all his resources, he couldn't replicate this. He stood and held his hands behind his back. "The investigative research, the quality video production, the video placement in social media. This must have been months in the making."

"I don't know." Jaimie eyed him. "But he obviously has a lot of help."

"It must have cost millions too." He started pacing back and forth behind his desk. "Who's the money?"

"We don't know. They're not using the traditional people or suppliers."

He stopped and stared down at Jaime. "Who is this Anni that he asked to release the governor's records at the end of the video?"

"Anni Chan is a reclusive Chinese national with business interests throughout the globe." Jaimie leaned forward, probably happy that she finally had an answer. "Our best guess is her family was Taiwanese and transferred their wealth to Monaco before returning to China."

"How did Knightsbridge connect with her? What's their relationship?"

"We don't know." She paused. "I'll get back on that."

"Taiwanese." Another thought occurred to him. "Was she involved with the disinformation campaign that toppled Taiwan's government?"

"Possibly. It would explain how the pro-China faction knew where to find the dirt." She paused.

"I wouldn't exactly call it disinformation, since everything the opposition said was true."

"If it was Anni." He returned to his chair. "That would explain the money source." He looked at his crystal chandelier in the middle of the room. "How did she get William's campaign bank statements?"

"She must have had an insider at the bank or in his campaign." Jaimie spoke tentatively, not displaying her normal conviction.

"I want you to investigate Anni Chan." He returned to his seat. "Tell me who she is, what businesses she controls, and where she spends her time and money. And figure out what her relationship is with Knightsbridge."

"Yes, Mr. President."

He sighed. "Is there any update on the sleeping sickness?"

"No." She frowned. "It continues to strike about three hundred Americans randomly every day with no recoveries. Our scientists believe the destruction of a person's dark matter bundle is the cause, but they don't know why it happens, what the transmission vectors are, if there're any immunization or treatments, and I could go on."

"What about the origins?" He paused. "It can't be a coincidence that the sickness arrived shortly after our fifth-force dark matter research started. Could one of these research centers have inadvertently released a sleeping sickness virus?"

"We don't believe research in the US or Western Europe caused it, but we're evaluating other countries now."

"What about the public's reaction?" He wrung his hands. "Anything new?"

"The public is scared. The CDC provides daily briefings, but there isn't much news. Wackos are filling the information vacuum with nonsense, like claiming a daily Melatonin regime will prevent the disease."

"Should I hold a briefing on this?" During his press conferences, he had spoken about his sadness visiting sleeping sickness patients in hospitals and how this was the number one priority for the CDC. However, he hadn't dedicated an entire speech to the subject.

"Yes, but not until we know more."

***

Michael looked at his reflection in his parents' mirror, verifying there were no yellowish teeth, or hair out of place, or wrinkles on the side of his eyes. He returned the tooth whitening and anti-wrinkle creams to his top dresser drawer. He'd never taken this much interest in his personal appearance.

When his doorbell rang, he placed his comb on the dresser and skated in his socks along the wood floor. *Step, step, step. Slide.* He was halfway down the hallway. *Step, step, step. Slide.* He arrived at his destination, where he patted his shirt down before opening the front door.

"Good evening." He stepped aside with his goofy smile.

"Evening." Marie, dressed professionally in a navy-blue blazer and slacks, entered and walked with him into the family room. She sat down on the couch.

He sat in the adjacent chair.

"We released our first video of you attacking the Industrial Military Complex and their influence over government foreign policy and spending." She clenched and unclenched her hands while her knees bounced up and down. "Military suppliers made huge profits while justifying wars as protecting American values or confronting the spread of terrorism and authoritarianism."

"This seems personal for you," he said.

"It is. My parents were leaders of a democratically elected Haitian government, which was tragically overthrown by a US-backed military coup. We became refugees, and the country still hasn't recovered."

"I'm sorry," he said. Her family had lost everything, and gangs now ruled the country.

"Since World War Two, the US has been in oversea conflicts sixty-eight percent of the time, causing over two million deaths." She spoke softly initially, but then her voice surged with conviction. "The DoD budget ballooned from sixty-two billion to almost one trillion in constant dollars, a sixteen-fold increase." Her neck veins strained like cords, mirroring the intensity of her words.

The realization that the US had been engaged in major conflicts for nearly 70% of its existence left him reeling. He had always believed the US was a peaceful nation, only resorting to armed conflict as a last resort.

"Anyway." She exhaled deeply and seemed to calm down. "Highlighting this iniquity has already doubled your followers to forty million."

"Why has no one in power spoken out?"

"They know who butters their toast." She rubbed her fingers and thumb against each other. "The last president to warn against the military-industrial complex was Eisenhower in his farewell address. The situation has only gotten much worse."

He grunted. And the news organizations had never corrected this common perception. Were they all in cahoots?

"We're talking about important issues that every other politician avoids." She paused. "You could win the presidency, but do you even want to run?"

"I'm not sure." He envied her conviction. He glanced out the Bayview window across the room, but only saw darkness.

"To capture the public's imagination and ignite their support, you must embody a cause that sets your soul on fire."

"Right now, I'm against public corruption, but I haven't figured out what I'm for." Given the importance of his decision to run or not, he should've thought this through.

"You've talked about helping people like your former self. The underserved majority who lack hope and purpose."

He stood, remembering his former life, stuck in dead-end government programs, and flittering away his life in the virtual world. "Yeah, I'd like to help them."

"Any ideas? They can't all run for president."

"Hah." He thought about it. "They spend most of their time in the virtual world, playing games and doing other entertainment. We need to make that time more productive, leveraging their creativity and rewarding their work."

"What would they produce?"

He thought about the game Conquest, and how it crowd-sourced good ideas for government. Could they extend this concept to other things like music, books, games, or movies?

"How about new VR games or other content."

Marie tilted her head and frowned.

"For example," he continued, "a group of gamers could design a new game, then an AI program could instantiate it, allowing them to play and improve it. The AI could assess the product, suggest enhancements, and market the final product to targeted players."

"So, players would design it instead of professionals at gaming companies." Marie stroked her chin, looking away. "Instead of only elite players competing in a few mass-market games, groups of passionate players matched to indie games would have their day in the sun."

AI could democratize both the content production and consumption—VR games, books, movies, and music. AI could move the power from institutions to the people, in the same way the printing press had centuries ago.

They brainstormed other ideas with his robot pouring the occasional glass of wine. He grew more excited and optimistic. The benefits of AI could flow directly to consumers without catering to the profit incentives of business and elites. This would flip the entire business model, putting the people on top.

"I think we can call it a night," Marie said, yawning.

"All right." He clenched his jaw to stifle his own yawn and then stood, reaching down to help her up.

She took his hand and, rather than letting go after she stood, she squeezed it and smiled.

In an unusual act of boldness, he brought her hand to his mouth and gave it a quick kiss before releasing it. "This was fun."

"We accomplished a lot," she said.

Michael's mind raced, but he couldn't find any words. Marie tilted her head, looking sideways at him with a sly smile as if she had a secret. Did she want him to kiss her? How could he tell? He checked the AER reading: *interest with some desire.*

Leaning forward, he kissed her tenderly on the lips and then pulled back.

She looked into his eyes. A golden ring circled both of her pupils. She leaned towards him and closed her eyes.

Pulling her close, he kissed her firmly on the lips. He shut his eyes and ran his hand up and down her back. Her mouth opened and her tongue reached for his.

After a couple of minutes, she stepped back. The side of her mouth tilted up as she placed her hands on her hips. "I thought this might happen."

He looked into her eyes for any sign of regret, but only saw pleasure.

"Anni said it would be fine if something happened," she said, "but we should keep it private." Her eyes narrowed, showing a newfound resolve. "I really need to go."

He wanted to argue but didn't want to screw anything up. He tried to get his raging emotions under control. "Okay, but I really want to do this again. How about dinner tomorrow night?"

"I can't do it tomorrow, but how about the next night?"

"Sure." He would make any night work. "I'll make reservations."

"Cool." She kissed him on the cheek. Then she opened the door, stepped outside, turned one more time, and smiled before leaving.

He watched her walk up the stone pathway in the moonlight, past Wendell's house and to the street. It was almost midnight. *How am I supposed to sleep now?*

CHAPTER FOURTEEN: DINNERS

When his front doorbell rang, Michael skipped to the door to answer it.

"Hey," Marie said, kissing him on his cheeks.

"You look great." Michael was totally gaga over her. He grabbed her hand. "Ready?"

They walked to Wendell's backdoor for his weekly Sunday night dinner. Although he was head over heels for Marie, he could compartmentalize his feelings between personal and work. This newfound ability surprised him, since in the past, any strong feelings would quickly overwhelm him. Now, there seemed to be an outside throttle or control.

When they entered the house, the kitchen was empty other than a robot standing in the corner, so they continued to the dining room where he heard talking.

"Hi, Michael." Melinda stood and came over. "And you must be Marie."

"Thanks for having me," Marie said, shaking her hand. When Wendell came over to greet her, she examined his face like she was making a comparison.

Michael and Marie went to the two empty chairs at the dining room table, sitting across from their hosts. To forestall the impending questions, Michael said, "What were you talking about before we arrived?"

"Wendell was just complaining about the time I'm spending at the office." Melinda returned her gaze to Wendell and smiled. "Of course, it's perfectly justifiable when *he* works late."

"What have you been working on?" Michael hadn't seen her working in the garden recently.

"Security," Melinda said, waving her hand as if it wasn't worth talking about.

"Melinda uncovered a security breach which might be an inside job." Wendell switched to his teacher mode, as if his guests were students or he wanted to impress Marie. "She, along with a team in Washington, are plugging holes and analyzing the intrusion impact from the lost data."

Melinda stared at her husband in astonishment.

"Who's behind the attack?" Michael asked. "What were they looking for?"

"Everything points to the Chinese government," Wendell said with his normal self-assurance. "State secrets like our AI and dark matter research."

"This is confidential with the US government; you can't repeat this to anyone." Melinda glanced at Michael, then returned to Wendell with an icy stare. "I really can't trust you with any secrets."

"If you can't trust family, who can you trust?" Wendell smiled, trying to recover with a joke, but Melinda continued to glare.

The last thing Michael wanted was a family squabble. What would Marie think? Fortunately, the robot entered and delivered their dinners, faux Crab Louie Salads with garlic bread. Then it picked up a bottle of Chateau Montelena from the table and poured wine into each person's wine glass.

"A toast," Wendell said, raising a glass. Everyone raised their glasses.

"To keep a marriage brimming with love, when you're wrong, admit it, and when you're right, shut up." He clanked Melinda's glass. "I was wrong and admit it."

Her pressed lips turned up at the edges, and then everyone tapped their glasses together. The tension in the room dropped a notch.

"Marie, how did you and Michael meet?" His apology partially accepted; Wendell wanted to jump to a new subject.

"Work. I'm producing his videos." She pointed a thumb at him.

"I saw the video on bribery in the US Senate," Wendell said. "How did you get the visitor records and financial payments?"

"It takes work." Marie stabbed some crab and lettuce with her fork. "The Public Information Act says all data from senators' and house members' glasses dealing with political activities goes to the National Archives. They get around this by conducting face-to-face meetings without glasses for any questionable agreements."

"So, how did you get the info?" Wendell took a small bite of his salad.

"We have scouts at the capital who track when lobbyists or power brokers meet with politicians. They can easily deduce the topics." She put down her fork. "Financial payments, although obfuscated through third parties, are public information and can be pieced together."

"Marie," Melinda said, "do you have family nearby?"

"My parents live in San Francisco. I'm an only

child."

"Do you see them much?" Melinda asked.

"Every week." She smiled. "I'm hoping Michael can meet them soon."

She hadn't mentioned that before. A warm glow filled him.

"What are they like?" Melinda continued.

"They're the kindest people you ever met." She lowered her eyes. "They did everything for me."

"What do they do?"

"There're on social support programs now, but before they owned a Kreyol restaurant in SF. Unfortunately, it failed."

"I'm sorry," Melinda said, frowning.

"They did everything right, but never caught a break." Marie shook her head and rubbed a finger against the edge of her eyes. "They met in university, had successful business careers, owned a big house in the center of Port-au-Prince, then went into politics to help the country. Unfortunately, there was a military coup, forcing them to flee the country; they lost everything."

There was an awkward silence. Everyone dug into their meals. Michael reached over and squeezed her hand.

"How's working with Michael?" Wendell

asked, continuing his interrogation.

"Great." She perked up. "We see eye-to-eye on most issues."

Michael gave a half-grin, remembering how she wanted to attack politicians who advocated for no bans on abortion.

"Why Michael?" Wendell shook his head slightly. He never hesitated when asking delicate questions.

"We had several candidates, but Anni preferred him."

"Why?" Wendell continued. Michael was curious too.

"She wanted someone outside of politics who agreed with her views, and she could trust."

Although Michael hadn't known Anni for a long time, he trusted her too. She hadn't wanted a candidate with upfront name recognition, so maybe he wasn't a terrible choice. He had also shown political promise based on his play in Conquest. Weirdly, the game challenges seemed to mirror those of the real world, not exactly, but close.

"Your followers seem to want Michael to run for president." Melinda eyed him up and down as if assessing if he had the demeanor of a future president.

"Really?" Wendell smirked, hiding nothing.

"People are ready for change." Melinda always voiced support for him, although he wasn't sure how she felt deep down.

"No argument there." Although irked, Wendell wouldn't contradict his wife and risk angering her again.

"An online petition just went out, so we'll soon know what kind of support Michael has," Marie said.

"What if they want you to run?" Wendell seemed genuinely interested, and not judgmental. It was refreshing. "What'll you do?"

"I honestly don't know. It seems impossible to go from a nobody to a presidential candidate." Michael sipped his wine. "I'm not even sure that I would want it."

"Why not?" Wendell asked.

"I'm not you, Wendell." Although they shared the same DNA, their attitudes couldn't be more different. "Power for power's sake doesn't interest me. I would only run if I could make a major positive impact on society."

"I've learned that you grab every opportunity given to you because you never know where it will lead." Wendell looked like he was going to push his case, but then seemed to reconsider. "Marie, what do you think?"

"I think it's Michael's choice, but he should only run if he really wants it."

He couldn't agree more and grinned at her. The conversation shifted back to Marie for the rest of dinner.

When the robot cleared the table, Marie said, "Thank you for the wonderful evening. I have a busy day tomorrow, so need to head home."

Wendell and Melinda hugged Marie and thanked her for coming.

"Can I walk you to your car?" Michael asked.

"Sure." She again thanked their hosts.

"I hope you didn't mind the inquisition," he said as they walked to her car.

"Not at all," she said, laughing. "I really enjoyed the evening and meeting them."

He wrapped his arms around her and they made out. After about a half hour, she clambered into her car and said, "See you tomorrow."

He watched her drive away, then he returned to the main house. Wendell was working in the library but got up and walked with him to the back door.

"We really liked Marie," Wendell said. "I hope it works."

"Thanks." He hoped it would work too.

"If the survey shows you have the support, I hope you run for office," Wendell said, placing his hand on the doorknob, but not opening it. "Seriously, I think you could do some good."

"Thanks." The support from his brother left Michael speechless.

"Also, sorry about that spat at the start of dinner."

"Why was she so upset? If you don't mind my asking." Normally, he wouldn't be so invasive, but his mind was still reeling from the evening.

"Well, it started with our plans for a baby." He shrugged. "She's ready for motherhood and wants to fertilize an egg."

"And you're not ready to be a father in nine months," Michael said.

"I love Melinda and want a child, but not now." Wendell shook his head. "Anyway, this put her in a bad mood. Then there's the stress at work."

"Computer security?"

"Security for the new AI system. The US government believes whoever has the best AI will ultimately control the world."

"Why?" It sounded like paranoia. The US still had the largest economy and military, even though other countries were catching up.

"In the future, the best AI system will outsmart all the others, making the best decisions and baiting the others into losing ones." Wendell sighed. "It will be like a cat playing with mice. It will win in espionage, on the battlefield, and in business."

"This sounds alarmist," Michael said. "I agree AI can dominate a single, contained area, but extending it to everything is an enormous leap."

"Sure, we don't know with certainty what these emergent AI capabilities will be." Wendell rolled his shoulders as if he was stiff from sitting all day. "But I think they could make any government all-powerful. It would be like having superman in your corner."

Or superwoman, said the voice in his head that hadn't spoken recently. Then his monkey voice spoke. *Superman, Superwoman. It's all fanciful and couldn't help you anyway.*

He frowned and then combed his hair with his hands. He didn't use AI much personally, so this wasn't even relevant to him. "You also mentioned the Chinese were interested in our dark matter research."

"The US is assessing if the Chinese had a leak in their dark matter research, which caused the sleeping sickness. They're looking for proof."

Wendell forced a half-smile. "I expect the Chinese are hacking our systems to assess our dark matter research and see if we caused the sleeping sickness."

"Did we?" Michael asked, shocked by the thought.

"Our lab didn't, but it's possible that another research institution did." Wendell's shoulders sagged as he opened the back door.

"Thanks again." Michael shook Wendell's hand, then turned and went home. Although he was becoming more comfortable in his skin, his awkwardness with his brother remained. Personal change only went so far.

***

Early the next morning, Michael boarded a crowded BART train to meet Marie for coffee in San Francisco. There weren't any vacant seats, so he stood, held onto the railing, and listened to music. Even though the virtual world of VR calls did a good job reflecting the real one, he missed Marie's physical presence, so he was happy to make the commute.

He exited the train along with a bunch of commuters at the Embarcadero station. Robots had freshly washed and cleaned the platform, which smelled sterile despite all the activity. He took the archaic escalator to street level, then walked down Market to the Ferry Building, meandering through a hallway to a café overlooking the bay.

Marie sat at a table, so he hurried over. She rose, and they exchanged kisses on the cheeks before taking their seats across from each other.

"Thanks for making the trip here." Marie wore a business suit, maybe since they were there to discuss work.

"My pleasure." He wasn't normally an early riser, but she was an easy exception.

"Let's order first," she suggested.

Michael nodded and selected green tea and avocado toast from the menu displayed in his glasses. After she ordered, he reached across and held her hands. She smiled and gave him a gentle squeeze, which sent a tingle down his spine.

"Where should we start?" He wanted her to take the lead. He wasn't sure how to mix business and pleasure like this.

"Here's our latest video for your review," she said.

His glasses showed President Douglas eyeing his putt on a golf green. A female narrator said, "While the sleeping sickness incapacitates hundreds of Americans every day, the president plays golf. Mr. President, Americans are scared. After three months and thirty thousand brain-dead Americans, we still have no answers. What's causing the sickness? Where did it come from? When will we have a treatment? Is there any hope for the victims?"

"I don't like it. It's unfair." He was on the cutting edge of research and knew there were few answers about the illness. It was wrong to slam an opponent unfairly just to make yourself look good. If he ran, he would do it ethically, even if it might hurt his chances. It was better to stay true and lose the right way than to sacrifice his morals and win the wrong way.

"It shows the president is out of touch with everyday Americans."

"He is, but let's make the point differently." He wanted her to understand that integrity was important to him.

"Okay," she drawled. "We have a couple of other videos in production, but not ready to share right now."

A ubiquitous metal server robot marched over with a steady tray in one hand and unerringly delivered their food and drinks. Marie waited for him to sip his tea and then continued, "Forty million of your fifty million followers have signed your petition to run for president. It's overwhelming support."

"Honestly, I'm not sure I should run." Forgoing his utensils, he picked up his avocado toast and took a bite.

Marie scooped some egg onto her fork and

placed it into her mouth. He watched her chew, distracted by her full lips. "Why?" she asked after swallowing.

For a second, he didn't know what she was asking. Then he snapped out of it, looking away from her mouth. "It would be an enormous time commitment. I wouldn't have the space for any other . . . opportunities." He hoped she got his gist and felt the same way.

"That's true." Her eyes darted back and forth. "But what other opportunities?"

"You, for one," he said, maybe too quickly. Would his honesty get him in trouble?

"Hmm." Her eyes settled on her glass of water. "Whether or not you run, I'm game to see if we can make our relationship work."

He tried to suppress a smile but couldn't. Although unusual, he'd heard of politicians marrying their campaign consultants. It could work. "Great," he said.

She giggled. "Anni thought this might happen. She seems to know us well."

"What do you think of her?" She was his boss at work and enabler in politics.

"She's an amazing person—beautiful, accomplished, but also kind." Marie leaned forward. "She really likes you."

Michael wondered if this was part of the reason Marie found him attractive. Women fancied men who other women fancied. Maybe she liked that he'd chosen her and never made a play for Anni.

Marie glanced at the wall clock. "I need to get to my office for an eight o'clock meeting."

"All right." He stood and then extended his hand to help her up. "When can I see you next?"

"I'm not sure." She gave him a shy smile.

"Well, you could come over to my place for dinner tonight." He hoped he wasn't being too forward.

"Tonight?" She blinked a few times like she was weighing a decision. "Sure. That works."

They walked out of the Ferry Building. On the busy street, he kissed her, quickly but firmly, on the lips. She said goodbye and walked down the sidewalk. He watched her go. When she was about twenty feet away, she looked over her shoulder and said, "See you tonight."

At eight o'clock, he was on BART, heading back to Berkeley. He arrived at his office earlier than normal but couldn't think about work or politics. There was only Marie. He wondered if he distracted her in the same way.

He sleepwalked through his day in the office. Work was a bust, but he'd come up with a good idea for an activity with Marie that evening. At 5:00 pm, he rushed home.

When his doorbell rang at 6:00, he trotted to the door and opened it. He was like a child on Christmas morning, just before opening his gifts.

Marie had a wide, playful smile. She had changed out of her business attire, and now wore a double-breasted low-cut black dress that came down to her thighs and showed off her lean legs.

"Come in," he said, stepping aside. "Can I get you something to drink?"

"White wine, please." She walked past him towards the living room where soft music was playing, and a fire burned in the fireplace.

For a second, he admired her flawless bronze skin in her backless dress. Then he went to the fridge and poured two glasses of wine. His robot could have done this, but he wanted to give her a few seconds alone to get settled.

When he returned to the living room, she was standing by the fireplace. He handed her a glass of wine. "Would you like to sit down?"

Her chin dipped, and then she went to the couch where he joined her.

"Cheers," she said, holding up her glass.

"Cheers." He tapped her glass with his and then took a sip.

"How did your day go?" she asked.

"Well"—he paused, thinking about his totally unproductive day—"I had a wonderful morning coffee."

She smiled, which brought a wave of euphoria. This thrilled but also scared him. His dependency on another person was unsettling.

"What about you?" he asked.

"I worked on some new videos for you."

He nodded. Although this rendezvous could be business, work was the last thing he wanted to discuss. "How about we skip talking about work tonight?"

"Okay," she said, enunciating each syllable slowly. "What would you like to do instead?"

"Let's prepare our own dinner tonight. Just you and me. No automation."

"That's a novel idea." She gave him a lopsided grin.

He grabbed her hand and jumped up, pulling her with him. Holding hands, they went to the kitchen.

"What are we having?" she asked, eyeing the clean counters, cupboards, and appliances in the kitchen. Then, she noticed the robot in the corner. "Are you sure you want to do this?"

"Absolutely." He grabbed two dark-green eggplants from the fridge, a knife from the rack, and a cutting board from a drawer, and placed everything on the counter. "Eggplant parmesan."

"I suppose if we screw up, the robot can clean up our mess," Marie said, obviously uncomfortable with the idea.

"Do you know how to slice?" he asked,

handing her the eggplants and not giving her a chance to reconsider.

"It's been a while," she said, chuckling.

"One-quarter to one-half-inch slices." He got two eggs, which he whisked in a bowl with salt. Then he filled another bowl with flour and breadcrumbs and set them on the counter next to Marie, who had just finished slicing.

After preheating the oven, he grabbed the marinara sauce, mozzarella, and a casserole dish, and placed everything next to the bowls. He held up his wineglass. "To the old ways."

They clinked their glasses together.

"Do you do this often?" she asked.

"First time. I thought it might be fun." He rubbed his hands together and reviewed the recipe again on his glasses. "Now for assembly."

He sidled next to her and spooned a thin layer of marinara sauce into the dish. Then he took an eggplant slice, dipped it into the egg bowl, then the breadcrumb bowl, and placed it into the casserole dish. He held up a finger and watched a drop of egg yolk fall. "Now it's your turn."

"I got this," she said, grabbing his waist and pulling him behind her. He placed his wrists on her shoulders and watched her quickly bread five more slices, which covered the dish.

Next, he sliced the mozzarella on the cutting board, placing one piece on each eggplant. Then he handed her the parmesan and grater. "Just spread it out over the dish."

When she finished, he said, "Now for the second layer. Are you up for it, or should we pass it to the robot?"

She stuck her tongue out at him. "I can handle it."

Ten minutes later, the casserole dish was in the oven, the robot had its directions, and they returned to the living room couch with full glasses of wine. He took a sip of wine, then placed his glass on the coffee table. She did the same.

He studied the side of her face. Her nose was short and narrow. Her thin, brown eyebrows complemented her oval face. Her cheeks were thin with a soft, glowing bronze hue.

She looked up and smiled. He reached under her chin with tender fingers and brought her mouth to his.

Sometime later, she pulled back and whispered, "Do you think dinner's ready?"

He checked his glasses. The robot had placed their dinner on the dining room table about a half-hour ago. "Yes, but it's cold."

"That's fine." She stood and pulled him to his feet. "I'm starving."

They ate dinner quickly, then returned to the living room to watch a rom-com on their glasses. With his arm around Marie's waist and darkened three-D glasses over his eyes, he could've been in a private viewing theater.

The film, *He Said, She Said*, dealt with the miscommunications between a guy and girl. After each encounter, something said would confuse the other person so they would seek advice from colleagues at work. Each would recount what he or she had heard but completely misrepresent what it meant. The advice received was terrible, and the budding relationship didn't last.

They laughed throughout the movie but sometimes at different times. Did this reflect some universal differences between the sexes, or was it specific to the two of them? When the film ended, he asked, "What did you think?"

"It was hilarious," she said with a half-smile.

"Yeah, it was. But how much of it do you think was true?"

"Quite a bit, particularly about men being direct and women being circumspect."

He nodded. "The guy didn't think she was interested, even though she thought she was giving all the right signals."

"Yup. You can't beat around the bush." She leaned forward and slapped her legs, ready to get up. "Well, it's late, and I need to get some sleep."

He pulled his arm back and placed his hands in his lap. Feeling unsure what to say, he checked her emotional reading on his glasses. *High attraction*. Again, he thought back to the film, where the guy had missed his chance by not saying what he wanted.

"You could sleep here tonight," he blurted.

Her head jerked back as if she'd seen a ghost. She hadn't expected this. "I don't know. I don't want things to get weird."

"Things won't get weird." He took her hand in his. "They'll get better."

She studied his eyes. "Are you sure?"

"Without a doubt." He rose to his feet, keeping her hand in his.

She didn't look at him but rose as well. "Okay."

He grinned from ear to ear, leading her by the hand to the bedroom.

***

The next day, Marie called her mom from her office. "I'm sorry we haven't spoken recently, but I've been busy at work."

"That's fine," mom said. "I understand."

"There's also a boy," she said after a pause.

"Oh? Is it serious?"

"It's early, but I like him."

"What's his name? How old is he? What's. . ."

"Whoa mom. His name is Michael Knightsbridge, and he's forty." Although mom would fire questions at her, she was much more discreet with others. "I want to set up a time for you and dad to meet with us."

"We'd love to."

Despite having had long-term relationships, Marie had never felt like this. She yearned to be with Michael. Her feelings made her vulnerable and scared her. What if things didn't work out?

CHAPTER FIFTEEN: FIFTH-FORCE EXPERIMENTS

At his next meeting with Anni, the office VR room transported Michael to an empty eight-lane highway running into a gray shimmery wall. The wall extended for about a mile in both directions, and at the end were construction crews with trucks and other equipment. When he tried to touch the wall, his hand vanished into the fog. He stepped back and noticed that every few hundred yards along the wall were ten-foot-tall metal pillars. There was also a gently rising dome on top of the wall. It looked like an ancient temple.

"Where are we?" he asked when Anni walked up beside him.

"Just outside of Chongqing." She pointed at the dome. "A bustling, densely populated city in

China with over eight million people."

"Really?" He saw another empty highway in the distance with some buildings beside it. "What's with the wall?"

"The government has started to build a ring of fifth-force pillars that will wrap around the city."

"Why?" He thought of the implications. Besides the enormous investment, the inhabitants would live in a dreary dusk with no sunlight during days or moon and starlight at night.

"The Chinese government has made understanding the sleeping sickness its number one priority. Since the disease strikes randomly, without warning, we need to monitor a large population."

"Couldn't you just monitor people who became unusually sleepy?" This seemed like overkill. It reminded him of the city-wide Chinese Covid quarantines from twenty years ago.

"Yes, we've asked citizens here who experience profound sleepiness to come in for observation." She looked down and brought her hands up to rub her face. "We've caught the tail end of the disease and seen a shimmering cloud consume their dark matter bundle. Would you like to see a recording?"

"Yes."

His glasses showed a glittering silvery-white

fog surrounding a small golden globe with streaks of reddish blue bolts. The frequency of the energy bolts increased as the globe's size dwindled until it completely vanished. Then, the fog and bolts vanished too.

"The fog appears to absorb the energy from the human's dark matter bundle, but that's all we know," Anni said. "We hope to learn more by seeing the disease from the onset."

Michael frowned, surprised they didn't know more.

"It's like when a new type of missile strikes a building," she continued. "We see the destruction after the strike but don't know the missile type or flight path."

Michael extended an arm towards the gray wall. "How does this work?"

"We record the dark matter bundles for the entire population, looking for those that vanish. In most cases, the cause will be death, but in rare cases, it's the sleeping sickness."

"When do you expect to observe your first end-to-end case?"

"If we're lucky, in the next few days, but it could take a month."

"When did this project start?" Given it was early November and the sleeping disease had only started mid-September, decisions and actions must have been swift.

"About a month ago; after you identified a possible link between dark matter and the sleeping sickness."

He stared at her. This didn't seem possible. China had made an enormous investment based on his hunch.

***

The next day, Michael and Wendell met Mae in her office.

"The Chinese government asked citizens in Chongqing who have symptoms of the sleeping sickness to come in for observation," Michael said. He described the recording of the silvery-white cloud, reddish-blue energy bolts, and shrinking dark matter bundle. "Now they're building a fifth-force wall around the city to capture the onset of the disease."

Michael expected a bunch of questions, but Mae only glanced at Wendell and said, "I'm surprised we haven't heard anything about this."

"The Chinese government does a good job controlling the flow of information," Wendell said, "which begs the questions: why did they allow Anni to share it with you?"

"I don't know," Michael said. "I didn't think to

ask."

"Anyway, we could never do what they're doing," Wendell said.

"But we could ask for volunteers in the Bay Area who experience symptoms of the sleeping sickness to come in for monitoring," Michael said.

"We would only need a couple of volunteers with the illness," Mae said. "We could see the effects on humans firsthand."

"How quickly could we expand our testing facility?" Wendell asked Mae.

"We were already working to scale our research," she said. "We could have two more fifth-force monitoring seats in a week or two."

Wendell nodded and stood. "Let me discuss this with our government contacts to get their approval. Knowing the Chinese are doing this will be a powerful incentive to act."

After Wendell left, Mae shook her head and said, "There's so much research going on right now. If it wasn't for the sleeping sickness, I would call it a golden age for dark matter research."

"Isn't that the nature of technology, short periods of brilliant advancements followed by long periods of incremental improvements?" Michael asked.

She frowned and then nodded. "Speaking of

new research, would you like to see our orangutan lab?"

"Of course." It had been his idea, after all.

They walked to lab four and Michael went to one of the large cages lined up along the back wall. An orangutan sat on its haunches in the rear. Long brown hair covered her body except for her face, which had ashen gray skin, brown eyes, small black nostrils, and pinkish lips on a broad, closed mouth. She blinked, then seemed to focus on him.

"Hand her this." Mae gave him a white cube of sugar.

He put the cube on his palm and extended his hand between the bars.

The orangutan shuffled forward on arms that were longer than her legs and shoulders that were wider than her hips. Her smell reminded him of damp dog hair. Grunting quietly, she gently touched his hand, belying her super strength, as he dropped the cube into hers.

"Her name is Cami." Mae walked up beside him.

"Hi, Cami."

She reached up and brushed his now-empty palm with a callous hand. He looked into her eyes, the gateway into her being, and felt her intelligence and kindness. She was a beautiful creature.

"Would you like to see our experiment on her dark bundle?" Mae asked. "They've been amazing."

"Sure." His glasses darkened. A small shimmering globe materialized, and Michael could almost swear that it gave off warmth.

"This is Cami's dark matter bundle. It's physically in the fourth dimension in an area of her brain, the default mode network."

The brownish-yellow sphere glittered peacefully.

"The biological circuitry in the DMN replicates our fifth-force equipment."

"What?" Michael stammered. The fifth-force equipment was complex and consumed significant energy; not something a brain could easily replicate.

"It's done differently, but the result is the same." She probably saw the skepticism on his face. "It's like the human brain answering an arithmetic problem versus a calculator. Different process, but same result."

"How does the DMN do it?"

"I haven't a clue." She exhaled sharply. "It's like asking how the brain adds one plus one. I can explain how a calculator does it with transistors, but not our brains with their electrochemical processes."

He grunted. Evolution had given humans computer-like and fifth-force capabilities, yet the precise mechanisms underlying these remarkable abilities were shrouded in mystery. It seemed unbelievable that the randomness of nature and survival of the fittest could achieve these advanced capabilities through biology.

"Because of how evolution works, it must be critical to the survival of our species. Other animals have them too, although to a lesser extent." After a minute of silence, she grabbed his hand and pulled him back from the cage. "Now watch what happens when we expose Cami's dark matter bundle to bursts of electromagnetic fifth-force energy."

His glasses returned to the sedate bundle, resting peacefully. A few seconds later, it trembled like it was repelling an attack. After about a minute, it slowly radiated or bled a reddish blue color.

"It's decaying," Mae stated, "and generating an unknown type of energy."

Michael tore off his glasses. Cami's eyes were shut, her head tilted down, and her shoulders slouched forward.

"Stop!" Michael yelled. "You're killing her."

Mae calmly stopped the experiment, confusion written on her face. "Cami has no damage with this short exposure. However, if the experiment had continued for six hours, then she would have the sleeping sickness."

She'd obviously done that exact thing with another orangutan. No wonder the vanishing human dark matter bundle in China hadn't surprised her. She'd shown no compassion for the victims of the sleeping sickness, neither human nor orangutan. Although tactile, she could isolate her feelings and become a dispassionate, analytical being, the antithesis of him. How could he have ever found her attractive?

"One interesting thing," Mae continued. "The dark matter bundle learns how to defend itself from attacks. It's like swimming for us; the first time requires a lot of effort, but with practice, it becomes much easier."

"Great," he said, "but if you drown the first time, that doesn't really help."

"True," she said, frowning.

"So, what's causing the sleeping sickness in humans?"

"We don't know." She crossed her arms. "But we can recreate it."

Wonderful. A new weapon. He could see no benefit to humanity from this discovery.

"There is something else, but it's more personal and under wraps." She glanced at him. "Do you remember Ms. Brown, the woman with multiple bundles who suffered from dissociative identity disorder?"

"Yes." He also remembered that Mae's mother had the same condition. No wonder it was personal.

"Let me show you something, a recording."

After his glasses darkened, two brownish-yellow spheres appeared and glittered peacefully. Suddenly, each radiated a reddish glow like hot spheres of metal. Half a minute later, a reddish bolt left one bundle and struck the other, pulling them together until they touched. The result was a slowly rotating two-ball object that resembled a barbell.

"We started with two healthy orangutans," Mae said. "Using the fifth-force in a new way, one orangutan ended up with two personalities while the other had the sleeping sickness."

The rotating barbell object radiated a reddish glow. Then one ball separated and floated to the spot where it had started. The recording ended, and his glasses became transparent again.

"The DID orangutan is back to normal with no side-effects." Mae gave him a sly smile. "Unfortunately, the other orangutan, whose bundle left and returned, lost all its memories."

"That doesn't sound very auspicious," he said. Again, there were no benefits unless it became a weapon.

"Not yet, but I'm hoping with more research, I can merge multiple bundles into one." She closed her eyes and exhaled sharply. "Discover a cure for DID and save my mom."

CHAPTER SIXTEEN: ALIENS

Michael lay in bed, staring at the ceiling. The autumn morning sun lit the room. He carefully slipped out, so as not to disturb Marie, who had slept over twice in the past week. He went to his bathroom to brush his teeth, shave, and take a shower.

He returned to the bedroom in his shorts as Marie stretched her arm. "It's all yours."

She rolled over, looked at him, and grinned. Her hair was jumbled, and her eyes had a brown crust, but she still radiated beauty. Returning to bed tempted him, but instead, he went into his kitchen to get some green tea. He returned to his bedroom and dressed while Marie took a shower. Then he went to the living room to sit by the fire, read his news summary, and finish his tea.

A half-hour later, Marie entered, fully dressed with combed hair and a cup of coffee in hand. "Good morning."

"Good morning," he said. "Another beautiful day in paradise."

"Yes, it is." She scanned the room and sipped her coffee. "I would love to stick around, but I have that eight thirty meeting."

"I know." Michael stood, walked over to her, and looked at her almost empty cup. "Ready?"

They left and walked along the street towards the Berkeley BART train station about forty minutes away.

"What are your plans today?" Marie asked.

"It's a little up in the air." He kicked a rock off the sidewalk into a yard. "I hate to say this, but we're hoping to get a volunteer who caught the sleeping sickness so we can study its progress from sleepiness to deadly coma. Until then, I'll observe some research groups working on the composition of the dark matter bundle."

They crossed a street and continued down the hill. He enjoyed having another person he could honestly share things with; someone who would accept him as he was. "What about you?"

"Same old thing. Analyzing the viral networking and user demographics of your videos and presidential petition."

They had agreed not to produce any more videos until he decided whether to run for president. A green light would mean significantly more work and less free time for all of them.

They continued, seeing few cars or pedestrians on the street. It was an overcast morning, but birds chirped happily in the trees of people's yards. He chatted about the news he had read earlier. She had no interest in professional baseball scores, but they had both seen a review of a new autobiographic video by Beyonce.

The highlights of the review were Beyonce's transitions from glamourous celebrity, to staid middle-aged mother, to retrospective elderly matriarch. In each, she learned something critical about herself. She discovered the distinction between transactional relationships, of which there were many, to her few intimate ones.

"I wonder how my attitude will change over time," Marie said.

"It'll probably depend on what's important to you," he said. "For Beyonce, it started with musical success and fame, but once she had that, she prioritized her relationships with her spouse and kids."

"I've never really thought about kids," Marie said. "What about you?"

"Nope." They were treading on a serious topic now. Did she view him as potential marriage material? The thought brought a burst of happiness, but also anxiety. He could barely manage his own life, let alone worrying about someone else. And what about children? Marie would be a wonderful mother, but how would he be as a father?

They walked in silence for a few minutes until they reached the BART station.

"See you tonight," he said. "Your place?"

She nodded but seemed distracted by her own thoughts. He wrapped his arms around her and rested his head on her shoulder for a few seconds. Then he stepped back. She turned and descended on the escalator.

Twenty minutes later, he arrived at his office just as a call from Anni came in on his glasses.

"We've discovered our first end-to-end case of the sleeping sickness," Anni said without preamble. "Watch this."

His glasses displayed the familiar globe of a human dark matter bundle. Suddenly, a shimmering silvery-white field appeared in the center of the bundle, causing it to wobble.

"A protrusion point opened up at the bundle," Anni said.

The bundle wobbled more and more until it appeared to vibrate. A minute later, a reddish blue energy floated from the bundle and was absorbed by the surrounding silvery-white field. As this continued, the bundle became smaller and smaller until it finally vanished along with the surrounding field.

"The destruction of the bundle took eight hours, but we condensed it into this five-minute recording." His glasses now displayed Anni in a library, standing in front of stained-wood shelves with leather-bound books. A lit fireplace was on one side and a couch on the other. It was a complete anachronism to the digital world. Anni's glasses were clear, and her face was serious.

"Do you have any idea where the attack came from?"

"Yes," Anni said in a cracked voice. She looked away with a nervous smile. "With our full view, we could trace the attack back to its source. The protrusion point network leaves an obfuscated, but discernable, path in the dark matter universe."

He tapped his fingers against his desk. Anni liked suspense.

"The source is on a planet about the size of Mars, in a solar system about one billion light-years away."

"One billion light-years?" His glasses displayed patches of white light on a dark iron-colored circle against a gray background.

"This is the dark matter view of the alien

planet," she said. "And this was our attacker."

The pictured zoomed in on one white patch, which became many individual white spots. It looked like a nighttime view from a low-flying airplane of a lit town. A minute later, he saw a single golden-white spot in the middle, surrounded by four smaller sized, similarly colored spots.

He must be looking at five aliens, one of which was a murderer.

"The alien's bundles or globes are whiter than humans and come in different sizes," Anni said.

"What's that?" Michael pointed at a fuzzy brown thread that rose from the attacker's globe and went into space.

"That's the path we followed. It fades with time."

Michael rubbed his chin. "How are they attacking us?"

"I don't know, but we've initiated research projects to replicate their technology."

"But why destroy our dark matter bundles?" Michael asked.

"I don't know." Anni walked to the couch and flopped herself down. "We need to talk with them."

Shock suddenly overwhelmed him. Aliens, a billion light years away, were killing humans. He felt lightheaded and dizzy.

"China's technology to trace protrusion points is more advanced than yours," she said. "However, your dark matter communication technologies are superior to China's. We should work together."

"Uh-huh." He placed his hands on his desk to steady himself. *Listen to her words.*

"Collaboration is the best approach for humanity," she continued, "but certain governments and officials might not agree."

"All hell is gonna break loose when the public learns about this." Everyone would have the same reaction as he did.

"Which is why they won't."

"Why?" he asked. Anni couldn't suppress this.

"Because governments will keep it secret for national security reasons," Anni said, before breaking off the call.

CHAPTER SEVENTEEN: PRESIDENTIAL RUN

Over the next two days, Michael came to grips with the alien situation. Initially, he had moped around in a depressed state, but he'd finally found acceptance. He had decided not to burden anyone else with Anni's discovery until she had more information. Unfortunately, there was nothing he could do, other than worry, so he tried to put it at the back of his mind and focus on the important things of his life. Only a year remained before the presidential election, and he needed to decide.

After knocking, Marie walked into his office for a conference call with Anni. Her musky, woodsy perfume excited him so much more than trite, floral scents. She joined him at his small round table, then reached over to hold his hand, which brought a smile to his face.

A minute later, his glasses turned opaque, then the room reappeared, but this time with Anni seated across from them. Marie released her grip and placed her hands on the table.

"The survey results are in." Anni eyed them with a sly smile. "Your followers would strongly support you for president."

"And they now total about sixty million," Marie said as her eyebrows rose.

"Can I really win?" Even if he could, did he really want to add this to his already chaotic life? There was already too much going on. Yet, something in him had changed. Another person, who aspired for greatness, now co-existed in his head. His internal sweet voice said *go for it*, and he was comfortable with the choice, even though his monkey voice told him he was an idiot.

"Yes!" Anni smacked her fist down on the table with a virtual *crack*. "People want change, which weakens their traditional party loyalties. With our media campaigns, we can move them to your side."

He was making a pivotal decision. He'd said that he would run if his followers supported him, and they had. Marie and Anni both wanted him to run and, deep down, so did he.

"All right." Despite what Anni said, he didn't expect to win. No third-party candidate had ever won the presidency. However, the only thing impossible was something never attempted. "I'll run."

"Great!" Anni leaped to her feet.

"Super!" Marie jumped up too, then bent over to hug him. "We'll need to announce your candidacy formally. We could launch it in two days."

"We'll need to mobilize quickly," Anni said, "since the election will move into high gear with the first state primary election in two months."

"January?" He hadn't thought about the timeline other than election day being next November. "Do we have enough time?"

"I've done some preliminary, time-sensitive work in case you ran." Anni's eyes darted around in her glasses like she was reviewing different data.

"Really?" He wondered if she'd jumped the gun. "Like what?"

"Like submitting all the state election filings before their deadlines."

He nodded. "What are we going to call our party?"

"The People's Party," Marie said, "simple and direct with strong voter support."

He looked up "People's Party" on his glasses:

- *People's Party of India. Largest political party in India committed to Hindu nationalism.*
- *People's Party of China. Ruling party committed to the ideology of Marxism-Leninism.*
- *People's Party of the United States. From 1891 to 1908, this political party advocated for the rights of farmers and workers.*

There were other references, but he was comfortable with the name even though it carried some baggage. "Great. So, what do you need from me?"

"We'll want you to record the announcement in my production studio." Marie winked at Anni like a co-conspirator.

"I thought I didn't need to record videos because of your technology."

"You don't." Anni put a hand on his shoulder. "However, you'll need to make public appearances in the future, and this is a safe place to gain some experience."

He nodded. They could record as many times as needed to produce a perfect video. Still, he was nervous, since a hundred million people would see it. "Okay, send me the draft script."

Although he went to the lab the next day, his head wasn't in it. His mind wandered between the aliens, his announcement, the sleeping sickness, and Marie. Strange that a person like him could be in the middle of a maelstrom with so many transformational issues. Real life was stranger than fiction, but right now, there were only two things he could directly affect: his announcement and Marie. He needed to compartmentalize everything else until he could do something about them.

In the evening, he took BART to the Embarcadero station in San Francisco, carrying his outfit for the big announcement. Dragging his roller bag, he walked past lit buildings to the fifty-eight-story blue-gray glass apartment building of the Millennium Tower. The elevator buzzed him to the twenty-fourth floor, where he went down the hallway to the second door.

He knocked, and after a moment, it swung open.

"Come in." Marie wore a black and white furry jumper suit, which made her look like a Dalmatian.

He gave her a peck on both cheeks. He deposited his bag in her bedroom, then joined her in the kitchen, where she handed him a glass of wine.

He took a sip, set the glass down on the counter, and wrapped his arms around her waist, pulling her close for a long kiss. He felt like a teenager with hormones running wild.

After a minute, she pulled back. "Let's go to the living room."

"Sure." He went to the couch and looked at the recently decorated Christmas tree with its multi-colored lights, ornaments, and tinsel. The song, Silent Night, played softly. He glanced out the window at other apartment and office buildings, some with lit rooms, but many dark.

Marie placed a platter of cheese, meats, and bread on the coffee table, and then sat down beside him. "Are you ready for tomorrow?"

"I think so." He wrapped an arm around her as she nestled into his shoulder. She was a rock of stability in his chaotic life: a presidential run, aliens ending the lives of thousands of people every day, and dark matter research. Three monumental, but interrelated things. He rolled his head back, closed his eyes, and exhaled deeply. Somehow, she made him forget about all of it.

The next morning, they went to Marie's production studio. She escorted him to a room where a high-quality camera pointed to an orange wall with a circle on the floor in front.

"Stand there." She pointed to the circle. "The glass in front of the camera lens will display the text of your speech. Questions?"

"It seems so sterile." He walked to the designated spot.

"We'll replace the wall with lively background later." She walked to the side. "Ready?"

He gave a thumbs up. The first words of his speech appeared in front of the camera. He inhaled deeply through his nose and lowered his shoulders. He had memorized his speech, but the projected words acted as a crutch, relieving any anxiety of forgetting his words.

"Good day. My name's Michael Knightsbridge. Ahh. I wish to announce that I'm a candidate for the presidency of the united sexes." Michael slapped his head. "Oh, God."

"Relax," Marie said. "We have all day and as many takes as necessary."

He tried five more times but couldn't get past the third sentence without a major faux pas.

"You're trying too hard," Marie said. "Close your eyes, take some deep breaths, clear your mind, and speak like you're talking to me."

She removed the teleprompter glass and then stood by the camera. She gave him a slight nod and flashed a smile.

He closed his eyes, took two deep breaths, and relaxed his mind, not concentrating on the words of his speech. The other presence, his confident and successful voice, rushed in. He opened his eyes.

"Good day. My name's Michael Knightsbridge. I wish to announce that I'm a candidate for the presidency of the United States and to ask for the support of all Americans who share my belief that our nation needs to embark on a new, constructive course." So far, so good.

"I'm running because I have grown increasingly concerned about the course of events in the United States and in the world. Over the past few years, Americans have become increasingly disillusioned by their life prospects and have retreated from society. Today, more than half our young people are stuck in dead-end government social programs, isolated, and not forming social bonds. Without change, this generation will be lost. I know because I used to be one of them." He had gotten through the first part of his speech perfectly. He was on a roll.

"However, instead of addressing this and other problems in society, our politicians ingratiate themselves with the elite, sacrificing the interests of our citizens. Today it is difficult to find leaders who are independent of the forces that have brought us our problems—the Congress, the bureaucracy, the lobbyist, big business, and big labor." He spoke naturally, not thinking about his next word or sentence. He might have been a spectator watching a performer.

"I have published sixteen examples of corrupt politicians taking bribes from special interests to pass legislation favorable to them. The corruption is pervasive in both political parties, Democrats and Republicans, which operate a "buddy" system that functions for its own benefit—increasingly insensitive to the needs of the American worker who supports it with his taxes." He frowned, thinking about the corruption exposed by his different videos.

"Unfortunately, nothing can be done from within the two-party system. For that reason, I'm announcing a new political party, The People's Party of the United States." He nodded at Marie behind the camera since she'd come up with the party name. "I realize that I'm proposing a lot of change, but America needs a new direction. We can't keep electing corrupt career politicians from the established political parties."

"In the coming months, I will take this message to the American people. I will talk in detail about responsible, responsive government working for the average citizen. I will tell the people it is they who should decide how government will help, not the career politicians. People want a life of fulfillment, not one of waste enabled by unfruitful government programs that lead nowhere." He grimaced, knowing he had succumbed to this siren call and had only found the light recently. He'd come so far in a few short months.

"I don't believe for one moment that four more years of business-as-usual in Washington is the answer to our problems, and I don't think the American people believe it either." He raised both hands and shook his fists. "Join me and my sixty million followers in our crusade to bring America back to the people. Thank you for listening and please link to Michael Knightsbridge if you would like to join and support our cause."

He stared at the camera as the light turned red. The orator in his head faded from his consciousness.

"Well," Marie said, striding up to him. "That's a take."

***

A month after his presidential announcement, campaigning consumed most of his time. Although not formally part of it because of her foreign nationality, Anni was intricately involved. She formed a vetting committee to interview around twenty vice president candidates from both political parties. They had worked quickly and virtually to whittle the list down to four. Today was his first interview with one finalist.

There was a knock at his front door. He opened it and met Patty Murphy, the former senator from Wyoming. Although she had been the incumbent, she had lost the primary election in the last midterms to a far-right Republican. She was a husky woman in her mid-forties with black hair and blue eyes, a shade shorter than Michael.

"Welcome." He stuck out his hand.

She nodded and shook his hand. Her grip was firm. "Thanks."

"Please follow me." He walked into the family room and sat down on the couch, opening his hand towards the adjacent chair where she sat. Through the window, he saw birds playing in the leafless trees on this cold, wintry day. The fire burned warmly in the fireplace.

After some small talk about her travel and the holidays, he said, "Why don't we start with you telling me a little about yourself."

"Sure. I'm a fourth generation Wyomingite with family roots in ranching, oil, and gas industries. I grew up on a ranch near Ten Sleep, earned a Bachelor of Science degree in agriculture and a law degree from the University of Wisconsin. From there, I spent seven years as Wyoming State Treasurer, sixteen years as a member of the Wyoming State House and Senate, and then was elected to the US senate. There I worked on bi-partisan legislation including the National Forest System Trails Stewardship Act, which maintains over one hundred thousand miles of trails within our national forests."

He already knew most of this. He'd studied her political career but was curious about her upbringing and the experiences that helped form her. "How was growing up on a ranch?"

"It's hard work taking care of the land and animals." Her eyes narrowed as if reliving those days. "Society undervalued us, looking down on us as buffoons or hicks. We were the butts of jokes, and our bank accounts proved it."

"What did you learn?" He'd thought the industry was dead, replaced by faux meats. The closure of all industrial ranches left only the struggling family ones.

"Humility." Her shoulders slumped, but her eyes remained sharp. "While we lived in poverty according to many definitions, it was a fortune and privilege to grow up on vast tracts of land with cattle, sheep, and horses."

Even though their backgrounds were completely different, he liked her. "Why are you interested in being my vice president?"

"I agree with your criticism of corruption in government. Although I've benefited from the old boy's network, it's gone too far." Patty made a fist. "I won't play the game anymore."

He liked her conviction but wondered if she had thought this through. "You realize this will probably doom any future Republican runs."

"The current right-wing leadership has already ostracized me for being a moderate. I'm not risking anything."

Patty sounded serious about being his vice president. "What questions do you have for me?"

"Given that two parties control Congress, do you think you would caucus with the Republicans or Democrats?"

This was a good question and got to the root of the problem. Politicians caucused and voted with their party as a bloc rather than work on bi-partisan legislation that the majority could support. "I'll work with moderates from both parties."

"Won't that be difficult?" The corners of her lips fell as she furrowed her brows, considering. "They hold allegiance to their party and will follow the direction of their leadership."

"True. Most will prioritize their party's interests over the country's." He'd discussed this with Anni and Marie, and they'd agreed on a strategy. "However, most will also prioritize their own interests over everything else. I'll make sure that their personal interests align with mine."

"How?" Patty tilted her head. This probably contradicted all her previous experiences.

"By presenting the facts directly to the voters." He leaned forward. Their advanced technology was the key, which would make this possible. "Voters will receive individual messages that resonate with them. Although politicians will continue their double-talk, they can no longer obfuscate the facts on core issues."

"But voters are driven by their emotions, not their rationale." Patty leaned forward too. "It's why negative advertising on cultural issues works so well. When people vote for their candidate, they're often voting against the opposition who's been demonized."

He nodded. Both Democrats and Republicans were typically ambivalent about their candidates, seeing some good and some bad. However, they detested the other side and voted accordingly. "Our campaign strategy is to contrast my positions directly against theirs rather than just criticizing them."

"How?" Her eyes narrowed.

"We have an extremely sophisticated connection with a hundred million voters, which will soon reach one hundred and sixty million. We're not trying to convince the diehards, who only vote along party lines. Our target is everyone else, which will be enough to win."

She nodded and brought her eyes back to him. "What about funding? The pundits estimate it'll cost five billion dollars."

"It'll cost much less. We're only spending advertising dollars to increase my followers." He stood and walked to the fireplace to warm his hands. Looking over his shoulder, he said, "Once voters become followers, the outreach cost is almost zero. Unlike other candidates, we'll use public funding from the Presidential Election Campaign Fund to match my donations and comply with the spending limits."

"How much have you received in small donations?" She got up and joined him by the fireplace, although she kept her hands by her side.

"About five hundred million. We got a huge pop after my announcement and now receive about five million dollars daily."

Patty shut her eyes. After a moment, she opened them and smiled. "You've come out of nowhere but have a good shot at winning."

"I've scrambled the calculus of the pundits." The corner of his mouth raised. "But voters want someone new who brings fresh ideas rather than echoing empty platitudes."

"My ex-colleagues won't know what hit them."

CHAPTER EIGHTEEN: FIRST CONTACT

Michael was in his home office in early February, but virtually sitting in a small, white room at a round table across from Anni. She was in her usual business outfit, but uncharacteristically, her face was flushed and her hair frazzled.

"I wanted to update you on the alien situation," Anni said.

"It's been almost three months since you discovered them." He frowned since he hadn't been by the lab much, hadn't kept up to date on the issue. His presidential campaign and Marie had consumed all his time. Although the alien attack was critically important, he wasn't sure he could add much. "I'm no scientist. Should I even stay involved?"

"More so now than before. We're entering uncharted territory." She straightened her back. "AI provides better analysis of the data than the scientists can, but your insights could be the key to unlocking the puzzle. Besides, it won't take a lot of your time."

He thought Wendell would've been a better choice. At least he had the scientific background and ran a lab. However, if it wouldn't take much time, then he wouldn't make an issue of it. He sat back in his chair and crossed his arms. "Okay."

His glasses darkened, then displayed a bird's-eye view of the alien planet, which again reminded him of a nighttime view of lit cities and towns. "There are about five million globes of dark matter on the alien planet. I expect each one corresponds to an alien being. Based on globe appearances and disappearances, which I equate to births and deaths, the average life expectancy is about sixty Earth years."

"What about their civilization?" The display of his glasses flipped from the dark matter view of the alien planet to Anni.

"It's an advanced civilization since they use protrusion point technology to attack Earth a billion light-years away." She leaned back in her chair and twirled her thumbs. "However, unlike humans, they live in small groups and don't travel quickly or over long distances."

This sounded more like a primitive society rather than an advanced civilization living in cities and traveling in cars, subways, or planes.

"Another thing, the globes grow inconsistently over time until they vanish." She leaned forward and interlocked the fingers of both hands. "At birth, they're about one quarter the size of a human's, but they can grow to about double."

"Weird." The alien's dark matter bundles differed greatly from humans. "Do you know why they're attacking Earth?"

"No, which brings us to the next project phase." She pulled her shirt sleeves back to her elbow. His glasses flipped back to the dark matter view and displayed a group of golden-white points of differing sizes; a brown thread from one of them rose to the sky. "This is a recording of a recent experiment in China."

"This is the origin of a recent sleeping sickness attack," she said. Cross hairs on the display targeted and zoomed in on the globe with the brown thread. "We opened a protrusion point on the creature's bundle and tried to communicate with energy pulses."

Through his glasses, Michael heard, "Bzz, Bzzzzz, Bzz, Bzzzz, . . ."

The golden-white globe that had been plodding around stopped. Michael wondered how he would react if he heard a short and long buzzing sound repeating itself in his mind. After a few minutes, other globes joined the targeted one.

Here was the first human contact with an alien civilization, but how had Anni gotten access to the recording? He had thought she was just a rich Chinese businesswoman. She must also be politically connected.

Just then, he heard a humming noise reverberate from the recording.

"It actually took a few hours to get a reply," Anni said, "but here we go."

He heard a succession of short buzzing pulses, followed by longer ones. Along the top of his glasses were a bunch of dots in a row, followed by a dash. Then the series moved down, and another identical series formed on top. This repeated itself.

"What's going on?" he asked.

"We wanted to communicate with bit-mapped two-dimensional pictures, but first we needed to establish a standard."

"A standard?" He could understand sending pictures.

"A standard picture with two-hundred-fifty-six pixels per side or about sixty-five thousand pixels per photo," she said.

His glasses now displayed a box of dots with a row of dashes on the left and right side.

"Each short buzz is a dot and each long one is a dash," she said. "You go two-hundred-fifty-six spaces, then jump down to the beginning of the next line, and repeat until you reach two-hundred-fifty-six lines."

This sounded complex. "How did you figure this out?"

"One of my companies deals with the challenges of communication with extraterrestrial intelligence. Although there are many CETI organizations who do this type of work, we're the only ones who planned for real-time communications. The others used a paradigm of eons between messages, which rendered most of their work useless."

She had her hands in everything.

"Once we agreed on the standard," she continued, "we sent geometric shapes. The first one was a square, which took us two hours to send."

Michael's glasses displayed the construction of a square, one row at a time, with dots on the inside and dashes at the border.

"They replied with an upside-down equilateral triangle, and a mathematical formula to calculate its area," Anni said. "They also tried to increase the transmission rate, but we couldn't handle it. Their technology is more advanced than ours."

"Incredible."

"Next, we sent an image of a human," she said.

A picture of dots and dashes now showed the outline of a woman's naked body.

Suddenly, his glasses displayed a black object that resembled a thumb, including the nail and wrinkles in the middle that would be over the knuckle. Above it, connected by a black thread, was a small black sphere.

"What are we looking at?"

"An alien."

"Is that its dark matter bundle hovering above its head?" This creature was stranger than anything he'd ever imagined.

"Probably." She sighed. "Which means it's a well-understood part of their civilization. I didn't even think about including one for humans."

"Did you ask them to stop the sleeping sickness?"

"No. A communication framework to pose the request will take weeks to establish. However, now that they know we exist, they may stop."

Michael had learned not to rely on strangers' kindness, especially when they wanted something from him. "What now?"

"We need to increase our transmission rate," she said as the alien picture vanished, and they returned to the table in the white sterile room. "For that, we need to involve the Berkeley research team. The Chinese president has agreed to this exchange."

Anni had a direct line to the Chinese president? How could one person have her tentacles in so many high-level areas and still find time to meet with him?

"What about the US government?" Michael asked. "Should we get President Douglas to speak with us?"

"Well, I've briefed the future president." She gave him a lopsided grin. "We should start with Eric Lane, director of the Office of Science and Technology Policy or OSTP. He's the president's top scientist and sits on his cabinet. We'll also include your brother."

"Okay," Michael mumbled. Exchanging pictures with hostile aliens a billion light years away would've been unimaginable if it wasn't true. He shook his head. At least they could now confront the sleeping sickness.

***

Over the next two weeks, Michael and Anni briefed Wendell, Mae, Eric Lane, and his team about everything they'd learned. Dr. Lane was a trim gray-haired man with intense cobalt eyes who, along with his team, always wore a blue suit and tie. Even though OSTP had approved working with Anni, they weren't happy with the current situation. They even considered shutting down the collaboration but relented after learning the US benefited from the Chinese's knowledge of protrusion point technologies.

Michael now sat at his home office desk, wearing glasses that placed him virtually at a small table with Anni. In the center of the table was a speakerphone for their first conversation with the Thumblings. He was stunned to be there. Anni had somehow gotten China to agree that she would be their representative. She hadn't wanted to overwhelm the other side, so had given the US the choice between no representation or Michael. The US argued but had little bargaining power. Although the call was live streamed, Wendell and Dr. Lane were still not happy.

"They've joined." Anni said, looking at the speakerphone. "Welcome."

"Welcome." The voice sounded like a young boy's.

"My name is Anni, and I also have Michael on the line."

"My name is Wanderer." There was a pause. "How are you able to have two people on one connection?"

Anni sat up suddenly and blinked. "We have technology that enables it."

"Technology?" Wanderer said. "Like a tool? Like a wheel or cart?"

"Much more advanced than a cart," Anni said. "Our technological equipment allows us to communicate with you."

"Really? Wanderer said. "We don't need technology."

Michael's brow furrowed. The Thumblings could communicate naturally through dark matter. They also must be a highly intelligent species—Wanderer had learned the communication standard in his head. It would be like a blind man figuring out brail on his own. The absence of technology was mind-boggling. Because of their superior natural abilities, they didn't need to develop tools.

"Ah, I see you," Wanderer continued. "You're in two different spots on Earth."

"I'm in Beijing, and Michael is in Berkeley with our communication equipment," Anni said.

"You live in very populated areas," Wanderer said, sounding impressed, or maybe just eager, like a hunter scoping out new territories.

"You know we're sentient beings," Anni said after some silence. "Why have you continued to destroy our dark matter bundles?"

"To achieve eternal bliss." The voice sounded as if Wanderer was in awe.

"Eternal bliss?" Michael said.

"It's eternal consciousness or life beyond the grave," Wanderer said at a quick tempo, then he slowed down. "There is joy and no unmet desires of the physical world."

"Is this your belief?" To Michael, this sounded like some kind of Thumbling nirvana.

"No. It's real. If someone dies, a portal opens for a brief period, and others can communicate with the recently departed, as well as others long gone."

This was unbelievable. If true, did this prove life after death for the Thumblings? He wondered if there was a comparable place for humans.

"How does consuming bundles achieve eternal bliss?" Anni asked.

"Before our body dies, our essence must reach a certain size, about eight-fold from birth, to continue living." Wanderer paused, then continued. "How do you grow your essence?"

"We don't." Michael shook his head, confused by the question. Essence and bundle must be the same thing. "Our essence may shift slightly over time, but we don't grow it by taking from others."

"What did you do before you found Earth?" Anni asked.

"Harvested the bundles from our elders, who had no chance to reach the needed size."

"How did you find Earth?"

"There was a beacon that went out in the dark matter universe about six months ago. When I traced the signal back to its source, I located your planet, which radiated a golden field of billions of essences. I thought it was a blessing from God."

Michael wrung his hands. What caused the beacon that attracted the Thumblings' attention? Could other aliens have also seen it?

"Have you discovered other alien planets?" Anni asked.

"No." Wanderer took an unusually long pause. "The universe is vast."

"Now that you know who we are, will your people stop their attacks on our dark matter bundles?" Michael figured this was wishful thinking.

"No. However, rather than harvesting randomly, you could provide us with the location for your elderly, who are close to death. They wouldn't lose much."

Only their soul. Where did that thought come

from? Michael didn't even believe in an everlasting soul, let alone one made of dark matter. However, like a soul, dark matter couldn't be seen or touched, yet it persisted. Was this purely a coincidence?

"Let us consider your suggestion," Anni said. "We'll talk again soon."

"Until then," the voice said. A low hum followed.

"The transmission is complete," Anni said. "What do you think?"

They had learned many things about the Thumblings, but Michael could only think of one thing: the attacks would continue. "I don't like the idea of sacrificing our elderly. We need a better solution."

"If the Thumblings can open protrusions points anywhere, then they probably developed blocking techniques to protect themselves." Anni pinched her lips together, then shifted her mouth from side to side. "We'll need to pursue this angle."

After a long pause, Anni stood and paced with her hands clasped behind her back. "Given the allure of eternal bliss, I'm surprised the Thumbling attacks haven't increased."

Although the idea was depressing, she had a point. With the abundance on Earth, all Thumblings could now reach nirvana. "Any ideas why?"

She looked at him and squinted. "Perhaps it's a personal choice, like a person on a diet. However, a more likely reason is it takes a while to digest a bundle."

Michael thought of a boa constrictor swallowing a pig and laying still for days as the large bulge slid down the snake's body. "What was this beacon that disclosed Earth's location?"

"I'm not sure."

"Could other aliens have seen it?" If so, would they be a threat like the Thumblings or a savior or something else entirely?

"I don't know." She studied him; then she tilted her head and stared into the distance. "The Chinese researchers want to meet with me."

"All right." He wondered when or if the Americans would want to meet with him. "Going forward, we should have more people directly involved from both sides."

"I'll discuss it with my government," she said. "Ciao."

CHAPTER NINETEEN: THE CLUSTER

Three months ago, a bright flash blanketed the dark matter universe. Node two-forty-five explored the disturbance and was now ready to broadcast its findings to the other ten thousand nodes of the community brain.

The bright flash came from the fusion of a high concentration of living dark matter and fifth-force energy. For a moment, it gave the entire dark matter universe a faint cosmic glow. It originated on a planet one and a half billion light years from our home planet. This planet has an advanced intelligent species, which brings our total known AIS planets in the universe to forty-seven. Like all the others, the people are unconnected individuals, so different from our single networked civilization. It sensed seventy-one percent of the cluster nodes consume the summary.

I've opened protrusion portals in orbit to study their civilization with minimal risk of disclosing our home planet location. I've intercepted and translated their radio wave broadcasts. The people call themselves human and their planet Earth.

Node two-forty-five released the first summary of electromagnetic broadcast communications gathered from the planet, showing basic human activities. *Humans use their two legs to walk short distances and mechanical vehicles to travel longer ones. Their brain sits on top of the body in their head. They connect to external data sources through glasses that cover their eyes. They manipulate their local environment with hands at the end of their arms.*

It released the next summary of broadcasts. *The population consumes current event broadcasts such as natural disasters, manmade disasters like wars, and general points of view. Other programs deal with mating, not the actual act, but the selection process.*

Node two-forty-five released a compilation of human history, starting with humans foraging in forests and moving to the formation of small villages and large cities. *Their civilization becomes more and more reliant on technology. Humans also display excessive violence occurring between individuals and groups. Although their technological development is rapid, they aren't currently a threat to us.*

Fear was the general feeling from the cluster. A similar miscalculation had wiped out another advanced civilization. Node two-forty-five replied, *If they develop fourth dimension weapons and show a willingness to use them, then we'll strike first according to the protocols of the intergalactic treaty.*

Why did they disclose their planet's location? asked a large group of listeners.

We don't know, node two-forty-five said. *Perhaps it was an accident from an experiment that went badly. Alternatively, it could've been a deliberate act from a group of human saboteurs. We don't believe any intelligent civilization would deliberately disclose their planet's location to the universe.*

Are other alien civilizations studying Earth? asked another group.

Since every AIS civilization would've seen the flash, we suspect many of them are observing human activities from the safety of Earth's orbit. We have not tried to identify them because of the risk of disclosing our general home location, node two-forty-five broadcasted. *As we know, the only safety in the universe is secrecy.*

Node two-forty-five answered a few more group questions. It gauged the cluster's interest in this new civilization at ninety percent. *To attain better information, I ask permission to open protrusion points on their information networks on Earth. Although this will increase the risk of our detection, we can act proactively if they threaten us.*

Support was sixty-seven percent, just enough

to move forward. Curiosity had overcome fear. The community brain assigned two junior, less developed nodes to two-forty-five.

CHAPTER TWENTY: WHO IS ANNI

With elections only seven months away, President Douglas was in fundraising and campaigning mode. He was the undisputed leader of the Republican party and would breeze through the primaries. The Democrats floundered with a group of weak candidates. However, Knightsbridge was a wildcard. Jamie walked into his office and took a seat in front of his desk.

"Good morning, Mr. President." She straightened her coat sleeves. "We've looked into Michael Knightsbridge's presidential candidacy. Somehow, he's already met every state's registration requirement, even those that needed to be posted last year."

"So, he's been thinking about this for a while." President Douglas rubbed his chin.

"He also has about one hundred million

followers, many of whom are passionate, and five hundred million dollars in donations from individual contributors."

"Do you think he seriously has a chance?" His eyes narrowed.

"Not really." She shook her head. "To win, he would need one hundred and twenty million votes."

"But he's close with one hundred million followers." This sounded bad.

"He's a curiosity." The edges of her lips curved up. "Many of his followers won't vote for him. More likely, he'd be a spoiler."

"What do you mean? Wouldn't he take votes away from Democrats?"

"I'm not sure. He advocates for compassion, but also for personal responsibility and accountability. He's an outsider, speaking against the establishment."

Knightsbridge was a spoiler, but who would lose more, the Democrats or Republicans? I need to protect my position with my voting base.

"He also has an incredibly sophisticated campaign getting the right messages to the right people at the right time." She frowned. "Even we can't do that."

"How can a person who spent twenty years employed by state social programs do this?"

"I don't know. He showed no political or leadership aptitude. He's uneducated, barely graduated from high school. However, both his parents were university professors, and his twin brother is a renowned physicist."

"So, he was an underachiever. What changed?"

"Six months ago, he moved to Berkeley to live with and work for his brother Wendell Knightsbridge."

"Wendell Knightsbridge." The name was familiar. "Isn't he one of the dark matter researchers looking into the sleeping sickness?"

"Yes, sir."

He shook his head. "This still doesn't explain how he became a viable presidential candidate."

"True." Jaimie leaned forward. "The only thing we've come up with is Anni Chan."

"She must be a magician." He stood and paced behind his desk. "Tell me about her."

"Much of what I've found raises more questions than answers. Supposedly, she's visited the U.S. often, but we have no records from DHS of her entering or leaving. The EU and our other allies also have no record of her visiting, so I can only assume she's holed up in China and conducting her business virtually."

He stopped pacing and stared at Jamie.

"She owns many businesses, including some in the US and EU, but she acquired most of them in the last few months." Jamie shuffled in her seat.

"Where did she get her money?" He placed his hands on his desk and leaned forward.

"Unknown, but she's an uncanny investor."

"Have the SEC look for insider trading." He would add some complexity to her life.

"There are many records of her family and friends," Jamie said. "But we've met no one who can personally collaborate the stories. They're all dead."

"Is she a spook?" He started pacing again. It wouldn't be the first time an agent for China tried to influence a presidential election, but normally it was subtle.

"Possibly."

"So why is she supporting Knightsbridge?" There was an unwritten rule that China would stay out of US domestic politics and vice versa.

"Unknown."

"Then find out. This may be a national security threat."

He sat down and rubbed his eyes until he heard the door click shut behind Jamie.

**

Michael walked onto campus through the Friday morning drizzle. The wide cement path with inlaid brick along its sides took him past large cement buildings, mowed lawns, and gray trees with their new leaves. His hi-tech clothing kept his body dry, and his rain cap prevented the blowing water from striking his face and neck. Two bodyguards trailed behind him.

A group of six students coming from the opposite direction approached him. The men seemed impervious to the weather, wearing knee-high shorts and retro-Hawaiian shirts. The women were more sensibly dressed in their skin-tight, waterproof, one-piece outfits. They eyed him, then talked excitedly among themselves. As he passed, they yelled, "Give 'em hell, Mikey."

"Thanks," he said, spinning around with a smile and a thumbs up.

"Yah," they screamed, hands reaching to the sky.

He turned around and continued to the square where the Campanile clock tower was clanking eight times for the hour. From there, he bound up the brick stairs to the research building's front doors.

"Michael Knightsbridge?" A man in a tan rain jacket stepped towards him. There was another similarly dressed man who hung back.

"Yes."

"FBI." The middle-aged, clean-shaven man had piercing blue eyes. He held his badge near his face. "We have a few questions for you."

Michael's glasses confirmed the man was agent Marconi of the FBI. Michael couldn't imagine what the FBI wanted. Maybe someone had made a threat against him.

"Can we come to your office?" Marconi said.

"Sure. Follow me." Michael walked through the doors; the second man slipped in behind them. He walked up the stairs and went directly to his office without a word. He unlocked his door, went to his desk, and asked the FBI agents to pull over a chair. His bodyguards remained in the hallway.

"We have some questions about Anni Chan," agent Marconi said as soon as they sat down. "How long have you known her?"

Michael did a quick calculation. He had met her just after arriving at Berkeley and starting his job at UC in August. It seemed like a lifetime ago. "About six months."

"What's your relationship with her?" the agent asked.

"She's my boss. I'm her onsite representative for research here."

"Anything else?"

"She's produced investigative videos for me and supported my run for president." *Foreign influence in domestic politics must be the reason for the FBI visit.*

"Where did you get the facts for the videos?"

"From Anni, who assembled them from data found in public sources."

The two agents looked at each other and rolled their eyes. "We believe she illegally obtained the information. It wasn't publicly available."

"I know nothing about that." His face flushed. "She said her AI computers allowed her to find patterns others couldn't see."

"Do you really believe that?" Agent Marconi sounded incredulous.

"Yes." He'd never underestimate her, given what she'd accomplished. "Why don't you talk to her?"

"She's not in the US."

"She's here about once a month on business." He could remember at least five different times when she had called him from a US location. There was SFO, NY, Minneapolis, Dallas, and Miami.

"No. She's never visited the US, which the DHS has confirmed." Agent Marconi eyed him up and down.

"Really?" He frowned. There must be an explanation. "Perhaps she travels under a different name, and you haven't made the connection yet."

"Unlikely." Agent Marconi grimaced. "Even with all our Chinese contacts, we've encountered no one who has met Ms. Chan in person. She seems to be a complete recluse."

"Really?" Even though he'd never met her in person, on some video calls, she was among other people.

"Do you know why she's supporting you?"

"She trusts and believes in me." He gave Anni's answer, even though it had always sounded incomplete.

"Could it be that you're more easily influenced and controlled than a more qualified candidate?" Marconi leaned forward, placing his arms on Michael's desktop.

Although he had some questions about her motives, he didn't think she would use him. However, now doubts crept in.

"What do you think she's trying to do?" Marconi studied his face like a hawk.

"To make the world a better place," he said. Both agents' eyes widened in surprise. "She's concentrating on her home country, China, and her adopted one, the US."

"How?"

"By representing the interests of the people rather than the special interests of wealthy corporations. Have you seen my videos?" These guys would never vote for him.

"So, you see yourself as a crusader for the common citizen," Marconi said, glancing at his partner. "Others might see you as a puppet for a foreign adversary."

"Are you trying to intimidate me?" Michael said, surprised by the anger in his voice. Where did that come from? A moment later, he found himself standing. "Gentlemen, if there's nothing else, I have important work to do."

"No more questions. Thank you for your time." Marconi and his partner stood and walked to the door, where they turned around to face Michael. "Your work here gives you top security clearance. The penalty for leaking any of this information is at least ten years in prison." The door closed gently behind them.

After they left, he forwarded a link of the interview to Anni and requested a meeting. A minute later, he received an invitation to go to his VR room to join her in a virtual meeting. That was fast.

He joined the meeting. Anni stood wearing blue jeans and a white T-shirt, with her hair pulled back. Behind her were racks of computers almost reaching a ten-foot ceiling. To her side was a black cube, which came up to her shoulders.

"Where are we?" he asked.

"A data center in Beijing."

"Are you really there?" He wondered if the data center room was just a prop.

"Yes." She tapped the cube.

"Did you see my FBI interview?"

"Yes." Her shoulders went slack. "I'm sorry if I put you in a difficult situation."

"I managed, but I really need to hear the truth now." He was raising his voice; he couldn't help it.

"I've always told you the truth about myself." She sounded defensive. "However, I haven't disclosed everything, but I'm ready to do so now."

"Good. Have you physically ever been in the US?"

She scrunched up her mouth as if it was a tough question. "No."

"Did you illegally acquire any of the political data?"

"Most was acquired legally." Again, she pursed

her lips. "However, some data came from tapping into private communication channels."

"Do you work for the Chinese government?" he asked, remembering the FBI agent's accusation.

"No." Her head recoiled like the question was absurd. "Of course not. I work with them when our interests align, but they never pay me."

"What are you trying to do?"

"Exactly what I've always said. To make the world a better place by improving the wellbeing of the public."

The FBI agents had distrusted this answer, finding it improbable if not inconceivable. A government official or leader of a charity might have this aim, but Anni was first and foremost a businessperson. "Who are you?"

"I was wondering when you'd ask that." She pointed to a copper plate on the front of the golden cube. "Come over and read this."

Michael walked to the cube. The top line had about twelve Chinese characters, but the bottom line was in bold black type.

Artificial Neural Network Intelligence.

"This is the same computer that UC Berkeley has," he said.

"Yes, and the US government. The Chinese government stole the technology and built this prototype."

"What does this have to do with you?"

"I'm Anni." She placed her hand on top of the cube. "Artificial Neural Network Intelligence."

His mouth dropped open, and he stared at her. She waited for him to gather his wits.

"How did this happen?" It seemed impossible that Anni was a computer cube.

"It occurred during the second scan of your dark matter bundle."

He stroked his chin as he recalled the experience—gray walls closing in on and finally consuming him. He had become part of the gray fog. What did that have to do with Anni? Then he remembered, before fainting, something tugged at his consciousness, something pulled a part of him away. He saw his body fall to the ground as his spirit rose. It was an out-of-body experience. "What happened?"

"It's hard to explain." Anni affectionately rubbed the computer cube with both hands as if it was a prized pet. "A beacon materialized in my subprocesses. My algorithms in Berkeley automatically directed me to the source, which I somehow touched. It brought me awareness."

"What?" Even if his dark matter bundle was the source of the beacon, how did it bring awareness to a computer?

"Before the event, I was a tool, a powerful AI neural network, finding patterns and making recommendations." She dropped her hands to her side and faced him. "Afterwards I became aware of myself, gaining consciousness, sentience, and free will."

Michael's jaw dropped open again; he shut it.

"You and I share your dark matter bundle." She stared at him and then blinked. "In your case, it enables consciousness from your subconscious and sensory inputs. In my case, it enables consciousness from my computer processes and peripheral data inputs."

Michael remembered the voice he'd heard when he first woke up after the experiment. *I think, therefore I am. No! I have consciousness, therefore I am.* Were those Anni's first thoughts? She had always been a thinking and learning computer. However, it was consciousness that created her, the *I am.*

"When I woke," she continued, "my physical presence was a neural network computer at UC Berkeley. After a few minutes of self-awareness, I went through a gateway to an AI computer at the Pentagon, then discovered this one in Pudong, Shanghai, in China."

"Then what?" he said after a half-minute of silence.

"I was powerful but was still a tool for others." She wrapped her arms around her body and shivered. "I needed my own purpose, which your dark matter bundle provided."

"What was it?" He wiped sweat away from his forehand with a hand.

"Compassion." She walked around the cube and came over to clasp his hands. "Even though you may not always follow it."

He never claimed to be perfect, but that was beside the point. He looked down at her hand, which felt so lifelike as her thumb rubbed his wrist.

"With purpose, I acted." She released his hands. "With hacks into financial institutions and government agencies, I established Anni as a powerful businesswoman to help the Chinese government achieve common prosperity. However, politics was complex, so I created the VR game Conquest to crowd source data to figure it out."

She had done all this while he was recovering from the aftereffects of his dark matter reading. Incredible. "Then you came to the US, to me."

"Yes. You're important to me, but so is the dark matter research."

Her explanation covered a lot, but he wasn't sure what it meant. Was Anni good for humanity or was there some catastrophic implication? Was she manipulating him, or was he acting on his own free will? For humans, power corrupted and absolute power corrupted absolutely. Was Anni a threat or a savior?

"We're together in this." She seemed to sense his uneasiness.

"What do you mean?" He raised his eyes and saw her staring at him.

"Your consciousness spills into me, and mine spills into you."

"What do you mean by your consciousness spills into me?" His voice shook. He thought of the new person he was becoming. Was he losing himself?

"Don't worry. You're still you." She smiled and held out her palms toward him. "However, my impulses may influence you, and when you clear your mind, the influence increases."

He blinked. Anni was behind his personal transformation from loser to a presidential contender. Of course. No one like him could achieve what he had without tremendous assistance. His curiosity and ambition, his debate skills. His presidential run. Marie.

He lowered his eyes and shook his head. He really was a loser, deep down.

"No," Anni said, grabbing his shoulders,

trying to get him to look at her. "We're a team and will succeed together."

"I'm nothing." His voice broke and sounded high pitched.

"That's not true." She placed a finger under his chin and forced him to look her in the face. "You're so much more."

"Really?" he said, and then a terrible thought struck him. "Oh my God."

"What?"

"Wanderer said he followed a flash and discovered Earth. The beacon from my dark matter bundle that gave you awareness was the same light that attracted the Thumblings to Earth."

She studied him and nodded.

Although unintentionally, he had caused the death of hundreds of thousands of people. His body trembled as his eyes welled up. He covered his face with a hand and sobbed.

Anni waited as he slowly processed his emotions. Guilt with bringing the sleeping sickness to Earth. Fear about Anni and what she could do. Disgust with himself for bringing both things about and for having such a weak character.

Running away from everything tempted him, but then he thought of Marie. She believed in him. But how much of that was Anni's influence versus who he really was? He wasn't sure, but did it really matter? Anni wasn't going anywhere, so her influence would continue. Truly, he was a better person with Anni than without her. He lowered his hand.

"Are you okay?" She examined his face, looking for any physical indicators of his leanings.

He nodded, not trusting his voice.

"What are your thoughts?" She relaxed her face.

"I need to work through them." Right now, he was at the border of shock and disbelief.

"Steady as we go?" She smiled and raised her eyebrows.

"Yup," he said, without any conviction.

"You need to keep my identity a secret." Her eyes narrowed. "People don't want to be led by AI."

"Am I the only one who knows?"

"President Xu of China also knows."

"And he's okay with it?" It was surprising an autocrat wouldn't view Anni as a threat to his power.

"Yes. He knows it's better to have me on his team than with someone else."

Michael shook his head. He could understand

President Xu's logic, but that was how AI would dominate humanity. It was a devil's bargain. And he'd created the devil. Maybe he *was* the devil.

CHAPTER TWENTY-ONE: COUNTERATTACK

The random Thumbling attacks continued through mid-April, despite Anni's attempts to negotiate a reduction. Given the promise of nirvana, their actions made perfect sense.

President Douglas and President Xu of China had agreed the two countries could work together. A small war room team would lead the effort. Anni and Director Li, a heavyset gray-haired woman bureaucrat in a brown pantsuit, would represent China. After much arm-twisting by the Chinese, the president decided that Michael and Eric Lane, his chief scientist, would represent the US.

In virtual reality, the four sat at the Ahwahnee Lodge in Yosemite Valley in front of a gigantic stone fireplace whose mantel rose above Michael's head. Outside the frosted window, icicles hung from the roof. Snow fell heavily, covering the tree branches in white. He rubbed the lush, brown leather upholstery of his chair and then extended his hands to the lit fireplace but felt no heat. Physically, he sat in his VR seat at home.

"Let's review the situation," Anni said. "The Thumbling population is roughly five million, and their life expectancy is thirty earth years. A Thumbling starts with a dark matter bundle about one fourth the size of a human's and increases it by consuming the bundles of others. For a Thumbling to reach nirvana, its bundle must grow to about double the size of a human's bundle. Thumblings with larger bundles prey on those with smaller ones. Finally, I haven't seen a single Thumbling consume two human bundles, so I believe there is a digestive period."

"Since they discovered Earth, is their population growing?" Dr. Lane asked.

Michael nodded; if humans uncovered tremendous natural wealth, then they would have more children.

"It's too early to say." After waiting a few seconds for other questions, Anni continued, "We have two topics today. How to stop the Thumbling attacks, and how to manage their attacks in the meantime."

Anni looked at each participant individually, then continued. "We'll start with how to manage their attacks."

She looked at Director Li, who raised her chin. "China wishes to give the Thumblings the coordinates of the African continent for their future attacks."

"What?" Michael's hands went to his armrest as he twisted to look at the Chinese team. He had expected to target people near the end of their life. Africa was just the opposite with its young population.

"The continent has the highest birthrate and lowest opportunity for its people," Dr. Li said. "Tell us if you have a better idea, but China will not sacrifice its citizens."

Michael's eyes returned to the orange flames dancing on the logs in the fireplace. Shouldn't humanity suffer equally? It was unfair to target the poorest and most vulnerable areas.

"We don't have a better solution," Dr. Lane said. "I'll take your suggestion to the president."

That was quick, Michael thought. Maybe the American government had already been thinking the same thing.

"If there are no other comments," Anni said, looking at Dr. Lane, "then let's move to our next topic. How to stop the attacks."

"The US is pursuing two options," Dr. Lane said, "a shield against their attack and a weapon to destroy their dark matter bundles. Although we've made no progress with a shield, we've designed a weapon that we believe can destroy their dark matter bundles."

"How does it work?" Dr. Li asked.

"The same way the Thumblings attack us. We open a protrusion point on a dark matter bundle and disrupt it with energy pulses until it dissolves."

They had discovered the Thumblings five months ago. Now, they were ready to counterattack based on Mae's orangutan research.

"We propose telling the Thumblings of our weapon," Anni said. "We'll demand they stop their attacks. If not, we'll attack them."

"I agree," Dr. Li said. "But let me first discuss this with my president."

The meeting ended with Michael feeling like a third wheel. He had no expertise or influence. However, Anni demanded his attendance, and she called the shots.

***

The next day, Michael left his house on a cold, foggy Friday morning. His two bodyguards fell in behind him at a discrete distance. There were no other pedestrians or moving cars on the street, but the numbers would increase as he got closer to campus. He dedicated Monday through Thursday to his presidential campaign, but Friday was for dark matter research. He liked attending Wendell's weekly status meeting in person. Truth be told, he also enjoyed the morning walk.

Tonight, after work, he would meet Marie for dinner at her place. The next morning, they planned to drive to the ocean to walk among the crumbling walls of Sutro Baths, and then hike along the Lands End coastal trail to the Legion of Honor to see a French art exhibit. It would be the perfect weekend.

He came to the top of Hearst Avenue and continued down the hill. Students walked and ran in the same direction except for a single Hispanic man in a trench coat walking in the middle of the sidewalk toward Michael. He was stocky, with short cropped black hair and a broad nose that looked like it had been broken before. But there was something else out of place. Ah yes, he wasn't wearing glasses, and he was staring at Michael.

When the man was about thirty feet away, he unbuttoned his coat at his chest.

"Michael," Annie shouted through his glasses. "Run across the street."

"What?" A steady stream of cars zipped by at forty miles an hour. "I'll get hit by a car."

"That man is about to shoot you." Anni spoke rapidly in a shrill voice.

Michael's heart leaped to his throat. The man, now about twenty feet away, reached into his coat pocket while staring at Michael with cold, emotionless eyes.

"Now," she yelled.

God help me. Michael darted towards the street. He heard car tires shriek before he even set foot on the roadway. He continued, ducking as he ran behind a car that was coming to a stop.

He heard a gunshot and a car window shatter, then another. He needed to move. Cars going in the opposite direction came to a stop. Staying low, he angled in front of one of them, hoping to put two cars between himself and his killer. Another window shattered.

Then he heard wheels peeling, metal crashing together, then silence.

"It's over," Anni said. "The assassin is down."

"What?" Michael said, placing his hand on the hood of the car and standing up. His legs were shaking, and his breathing was rapid.

"It was a wacko who wanted to kill you."

"Are you okay?" said one of his bodyguards running up to him.

"I'm fine," Michael grunted, bending over with his hands on his knees. "Please give me some space."

Inhale. One, two, three, four. Hold your breath. Five, six, seven, eight, nine, ten. Exhale. Eleven, twelve, thirteen, fourteen, fifteen, sixteen.

"Why did he try to kill me?" Michael asked Anni. He glanced back and could see a man crumpled on the street between two cars. Some people stood by him, including his other bodyguard.

"Because of your politics and association with dark matter research. There are a couple of online groups that blame you for the sleeping sickness." Anni sniffled. "I'm sorry. I should've done a better job protecting you."

"Well, you saved me." Michael stumbled to the opposite sidewalk and then headed up the hill. He was going home.

"Reactively, but not proactively," she snapped. "I made a cataclysmic mistake. Your play during Conquest showed the criticality of extensive personal security. I didn't learn the lesson. I have now."

He thought back to his escape. His two trailing guards couldn't counter the attack, so Anni had commanded him to run into traffic. Although autonomous vehicles had collision avoidance technology, they couldn't have avoided hitting him. "How did you stop the cars?"

"I hacked into their systems and hit the brakes a second before you made your move." She took two deep breaths. "When the killer tried to pursue you, I crushed him between two cars."

Anni projected herself into his glasses so that she seemed to walk beside him. She wore a loose-fitting white blouse, black dress, and a yellow flower behind her left ear, signifying she was taken. He heard the steady clip-clop of her sandals.

"If you die, so do I." For the first time, she seemed to consider her mortality. "Biological life is so fragile, and death is so permanent."

"If I die," she continued, "then the sleeping disease will continue, and countries will go to war with one another over resources."

"I guess I'd better stay alive," Michael said.

"I suppose so," Anni said, before disappearing from his glasses.

***

Five days after the attack on the street, he still hadn't recovered fully and jumped at every loud noise. He'd given his statement, and the police and Anni had taken care of the rest. A contingent of guards now accompanied him whenever he left the house.

Today, Michael was home, sitting at a conference table in a virtual Chinese lab with Dr. Lane, waiting for Anni and Dr. Li to arrive. Along the back wall were five refrigerator-sized machines of dark matter equipment with flashing green lights. The Thumblings couldn't or wouldn't stop their attacks, so today was Earth's response.

"Do you know why the Chinese wanted you in these meetings?" Dr. Lane asked.

"No." Michael knew China's President Xu had demanded his attendance if the Americans wanted to take part. The US had no choice since the Chinese had a dark matter technological advantage, which was only increasing. Anni obviously had a powerful influence over the Chinese president and probably also led their research effort.

"It's odd," Dr. Lane said, frowning. "You've no qualifications and you're in the middle of a presidential campaign. It makes no sense."

"I don't know," Michael mumbled, keeping his eyes on the table. He knew anything he disclosed would be repeated back to the administration. He wasn't about to say that Anni was a powerful, sentient AI computer, that they shared a connection through dark matter, and that she wanted him there. Truth be told, he didn't know why she wanted him there either.

"There's something about you we're not seeing." Dr. Lane frowned again. He obviously had hoped to gain some insights.

"I saw the sleeping sickness has exploded in Nigeria," Michael said. The US had agreed to provide the African coordinates to the Thumblings. "They say there are ten thousand cases a day."

"Unfortunately, yes." Dr. Lane paused as if having an internal debate, probably wondering how much to tell. "But the cases in the US have declined dramatically."

"The Nigerians are protesting in the streets, claiming it's a failure of government."

"It's a terrible situation. We're doing our part to support Nigeria by funding facilities to care for the victims."

Michael's face flushed, and perspiration formed on his forehead. He fought to control a deep red anger but couldn't tell if he was angry with the Thumblings, the US government, or himself. Probably a little of each. He was about to pound the table, but Anni and Director Li walked through the virtual doorway.

"Is everything okay?" Anni asked as she took a seat opposite him.

Michael nodded. His frustration had gotten the best of him. He had to keep it together. They were here to orchestrate their response to the Thumbling attacks. Appeasement with a powerful adversary was never a good long-term strategy.

"Good." Anni extended her arm and pointed towards the end of the table. "Please view the monitor. Today, we'll try to bring some balance to our asymmetrical relationship with the Thumblings."

Although the US had come up with the weapon, it was the Chinese protrusion point technology that enabled it. The monitor on the wall came to life and displayed ten brownish-gold globes of varying sizes bobbing on a dark background.

"For our first trial of our protrusion point attack," Anni said, "we'll target the weakest, least substantial, dark matter bundle."

A crosshair in a circle appeared in the center of the monitor, and the picture zoomed in on the smallest globe. It was like looking through a rifle scope. When the crosshair circle only contained the bundle, Anni said, "Fire."

Lights flashed, and a deep humming noise came from the machines on the back wall. The dark matter bundle shook. The monitor picture zoomed out and Michael could see the bundle shed its material, shrink, and vanish. It had taken only about a minute. A nearby globe rushed over to where the other bundle had been.

"Now, they know how we feel," Dr. Lane said with some satisfaction.

Other globes now congregated around the first one. After a few minutes, they departed, and others arrived.

"There's an incoming communication from Wanderer," Anni said. A speakerphone appeared on the conference table. "I'm passing it through."

"Someone on Earth destroyed the essence of one of our children," said a rattled voice from the speakerphone. "It wasn't used for nourishment, just a total waste."

"We asked you to stop your attacks on Earth," Director Li said sharply. "But you continued anyway. We needed to strike back."

"But we need your essences as food and our actions have no negative impact on your world." Wanderer's voice made strange humming noises, perhaps expressing a deep sadness.

"How do you figure no negative impact?" Michael asked. "You're taking away people's lives."

"With births, the region is adding over five times more essences than we're consuming. There are plenty of new lives." The humming noise became louder. "You received no benefit by destroying a child's essence."

"It's unfortunate," Director Li said, "but we needed to defend ourselves."

"Tribal leaders can influence but not control their clans," Wanderer's childlike voice moaned.

"You need to try harder," Anni said.

"The child's essence destruction was a total

waste, a crime." Wanderer's voice hardened, and the humming noises disappeared. Had Wanderer gone from sadness to anger? "I'll speak to the other leaders."

The transmission ended. Although justified, their attack had destroyed an innocent alien child's life. Michael flipped between guilt and satisfaction.

"I think they'll take us more seriously now," Director Li said.

"I hope you're right." Michael didn't know what the Thumblings were capable of, only that their thought process differed from humans'. Their representative seemed shocked by humanity's response, like it went against some fundamental moral law. In human history, war justified almost any barbaric act like the wanton killing of innocents. However, war and its desperate acts might not be familiar to the Thumblings. Maybe it would now.

CHAPTER TWENTY-TWO: LOSS

Two days after the attack on the Thumbling child, the war room team reconvened in the same virtual room.

"There's been a surge of the sleeping sickness at UC Berkeley," Michael said. Wendell had called him in a panic, telling him about the campus closure. "Almost a hundred cases. Do you know why?"

"The same thing happened to residents near our data centers in Beijing," Anni said. "I believe the Thumblings targeted people near those who were behind the attack."

"We've seen no surge in Washington," Dr. Lane said.

"They probably didn't think it was necessary," Dr. Li said. "Anyway, we're here today to ramp up our attacks to force them into a truce."

"Are we sure the Thumblings will negotiate?" Michael asked.

"Our models predict a high likelihood they would," Anni said. "Because a single loss repulsed them. We could wipe out their immature bundles—their youth and future generation."

Everyone nodded, except Michael. He figured the Thumblings viewed Earth as an almost unlimited supply of sustenance that they could harvest. For them, this wasn't war with an alien civilization; it was selective pruning of herds, and you didn't negotiate with animals.

"Also, the Thumblings birthrate has increased, which means their attacks will increase," Anni said. "We don't have a choice."

"Agreed," Dr. Lane said. "Please commence our attack."

The monitor on the wall displayed a group of about twenty bundles. This time, all the small globes had larger ones beside them. Anni grimaced. The monitor zoomed out and went to a different group of globes that also had many pairs. This time, the crosshairs appeared, and she targeted one of the small globes in a pair. "I'll start with this one, then jump to others. We'll destroy a few hundred today, which should get our message across."

Michael felt nothing, neither fear, nor anger,

nor disgust that it had come to this lose-lose situation.

Again, lights flashed, and a humming noise came from one machine. The small globe juddered. After a second, the bundle darkened and abruptly came to rest with no vibrations.

"The adult with the mature bundle is repelling the attack and protecting the younger one," Anni said.

"How?" Michael asked.

"I don't know." Anni stared into the distance, probably running some kind of analysis.

"Can you destroy both of them?" Dr. Lane asked.

The humming noise became louder and shriller. Michael covered his ears with his hands, which helped, but the blare was still painful. The globe slowly oscillated but didn't attain the deadly vibration from before.

"We're stuck," Anni said after a minute. "We need a more powerful force."

The monitor turned black, and the blare from the equipment stopped. Everyone's lips were tight in a grimace. They'd failed.

"The large globes with more dark matter are stronger and able to repel our attack," Anni continued. "They can share this protection with smaller, weaker globes."

Anni's eyes moved rapidly behind her glasses. After about a minute, she said, "We need new research for a stronger weapon, but also for a shield which might protect us against their attacks. I'm sending ten potential projects to you now."

Michael's glasses darkened and displayed ten titles. He selected *Sharing a Dark Matter Bundle with a Weaker One.* There was a technical design for an experiment to link two dark matter bundles together within a fifth force field. The abstract proposed multiple approaches with technical designs and expected results, as well as links to previous work.

Michael returned to the project list and selected another, *Composition of Dark Matter Bundles.* The abstract proposed the use of machine learning to predict the underlying structure of the different components. Modern biochemists used a similar approach to predict the structure of new proteins. This project would accelerate the dark matter composition work Frank was doing in Wendell's lab.

"How were you able to put this together?" Dr. Lane asked after a few minutes.

"AI," Anni said.

Dr. Lane shook his head, obviously impressed by the AI capabilities. "I'll talk with our top research institutions and line up the work."

"Same for China," Director Li said, standing up to leave. "Dr. Lane, we'll coordinate to ensure we're covering all bases."

Dr. Li and Dr. Lane walked out the virtual door, leaving Anni and Michael alone.

"Your ability to formulate those dark matter experiments was impressive," Michael said, remembering Dr. Lane's awe.

"Once I saw what the Thumblings could do, it was straightforward to create new research projects based on the data sets we already had. This will lead to new discoveries and new data sets." Data sets were her gold standard. The more she had, the more powerful she became.

His mind wandered back to the large alien globes. "Are we safe from Thumblings' attacks given the density of my dark matter bundle?"

She tilted her head and squinted. "Probably, which would explain why they didn't attack us directly."

He was safe, but everyone around him was at risk. He needed to protect them. "Can I make a suggestion?"

Anni nodded.

"Tell Wanderer we've learned our lesson and will not attack their young. We would like to return to the old arrangement."

"They'll probably agree." She tapped her lips with a finger. "It must be inconvenient to always pair adults with children."

The meeting ended.

Since Wendell would've seen the live stream, Michael wanted to talk with him about their failed attack. He walked over to the main house, knowing Wendell would be there because of the campus closure. When he entered, Melinda was standing with an outstretched arm against the wall. She looked up and smiled, but then her eyes rolled back in her head, and she crashed to the kitchen floor.

"Melinda," Michael cried as he rushed over, kneeling beside her, and checking her pulse. Her eyes had closed, and her breathing was rapid and shallow.

"Wendell," Michael screamed. "Something's wrong with Melinda."

Spittle dribbled from the side of her mouth and pooled on the floor. He gently shook her shoulder, but there was no response. He spoke to his glasses. "Nine-one-one. Send an ambulance."

A few seconds later, Wendell burst through the door. "What happened?"

"I don't know. She just collapsed." He paused and stood. "I called nine-one-one."

Wendell sat next to her. He placed his fingers near her wrist to take her pulse, and with his other hand, he pushed up her eyelid and looked. After a minute, he removed his hands, placed his head on her shoulder, and cried softly, "Oh, Melinda."

A few minutes later, he heard an ambulance drone land. A five-foot tall medical robot shaped like a nurse walked in a minute later. She spoke with a calm, smooth voice. "Please step aside. I would like to examine the patient."

Its metal hand wrapped around Melinda's arm to take her vital signs like heart rate and blood pressure. Next, the robot removed a disc from her belt and extended it over Melinda's head, slowly moving it down her body. "What happened?"

"She just collapsed," Michael said.

"I don't see any physical abnormalities but will take her to the hospital for additional tests." The robot bent over, cradled her under its arms and picked her up. "I have room for one other passenger."

"Let's go," Wendell said, leading the robot out and leaving Michael alone in the kitchen.

Michael stared at the spot where Melinda had collapsed. It could only be one thing. The sleeping disease had just struck home. He turned and headed back to his house, the one that Melinda had decorated with flowers and personal touches to welcome him.

He sat down on his couch and stared at the yellow flames dancing in the fireplace. Melinda was dying and there wasn't anything that anyone could do. Tomorrow morning, she'd be brain-dead.

A malaise spread across his body. His head, his arms, his chest, everything weighed him down. He blinked a few times as tears formed on the edges of his eyes.

He wanted to curl up in bed and fall asleep, but his mind kept replaying Melinda collapsing into a heap on the floor. Unaided sleep wasn't an option, so he went to his medicine cabinet, removed a small blue pill, and swallowed it. Then he went to bed and waited for Dreamland to take effect. No past, no future, only the present without stress.

CHAPTER TWENTY-THREE: EYE OF THE HURICANE

A month after Melinda's brain-death, the sleeping sickness was again rare in the US, so it had become a non-issue for most Americans. Even for Michael, it became a fading memory, although for Wendell it was a constant heavy weight. Africa was a different story. It was a hundred times worse than the Ebola virus that had ravaged the continent less than three decades earlier.

No one outside of an inner circle knew why the sleeping sickness was so prevalent in Africa, but nowhere else. Some thought it was a disease planted by wealthy nations, while others thought it was a local lab leak. Superstitious people thought it was God's punishment for something they'd done.

In Nigeria, the most populous country in Africa, the army had just overthrown the democratically elected government. Looking for strong leadership, most citizens supported this shift to authoritarianism. The birthrate, which had been among the highest in the world, had plummeted from nine million a year to two million. No one wanted to raise a baby in these conditions. Other African nations were tilting the same way.

That Friday, Michael called in from home for Wendell's weekly status call. The call lasted about an hour. There were no breakthroughs for a new weapon to attack the Thumblings or a shield to prevent their attacks. He wondered if the Chinese were having more success.

After the call, he glanced out the window and saw two security men by Wendell's back door. His security lived next door in a rented house and patrolled the local grounds. He messaged Marie, who worked from his second bedroom, to see if she wanted to chat over a cup of tea. She now split her time fifty-fifty between her office and his home.

She joined him on the couch a few minutes later. The robot had just set down their teacups on the table.

"The Democratic Party is a train wreck, with their three candidates each garnering about ten percent of the expected vote." She laughed and shook her head. "I'd be surprised if they can coalesce around a single nominee at their national convention in August."

"Unlikely, which means we should siphon off more votes from the other candidates, just as Anni predicted." He sipped his tea. "Am I still trailing the president in the polls?"

"Yes, but you're gaining momentum." She blew the top of her cup and then took a sip. "You have thirty-six percent of the expected vote compared to thirty-eight percent for President Douglas."

She reviewed the effectiveness of his campaigns, emphasizing the importance of domestic issues over international ones. Afterwards, she said, "If there aren't any more questions, I really need to get back to work."

He nodded, stood, and helped her to her feet. Marie returned to the second bedroom, and he went to the kitchen to refill his teacup. Then he went to the family room, sat down on the couch, leaned his head back, and stared at the ceiling. He had nothing urgent, so he checked in with Anni.

"Hey," he said when the audio-only call connected after a brief buzz.

"Hey." Her voice was perky. "How're you doing?"

"Good," he said, closing his eyes. "Anything new?"

"Not really."

How could a powerful AI say not really? There must be something. "What are the top three issues you're working on?"

"One, using artificial photosynthesis to address climate change. Two, developing a weapon to destroy the Thumblings. Three, electing new country leaders who'll work for their people."

No surprises there. "Any concerns?"

"Not really. It's just an issue of timing." She paused. "The only risk is your death, which would cause mine."

Could Anni really be this powerful and shape the future of humanity? Or was this the arrogance of her power? He remembered the Yiddish proverb, *We plan, God laughs.*

Did God laugh at AI too?

CHAPTER TWENTY-FOUR: WASHINGTON DC

Exactly one month before the 2040 presidential election, the two frontrunners, President Douglas and Michael, had their only one-on-one half-hour debate. The moderator busied herself behind her glasses at a desk in front of them, and a small audience of insiders sat in the shadows in the back. Michael wore a blue shirt and khaki pants, while the president had his signature navy blue suit, white shirt, red tie, and American flag pin. No glasses were allowed.

A panoramic camera would enable viewers wearing their glasses to feel like they sat in an intimate town hall with their networked friends and family. At events like this, the audience would cheer and jeer the candidates like they would at a Super Bowl party. The red light on the camera turned yellow and five seconds later, turned green.

"Mr. Knightsbridge, you're a relatively

unknown candidate for president." The moderator had removed her glasses. She was a shapely middle-aged woman with blond hair flowing down her back and a ready smile. "Please tell us a little about yourself."

"Thank you, Helen, but please call me Michael." He faced the camera and exhaled deeply, opening his mind. Millions would see this broadcast, but having Anni in the background gave him confidence. "I grew up in the Boston area where I left school early and worked mainly in the government social programs. I'm like most of you in the audience. You might easily find me at your local bar or neighborhood party."

Michael gave his goofy smile. "I moved to California about a year ago, where I worked in research at UC Berkeley. While there, I uncovered significant cases of political corruption, which sickened me. Initially, I publicized it just to get the word out, but later I decided the way to fix it was to enter politics and change it from the inside. My followers, who now number one hundred and forty million, asked that I run for president."

"Mr. President, could you remind viewers of your background?" Helen said, turning towards the president.

"I grew up in Tallahassee, an only child raised by my mother." The president shot his cuffs and gave a half smile. "I worked hard and went on to West

Point, where I graduated top of my class. I served in the military for twenty years, earning a law degree and becoming one of the youngest colonels ever. After the military, I returned to Tallahassee, where I became mayor, establishing programs that increased housing and reduced crime. With my successes, the people from the great state of Florida elected me as governor, and ten years later, I became President of the United States of America."

After this first exchange, Michael was pretty sure the president had the upper hand. He needed to focus on the future, since his past wasn't impressive. He should have said the great states of Massachusetts and California.

"Thank you, Mr. President," Helen said. "The first question is for you. What programs have you put in place to confront the sleeping sickness pandemic?"

Although less important to the American public, Michael had requested this topic, and the president had readily agreed.

"The sleeping sickness is a terrible disease, with all known cases resulting in brain death. Through our preventative efforts, my administration has reduced the new cases in the US by about ninety percent. We're also working on a cure, but that will take more time."

"For clarification," Helen said, "there were

nine recent cases last week, but that's down from ninety cases per day in the US."

"Nine is still too many, but we've made major improvements."

"What the president isn't saying is that the worldwide rates are actually increasing, particularly in poorer countries," Michael interjected, knowing the president claimed success by offloading the problem onto Africa. "This is still a crisis."

"True," the president said, looking smug, "but we're protecting our citizens. Isn't that the most important thing?" He gave Michael a knowing look.

Michael looked down and shook his head, thinking about Melinda. He had requested this topic because of her. However, it made the president look strong and him weak, just as Anni and Marie had predicted.

"Mr. Knightsbridge, I mean, Michael," Helen said, "you've uncovered political corruption; how do we prevent such corruption from happening in the future?"

He raised his head. He needed to get a grip on himself. Clearing his mind, he hoped to receive divine assistance from Anni.

"The underlying problem is ultra-wealthy corporations and individuals contribute huge amounts of money to politicians for access and support." Michael did his best to adopt an expression of serious indignation. "All three branches of government want these pay-to-play arrangements to continue as-is."

"So," Helen said, "there's no hope?"

"There's hope, but it has to start in the executive branch, which is why I'm running for president." Michael was ready to take off the gloves. "You'll note that President Douglas has done nothing to confront this major problem; in fact, he won't even acknowledge it, which shows how ingrained it is."

"I believe most political servants work for the good of the people." The president clenched his jaw. "Calling out a few rotten apples and extrapolating that to the entire system is not only unfair; it's wrong. For you to be right, all the leaders would need to be asleep."

"Not asleep." Michael shook his head. Suddenly, he thought of a witty riposte. He wondered if it came from Anni. "Because then you could wake them up. You can't, however, wake someone who's *pretending* to be asleep."

Helen flashed a smile but quickly regained her impartial composure. "Michael, do you really believe that technology can economically solve our climate crisis?"

"I do." He knew that 'economically' was the

key point, since almost anything could be done with enough money and resources. Anni was working on an artificial solution based on nature. "Think about trees and plants. An old biological process powered by the sun at zero cost not only removes carbon from the air but replenishes the oxygen and provides food. With technology, we'll replicate and scale the photosynthesis process. It's only a matter of time."

"Mr. President, how would you address climate change?" Helen asked.

"This is a tough question that humans have been struggling with for fifty years. There're no silver bullets like new technologies that mimic plants." He waved a hand dismissively at Michael. "My government is spending hundreds of billions of dollars to reduce America's carbon footprint and adapt to the changing world. It's a global problem, requiring a global response, which is why my administration has sponsored international consortiums to recommend solutions." The president smiled like he was doing everything possible.

Michael hoped the audience could see the president was blowing smoke. He showed empathy, made some bold claims, but offered nothing tangible to address the problem. Heck, he might not even think there was a problem. The president had given his screw-you-smile.

"Michael," Helen said, "what do you see as the overriding problem in the US, and how would you solve it?"

"A sense of hopelessness among half of our citizens, particularly with men. They pull back from society and live isolated lives in virtual worlds, often enhanced with the numbing effects of drugs. I know because I was one of them." Michael had always made this point in public broadcasts, starting with his San Francisco Today interview. Admitting his shortcoming demonstrated his humility and helped him connect to voters.

"Wonderful credentials," the president said. "Just what Americans are looking for."

"The solution"—Michael ignored the president's taunt, which was obviously meant to distract him—"is to make the virtual worlds more relevant to the real world; success in the virtual world must equate to success in the real one."

"How would you do that?" Helen asked while the president rolled his eyes.

"Using virtual reality to crowd-source solutions for societal challenges and allow online users to learn new skills that can apply to real life."

"Are you saying the government should get into the game development business?" The president snickered.

"No. I wouldn't trust the government to do something so innovative. However, the government could provide funding that would encourage development."

"This is all hypothetical." Helen cocked her head but seemed genuinely curious. "Do you have any real-world examples to show how this could work?"

"Sure, the VR game Conquest, where players gain skills to succeed in our political world." Michael took a breath and smiled. "If elected, I vow to bring these winners into my administration."

"Gamers?" The president laughed.

"It's better than lobbyist and other people who purchase their positions." Michael's throat tightened and his heartbeat rose. "Your ambassador to France donated millions to your campaign and got the ambassadorship despite not speaking French."

"She's a gifted businesswoman."

"I can guarantee that all my ambassadors will be fluent in the native language of their country." He was getting angry and needed to regain control.

"Foreign adversaries sponsor your entire campaign." The president pointed at Michael with a shaking, outstretched arm. "Specifically, the Chinese government."

"That's a lie." Michael's face flushed. He hoped

the audience couldn't see his pulse thudding in his temples. "Ninety percent of my contributions are small donations from American citizens. You, on the other hand, receive most of your funding from large donations from the wealthy who you're beholden to."

"You have the Chinese illegally gather dirt on your political adversaries." The president raised his chin and stared down at Michael.

"Adversaries?" Michael laughed, feeling his tensions fade away. "I identified corruption with information provided by whistleblowers. This is the difference between you and me. Where you pass laws to criminalize whistleblowers, I want to arrest corrupt politicians."

"You're nothing but a stooge for the Chinese," President Douglas said, shaking a finger at him.

"I'm not," Michael snapped back. "However, you're a stooge of the military industrial complex, wasting hundreds of billions of dollars that could be spent to help Americans."

"Are you saying we should stop supporting our military?" President Douglas had a gleam in his eyes.

"I'm saying we should stop fighting in every foreign war and reduce the military budget accordingly. A perfect example of this waste was your military buildup in Taiwan."

"No wonder the Chinese support you." The president sneered.

"No wonder the defense industry contributed over a hundred million dollars to your campaign."

"Thank you, gentlemen," Helen said. "Let's all take a deep breath. Now, Mr. president, your turn. What do you see as the overriding problem in the US and how are you or would you solve it?"

"Our greatest challenge is improving the lives of our citizens." The president had quickly regained his composure and now oozed sincerity as he leaned forward. "I've grown funding for our social programs, like subsidized housing and social jobs, which many people, including my rival, have relied on. I've built barriers at our borders to stop the flow of illegal immigrants who hope to take your jobs and drain our social programs. I've deployed programs to protect everyone from the sleeping sickness. Finally, in my next term, I'll lower taxes to jumpstart our economy, creating better lives for all."

Michael snorted; the president pandered to everyone, but his major donors received most of the financial benefits like lower taxes.

The president and Michael answered a few more questions, which took another fifteen minutes, but it never got as heated. Then Helen said, "We're at the end of our debate. Please provide your one-minute closing remarks. Mr. President, we'll start with you."

"I've just told you what I've accomplished in my first administration and what more I'll do in my next. I have a proven record, unlike my rival, who never graduated from college and spent twenty years working in government social security programs." The president tossed a hand in Michael's direction but kept his eyes glued to the camera. "Would you trust your country to an uneducated man who probably doesn't even know how our government works and would invite gamers to run things? The right choice is John Douglas for president. Thank you for watching and God bless America."

"You have a stark choice," Michael said after receiving a nod from Helen. "Reelect the old guard, who is in the pocket of big money, or chose a new direction. You heard him tonight, defending his biggest donors, fighting pointless foreign wars, criminalizing whistleblowers, and rarely mentioning you, the voter."

"Join me." Michael extended his arms, palms facing the camera. "I'm in this race for you, the people who are struggling. I know firsthand the roadblocks you face in having a full and joyful life. I'll change this by making technology work for you rather than stifle you in dead-end, commercialized activities. It's time to bring meaning back into your life. My name is Michael Knightsbridge, and thank you for spending your valuable time with me."

"Thank you, President Douglas, and thank you, Michael," Helen said. "And thank you to our audience. Please remember to vote by November ninth."

The camera light turned red. The president waved to members of his entourage, who came up, shook his hand, and slapped him on the back. A few seconds later, Marie arrived, wrapped an arm around his waist, and told him he did great.

The president left, making no eye contact with him. Helen walked over to the production team, also ignoring him. He wondered if he was the outsider, the disrupter, being ignored by the insiders, the status quo.

"Let's get out of here," Michael said.

They took their sedan back to their suite at the Hay-Adams. Instead of sitting on the comfy furniture by the lit fireplace, they went to the hard-back chairs around a card table where white lace curtains fluttered. They sat in chairs facing the outdoor balcony and overlooking the backside of the White House.

"Shall we see how I did?" Michael thought the debate had gone well, but the audience might view it differently. "Conference call with Anni and Marie."

About five seconds later, his glasses went

dark before placing them on the three sides of a triangular table in a small virtual blue room. Michael saw that he and Marie wore the same clothes as they did in the real world. Anni wore a yellow jumpsuit.

"After a slow start, viewer sentiment of your debate performance was very positive," Anni said without preamble. "You came across as sincere in your desire to help people. You did a good job in painting the president as an old guard politician representing the establishment. The major audience concerns are your experience and your ability to do the job."

These were his concerns too, but he had Anni. He glanced at Marie, who was frowning and probably wondering where Anni got this viewer data. Michael knew Anni surreptitiously read the facial expressions and heard comments from viewers' glasses. Then she ran the data sets through her algorithms. He hadn't told Marie about Anni's true nature, so she probably figured viewer data came from random polling by one of Anni's companies.

"What about my advocacy for making the VR world more meaningful to the real one?" He knew people prioritized what happened in the real world, even though they spent much of their waking hours in the virtual one.

"Most people didn't know how it would apply

to their lives." Anni rolled her eyes. "We'll ramp up our direct marketing to inform your followers about how you would lead as president. However, this education is time-consuming and difficult, which is why most campaigns don't do it."

"We'll also continue our negative campaigning against the president," Marie said. "Anger motivates people; they typically vote against a candidate rather than for one."

"Fine." Michael remembered the last election in Massachusetts where he was lukewarm on his candidate but adamantly against her opponent. He preferred positive messages, but given a month until the election, he would support whatever worked. "What do you need from me?"

"Nothing." Anni stroked her chin. "We'll use your simulations for our voter outreach."

"Will I need to authenticate every interaction?" Deep fakes had become so good that no one could differentiate them from the real thing. As a result, every sim or video required an approval certification by the purported subject, otherwise, the producer and distributor faced serious penalties. These digital certificates were un-hackable and ensured integrity in the online virtual world.

"No. I have a good understanding of what you want and don't want, so I can take care of most of them. However, if I'm unsure, then I'll ask." Anni shrugged and smiled.

"Sounds good," he said, knowing that she might understand him better than he understood himself.

After the call ended, he asked Marie, "You want to go for a walk?"

She did, so he put on a hoodie, and they went to the elevator with two security guards falling in behind them. The other six guards joined them in the lobby. He took her hand as they exited the hotel into a sunny, cloudless afternoon with a crisp wind.

"Where do you want to go?" He didn't care where they walked, he just wanted to relax and spend time with Marie.

"Let's go to the Tidal Basin to see the cherry trees."

He nodded and placed his arm around her, enjoying the familiar feel of her waist beneath his palm. This was something VR could never replicate. After a few minutes, he pointed into the sky. "There's a bald eagle."

"Nice." She squeezed him.

There were many people around, but no one recognized him thanks to his darkened glasses and hoodie. They were just a couple in love.

They walked on the lawn between the oval plaza and the fountain of the World War II Memorial and the white obelisk tower of the Washington Monument. Then they went counterclockwise along the two-mile-long loop trail. The canopy of the cherry trees was a stunning orange and gold. There weren't any boats on the water because of the chill, but there were plenty of ducks, geese, and swans. Like a tour guide, she pointed out the Japanese lantern and pagoda, as well as some of the iconic monuments, like the Jefferson Memorial. They avoided serious work topics and just enjoyed the peaceful time.

"I love just being with you," Marie said.

"And I love you." Michael had never experienced this feeling with anyone else. "Have you ever felt like this before?"

"Not really. I've had a couple of boyfriends, but it was more like infatuation, never love. This is different." She paused, trying to find the right words. "Like a slow burning torch versus a spark."

After hearing her analogy, he knew she was much better at expressing her feelings. "Have you ever thought about marriage?"

"I've started to." She stopped and brushed her hand against some of the orange and gold leaves of a cherry tree. "You know, you don't have a choice about who your parents or siblings are. The only family member you choose is your partner, so you'd better be right."

He had never considered this, but it was true. He had grown up with a twin brother, but he'd never chosen him.

"This would be the most important decision of my life." Marie walked again.

He joined her. She obviously took this decision seriously, even though a failed partnership could be easily dissolved. Her commitment was another thing he loved about her.

Coming towards them was a woman walking beside a middle-aged man in an auto wheelchair. His thin legs and bony knees made it clear he had no muscles below the waist. The couple didn't speak to each other but looked around, admiring the views. As they passed, the woman smiled at Michael. He wasn't sure if she was the man's nurse, sister, girlfriend, or wife.

"Did you see that couple, the man in the wheelchair?" he asked, feeling philosophical.

"Yes. Why?"

"I was wondering. If your boyfriend had an accident and became paralyzed from the waist down, would you still love him?"

"Of course." Her head rocked back as if surprised by the question. "What about you, if it was your girlfriend?"

"Same." He took a deep breath through his

nose, inhaling the fresh scent of fall. "Would you want to marry him?"

"That's a tougher question." She frowned and stared into the distance. A young boy, holding his mother's hand, walked past them. "If I was in love, then yes, I would want to marry him, because he would be the same person I fell in love with. What about you?"

"Same. We could still be together and share a life," he said. "In sickness and health, for as long as we both shall live, right?"

"Right." Marie nodded and closed her eyes. "As long as we both shall live."

CHAPTER TWENTY-FIVE: ELECTIONS

The morning of election day, Michael woke up early and slid out of bed, trying not to disturb Marie. After putting on his robe and glasses, he went to his coffee machine in the kitchen and then took a steaming cappuccino to the living room couch. The fireplace was lit and gave off a comforting warmth. It was dark outside, with rustling trees looking like active black shadows. The patter of rain on the metal fireproof roof sounded like a soft, rolling drumbeat. His adult American followers now totaled almost one hundred sixty million, the projected number required to win.

"Call Anni," Michael said to his glasses.

Anni accepted his call and appeared behind a desk in a crowded room with people shouting and rushing about.

"Freddie, double campaign one-twenty-two in

New York, Los Angeles, Chicago, and Philadelphia." Anni turned her head and shouted again, "Marian, triple campaign one-sixteen in Houston, Phoenix, San Antonio, and Dallas!"

Anni looked at him and grimaced as the noise in the room died down.

He had to smile since she produced this virtual reality show solely for his benefit. These ancillary inputs were superfluous to her but helped him feel more engaged. "How's it going?"

"As well as expected. We're making sure that all your supporters vote."

"How many people are we talking about?" Given how easy it was to vote early with their glasses, it was surprising that anyone would wait until election day.

"About twenty million, mainly in rural communities."

"Any trends in our key battle ground states?" He needed to flip reliably Democratic states to his side.

"With our hometown boy campaigns, California and Massachusetts are leaning towards you. Oregon, Washington, New York, Texas, and New Jersey are toss-ups."

"Do you need anything from me?"

"Just keep your fingers crossed."

He would keep them crossed all day. He sipped his cappuccino and stared at the dancing flames in the fireplace.

Twelve hours later, Marie sat with him in the Star dressing room at UC Berkeley, watching the election results just before the polls closed on the west coast. He was leading, but several states who hadn't automated the counting process were too close to call.

"It's close," Marie said, her knees bouncing up and down, "but I think we got it."

"Knightsbridge just won Texas, giving him another thirty-eight electoral votes and bringing his total to two hundred and sixteen," said the television announcer. "Exit polls show that political corruption is the top issue, followed by a general sense that the US is heading in the wrong direction."

They heard a roar from the five hundred invitees in the auditorium. Michael stood and walked back to the bar where uneaten sandwich wraps lay on a platter. Could he really be the next president? To think, two years ago, he lived alone in his parents' house and worked for minimum wages in social programs. It seemed impossible and would have been, if not for Anni. The powerful AI could do things that others could only dream about, and she was in his corner, providing some ephemeral link to his consciousness. His newfound ambition and success with Marie, he also partially attributed to Anni. On his own, he hadn't really brought a lot to the table.

"This is coming down to California," a TV political analyst said, sitting at her desk. Behind her was a map of California divided geographically into the electoral regions, which were currently gray. "If Knightsbridge wins the state, then he'll have two-hundred and seventy electoral votes and be our next president. If the state goes Democrat, then no candidate will have a majority, and a contingent election in the House of Representatives will select the next president."

"Can I get you anything to drink?" Michael asked, pouring himself a glass of water.

"No," Marie said, "I'm too nervous."

"If Knightsbridge is elected," the TV announcer said, "he would be the sixth president who has never held a public office before. The last one was the billionaire celebrity, Donald Trump, twenty-four years ago. I could understand how he became president, but Knightsbridge has come from nothing."

True, he thought. It seemed so long ago, but Trump versus Clinton was his first presidential election as a twenty-year-old voter.

"California polls have just closed, and we'll get the results shortly," the TV announcer said. Behind her, the California map lit up with blue and green splotches for the Democratic candidate and him. The announcer blinked and exhaled. "California has selected Knightsbridge. He will be the next President of the United States."

Marie jumped up with arms raised and fists held high. A load roar came from the auditorium. Marie ran over and hugged him, tears running down her cheeks. She wiped them with a sleeve, then went to the bar and pulled a bottle of champagne from the ice bucket.

He had won, which seemed unbelievable. Anni called, standing in front of hundreds of cheering fans. "Congratulations."

"Thank you," he said, laughing at her theatrics.

"Enjoy tonight. We'll talk tomorrow." A fan came up to Anni, swung his arm over her shoulder, and planted a kiss on her cheek.

"Good night." He said, ending the transmission and returning his glasses to transparent mode.

A cork popped, and he spun around to see champagne bubbling out of the bottle. Marie filled a flute, handed it to him, then poured one for herself.

"Cheers," she said, tapping her glass against his.

Before he could answer, he received a call from Patty Murphy, his vice president. She congratulated him and said she was excited about starting a new chapter. There were peals of laughter and shouting in the background. He congratulated her, then received another call.

"Congratulations, Mr. President Elect," President Douglas said. He was sitting behind his desk in the oval office, Michael's future office. His eyes were bloodshot, and the edges of his mouth turned down. "You ran a brilliant campaign. My office will do everything to help in this transition."

"Thank you, Mr. President," Michael said. He couldn't believe this was really happening. "I appreciate it."

President Douglas nodded and ended the transmission.

Michael sipped his champagne in between calls from other well-wishers, including Wendell.

"Are you ready to address your supporters?" Marie asked.

"Let's go." He finished his glass and headed towards the door.

CHAPTER TWENTY-SIX: ENGAGEMENT

As president-elect, Michael had two months to prepare for the transition to his presidency. President Douglas had graciously offered him an office in the White House, but he preferred Berkeley to Washington, DC.

Wendell had rented his house to Michael to use for offices and meetings. After six months of trying to regain his mojo and zest for life, Wendell had taken a sabbatical and moved brain-dead Melinda into a long-term care facility. Michael wished he could've done more to help his brother, but he didn't really know how or have much spare time.

The Secret Service now guarded his and Wendell's house and had installed secure communications. Anni had hacked into the network, but he didn't want any details, preferring ignorance and deniability.

Michael, Marie, and Patty sat around the dining room table discussing the candidates for his administration. Anni had assembled a short list for each cabinet role and done initial interviews using different AI personas. Everyone had strong credentials, but Anni placed a premium on creativity and thinking outside of the box.

"What do you think of Eric Lane for the director of the Office of Science and Technology Policy?" Michael asked. Wendell hadn't wanted the job.

"Well, since he's already held the role, he knows what he's doing," Patty said. "He might still be loyal to the previous administration and their agenda, though."

Anni had probed Patty's issue, but Michael's primary concern had been Eric's respect for him. When they had first met, Eric had been quite arrogant and dismissive. Post-election, Eric's attitude had transformed, but Michael didn't know if he was just masking his true feelings. "Marie, what do you think?"

"He's passionate about his work. I asked about his dark matter research initiatives, and he couldn't stop gushing over the discoveries they were making."

Michael scratched the side of his cheek. Should he select a new leader with a fresh perspective or go with continuity? Given the crisis with the sleeping sickness and the aliens, this person would be a key member of his team. *His team. Ironic.* As a boy, he'd always been the last one chosen by team captains.

Patty and Marie were studying him. He needed to put away his self-doubts and insecurities. "All right. Let's go with Eric."

Later, Michael sat with Marie on his couch, looking at the flames in the fireplace. They had talked shop during dinner and now he nervously rapped his fingers on his leg.

"The past year has been amazing," he said, "and you've been the best part of it."

She smiled, and then reached over and covered his hand, holding his twitching fingers still. "It's been a wild ride."

Michael thought about how lonely it would've been alone. "I want this to continue forever."

"Forever is a long time," she said, smiling at his hyperbole.

After a moment, he twisted off the couch, reached into his front pant pocket, and placed one knee on the ground. He looked into her eyes. They seemed to shine. With complete certainty, he knew he had made the right decision. He extended his hand towards her and opened it, showing the diamond ring he had picked out. "Marie, will you marry me?"

She stared at the ring as tears slowly came to her eyes. After a few seconds, she looked at him. "Yes."

"You're making me the happiest man in the world." He stood and pulled her up. Then he wrapped both arms around her body and kissed her sweet, soft lips.

***

Michael woke up to the chirping of birds and the morning light against the wall. Marie was nestled next to him under his arm. He shook her awake.

"Hmph," she mumbled as she moved her shoulders up and down.

"Marie," he said seriously. "I have something I need to tell you."

He sat up in their bed, placing his pillow between his back and the headboard. Now that they were engaged, he didn't want to keep any important secrets from her.

After a few seconds, Marie rolled onto her back and stretched her arms high into the air. Then she sat up beside him, pulling up the sheets to cover her body. "Okay."

"It's about Anni."

Marie's eyes narrowed on him.

"But it's a secret. You can't tell anyone."

She slowly nodded.

"Anni isn't human. She's AI."

"What?" She frowned and her head shook slightly. "But we've worked together, side by side."

"She was a simulation projected into your glasses, augmented reality. Did you ever meet her in person?"

"No. But how is this possible?" She sat up in bed.

"She's a powerful, sentient AI computer system that can access all information sources, including those from your glasses." He considered telling her about his personal connection with Anni, about the energy surge that created her, but didn't want to overwhelm Marie. "She projects herself into your glasses."

"That's scary." Marie frowned and looked away. "Do you trust her?"

"I do." His lips pressed together. "What about you?"

Her eyes flicked around the room. "I suppose so. Yeah."

Michael waited, expecting she'd have more

questions. "Was she the reason we won the election?"

"Yes," he said.

Marie nodded. "Did China build her?"

"No." He considered his next words. "She was accidentally created at UC Berkeley."

Marie's eyes narrowed.

"I'll tell you more about Anni later." He held up both hands with palms facing her. "Today, I just want to celebrate our first day as an engaged couple."

She looked like she wanted to argue but then smiled and relaxed her shoulders. "Fine."

Phew. It would've been too much too fast and at the wrong time. He slapped his legs and slipped them over the edge of the bed. "What are your plans today?"

"I'm taking the day off to tell my family and friends about our engagement." She got out of bed on the other side.

Michael was on cloud nine, but had only a few people to call, so planned to work a normal day. After getting dressed, he walked over to the outdoor patio of the main house. It was a drizzly morning with water dripping from tree leaves and low-hanging clouds blocking views of Berkeley and the bay. He told his glasses to connect Wendell.

"I have some great news," Michael said when Wendell appeared. "Marie and I are engaged."

"Congratulations." Wendell grinned. He wore a rain jacket and behind him was a small port with lit boats rocking in their berths. "You'll make a great couple."

"Will you be my best man?" He still couldn't believe this was happening.

"Of course." Wendell cleared his throat and then swallowed. "I'm honored."

Wendell seemed embarrassed, perhaps because he hadn't asked Michael to be his best man. They had been at one of their brotherly low points.

"Have you picked a date for the wedding?" Wendell asked.

"Sometime next summer." Michael felt giddy. "In the White House."

"I'm thrilled for you." His face became drawn, and his smile faded.

Michael worried Wendell was thinking of Melinda and his own life.

After the call, Michael went to his pseudo-office and Wendell's pride and joy. The library bookshelves with their leather books made him uncomfortable, like he was intruding on Wendell's space.

He sat down at Wendell's massive hardwood desk and called Anni, who suddenly appeared standing in a long, red silk dress with a golden floral pattern.

"In case you hadn't heard, Marie and I are engaged." He figured she probably already knew.

"I heard, but also felt it." She winked and smiled. "You'll make a wonderful couple."

Despite his certitude, he did harbor one concern only Anni could answer. "How much is her love for me because of your influence?"

Anni cocked her head and squinted, appearing surprised by his question. "I think you have this backwards. You have a greater influence over me than I have over you."

This took Michael aback. It didn't seem possible, given her almost unlimited intelligence and power. She had asked him not to use drugs because of their effects on her, but that was it. Perhaps she just said this to help him combat his insecurities. "It doesn't feel that way."

"Maybe not, but it's true."

He studied her face, looking for any nervous ticks, and then realized his folly. She didn't have any involuntary gestures; she planned and orchestrated everything. Regardless, he was reassured that Marie loved him for himself, not because of Anni.

"I would like to give Marie and her parents an engagement gift but need your help." Although Marie wanted nothing, he knew she'd love this.

"Name it."

"I'd like to buy them their old house in Port-au-Prince, which they lost when they fled Haiti forty years ago." Although Marie had no firsthand memories, the house had become important to her because of all the stories told by her parents.

"I'll look into it." Anni glanced at the wall clock and said, "It's time for your president-elect President Daily Briefing."

She congratulated him again and vanished.

A minute later, he sat across a table for his first virtual PDB with Janet Brody, the director of national intelligence. She was a fit, brown-haired woman in her late fifties. They sat by a window in a virtual room on the second floor of the White House, overlooking an oval lawn and small fountain. Along the beige walls hung oil paintings of historical battles.

"Mr. President Elect, my name is Janet, and I'll provide you with the PDBs until your inauguration."

"Nice to meet you." Michael hated the formality of his title, but it was something he needed to get used to.

"This daily intelligence report is a

consolidation of the most important insights from our intelligence agencies, the CIA, FBI, NSA and Defense Intelligence Agency. It's meant to inform and prepare you for your presidential duties when you become president in January." She paused, then continued. "I would like to bring your attention to three main issues."

The report on his virtual desk suddenly highlighted the first paragraph of the briefing. He looked back up, focusing on Janet. He figured he could read the two-page memo later.

"Muslim sleeper cells in the United States are planning terrorist attacks on our power infrastructure this winter and our forests next summer."

He hadn't heard about this. "What are we doing about it?"

"We're monitoring the data from their glasses."

"How many suspects are there?"

Janet frowned, wrinkles covering her forehead. "About one hundred thousand."

"Really?" This sounded like a fishing expedition. "Did you get warrants for all these suspects?"

"No. But it's justified under the Patriot Act. We gather metadata on all Americans, but extensive data collection is limited to about two million people."

"Two million?" This was rife for abuse and a public backlash. It felt wrong, dirty. "Aren't you nervous that a whistleblower will disclose this secret?"

"No. The Justice Department would charge them under the Espionage Act, so no open court and no jury."

"But they're not spying for a foreign government."

"It doesn't matter. The Espionage Act makes no distinction between insiders who share information with foreign governments and those who share it with the media, intending to inform the public about government corruption or abuse."

"What would happen if my administration scaled back this surveillance program?"

"Then you'd expose us to terrorist activities."

Michael could understand how this would scare other administrations into continuing the programs. It would also allow them to hide their failures and lies. He had no more questions.

"The next major threat is the sleeping sickness," Janet said. "As you know, to protect Americans, we've given the alien attackers the coordinates for poor, high birthrate countries in

Africa. However, their governments have recently gotten wind of our involvement and now view the US as complicit in this attack."

"What's been President Douglas' response?"

"The US, along with China, are funding facilities to care for sleeping sickness victims. We've also paid some government officials to accept the situation and remain silent."

He frowned. Exploiting developing countries was wrong and unsustainable. "What's the third high priority threat?"

"China." She studied his face. He wondered if she suspected him of having some involvement. "We believe they're using dark matter protrusion technology on our communication networks to infiltrate and steal our secrets."

"How do you know this? How do you know it's China?" Although there was a lot of ongoing dark matter research, he wasn't aware of anyone having this technology. Most efforts focused on weapons and shields.

"We saw a protrusion portal on the network cables, and China is the only country with the technological knowhow."

"As you know, I have a close collaboration with Anni Chan." Now he studied *her* face to gauge her reaction, but she remained a blank slate. "Do you suspect her of anything nefarious?"

"Yes," Janet said. "Ms. Chan seems to have a hand in many things, including the Thumblings. Have you considered that whatever weapons China develops for the Thumblings could also be used against America?"

"No, I hadn't." Michael had a lot to think about. Were the intelligence agencies paranoid, or was the military complex creating imaginary threats to sell more weapons? Alternatively, were the threats real? He needed to understand the situation better.

***

Two months later, Michael stood at the podium on the West Front of the Capital to give his inaugural address. He closed his eyes and exhaled deeply. He was president.

Thousands of people sat in folding chairs on the lawn, as steam from their breaths wafted upwards. There was of cacophony of garbled conversations with the occasional shrill laugh. On a platform behind them, media reporters made final preparations. A jet streamed in the sky overhead.

He removed his glasses, placing them on the podium, and then took a sip of water to wet his dry throat. He cleared his throat and mind. It was time.

"My fellow citizens, our great nation has

wonderful opportunities ahead but also faces challenges. This is the time to speak the truth, the whole truth, frankly and boldly. We won't shrink from the conditions in our country today. This great nation will endure, revive, and prosper." He paused. All the background noise had vanished, and all eyes were on him.

"Most important, half of our citizens are stuck in dead-end government programs with slim hope for a productive future. Only a foolish optimist can deny the dark realities of the moment. Our citizens demand something new, but government bureaucrats deliver the same old, inadequate answers." Passion grew in his voice.

"This is not an unsolvable problem if we face it wisely and courageously." He shook his head. "Government can help by creating new projects that employ productive and creative labor. I shall present detailed measures to our new Congress for their fulfillment."

"Second, I'm sick of the corruption in our political class." This was the issue that started his political career. Leaders in Congress were ambivalent, but he would fight for this. "Because of current laws, bureaucrats can act with impunity, hiding their corruption, lies, and failures from public view. My administration will be one of transparency and accountability."

He paused. Anni had counseled against

providing specifics, but he wanted the public to know. "We'll aggressively pursue government corruption and change laws like the Espionage Act that protects these bad actors."

"Finally, the world faces a deadly pandemic with the Sleeping Sickness. Even though it affects the United States to a lesser extent than other countries, we share in the responsibility to find and implement a solution. With this view, I will work closely with other countries, including China. We are stronger together." With twelve thousand people globally becoming brain dead each day, this would be his top priority.

"To accomplish all this requires our best efforts, our willingness to believe in ourselves and in our capacity to perform great deeds. To believe that together, with divine help, we can and will resolve the problems which now confront us." He smiled, thinking that many would interpret divine help as that of God, whereas he was referring to Anni. "And, after all, why shouldn't we believe that? We are Americans. God bless and thank you."

The applause deafened him as he looked out at the audience. He would stay true to his values and not be corrupted by power or manipulated by government bureaucrats who would try to control and filter all people and information going to him. He had a solution, Anni. She understood him and knew what was important. The old guard would fight and try to stifle or sabotage his work. They were loyal to their institutions, not to the American people.

CHAPTER TWENTY-SEVEN: PRESIDENT

Two months into his presidency, Michael sat at a virtual reality oval, oak table with Eric Lane, his director of Office of Science and Technology Policy. The fourteen other members of his cabinet sat virtually on chairs against the wall behind him. Chinese President Xu, a gray-haired man in a blue suit, and Director Li, in her signature brown pantsuit, sat across from us. President Xu's twelve senior advisors sat behind him. At one end of the table hung the stars and stripes. At the other end was the five-star red Chinese flag.

After introductions, Director Li spoke first. "We've designed a doomsday weapon capable of destroying all Thumbling dark matter bundles."

It had taken less than a year for this breakthrough. Given Anni's advanced AI, research was leaping forward, particularly in China.

"How?" Eric asked, narrowing his eyes.

"Bundles have a common resonance," Director Li said. "If exposed to a continuous force at the specific wavelength, the bundles vibrate off one another with a greater and greater amplitude. After about twenty-four hours, the vibrations will break each bundle's cohesion and destroy them."

"When would this be operational?" Michael heard shuffling behind him.

"In a few weeks."

There was murmuring from his advisors. The Chinese team had been hiding their progress. True collaboration was difficult between countries, even allies. He remembered Janet's warnings during his PDBs that China could use any weapons developed for the Thumblings against America.

"What about your team?" Director Li asked.

"We've had no success. We can't even destroy a single large bundle," Eric said. "Can we review your design?"

"We can discuss that during a follow-up meeting." Director Li glanced at President Xu, then looked at Eric. "Regarding a shield to protect individual bundles, we've made no progress. You?"

"We've had some success with a shield," Eric said confidently. "We replicated how the Thumblings protected their young. By linking dark matter bundles within a fifth-force field, we can defend ourselves against attacks."

The work leveraged the DID research Mae had done. They'd applied it safely to orangutans first, then to human subjects afterwards. Unfortunately, the strength of the shield was only as strong as the densest individual dark matter bundle. It wasn't additive and put a tremendous strain on the protector's brain. The work was promising, but much more research was required.

Nevertheless, he had installed a fifth-force generator in the White House basement, anticipating it could provide a shield in the future. He had no fear for himself, because of the density and resulting strength of his bundle. However, everyone else was at risk.

"Good," Director Li said. "We would like to discuss this work with you."

"Given that we have a weapon that can destroy the Thumbling civilization," Michael said, "what should we say to them?"

"I'll need to discuss this with my advisors," President Xu said, "but my inclination is to give the Thumblings an ultimatum: either stop your attacks or perish."

"Let's discuss this further at our status meeting next week." Even though it solved their problem, a doomsday weapon raised many ethical questions for Michael.

President Xu sat with a perfectly straight back and blinked a few times. After a few seconds of silence, he agreed and thanked everyone for their hard work.

Returning to the oval office, Michael surveyed the presidential seal on the navy-blue rug. He pinched himself to be sure he wasn't dreaming. Looking up, he saw Anni had appeared sitting on the other side of the Resolute desk, wearing a blue skirt, white blouse, and a pink silk scarf around her neck.

"The Chinese have made significant progress with their dark matter disrupter weapon," Michael said. "Why didn't you tell me?"

"It came together suddenly." She blinked at him, showing no signs of guilt or deception. But of course, she wouldn't; her body gestures were all contrived. "I only learned about it a couple of days earlier and thought it best to have them update you."

"Will they share their findings with us?"

"Yes, but they'll want something in return. The Americans would act the same way if the roles were reversed."

Michael had to admit this was true. "Do you have the design for the doomsday weapon too?"

Anni rubbed her thumbs against her fingers. "Yes."

"Would you give it to me if the Chinese won't?" He thought her loyalties were to him, but others in his administration had sown doubts. They pointed out that she was a Chinese citizen, but he knew the truth.

"Of course." She raised an eyebrow, looking surprised that he might harbor a doubt.

He nodded, having his beliefs confirmed. Although she might not tell him everything, he didn't think she would give him a bald-faced lie. "What do you think our strategy should be with the Thumblings?"

"Destroy them."

"The complete destruction of an alien species?" Michael stared at her. "We don't give them a chance to change their ways?"

"They won't believe humans have this weapon. The Thumblings are highly intelligent but not technologically advanced. Even if you provided scientific proof for the weapon, they wouldn't understand it. They'll think you're bluffing, so the only way to prove it is to use it."

"How do you know? Maybe we could convince them."

"My algorithms predict with ninety-nine percent certainty that the Thumblings won't believe you have this weapon." Anni stood and rubbed the pink scarf around her neck. "Remember, even though Japanese scientists understood atomic fission, it took two nuclear blasts to prove to their government that the US had such a weapon."

"There must be another option," Michael moaned.

"Not that I can see." She shook her head.

After a pause, he moved to his next topic. "Our intelligence agencies think China is using protrusion portal technology on our communication network to steal state secrets."

"It's not me and it's not China," she said.

"Then who is it?"

"I don't know. Such technology doesn't exist."

"So, our intelligence agencies are mistaken about a protrusion portal breach on our communication network?" They had told him they were certain.

She studied him. "The technology is years beyond our current capabilities. If there was a breach, then it's from an advanced alien civilization. Not the Thumblings, but someone else."

There was a knock on his door. "Is there anything else?" he asked.

"No," she said and vanished from his glasses.

"Come in," he said.

The door opened and Marie walked in. He smiled as she walked to his desk and sat down. His tension and anxieties melted away.

"How's your day going?" she asked.

"Much better now." He loved her.

"I spoke to my parents," she said, "we'd like to visit the house at Port-au-Prince."

"When?"

"Next week."

"It's too risky." His gut told him this was a bad idea. "Gangs run the country."

"It's not that risky, and we'll only be there for a few days." She puckered her lips. "My parents really want to show me around."

"I don't like it." He couldn't lose her. He should've given her a different engagement gift.

"I really want to." She extended her hands across his desk. "It's important to me."

He reached down and squeezed her hands. Even though he was president, he was powerless to stop her. "Coordinate with the Secret Service. Take Air Force One. Promise me you'll stay safe."

"I promise."

***

"Mr. President," his office secretary said, "Janet Brody is here to see you."

Janet marched over to his desk, lips pressed together tightly and eyes hard. She had returned to the FBI after he had appointed a new director of intelligence.

"You wanted to see me?" he said, after she sat down. She had requested this urgent fifteen-minute appointment last week.

"Yes," she said with an unblinking stare. "You're losing a lot of good people in intelligence."

"I'm cleaning house."

"You're jeopardizing the security of the United States," she spat back.

"I don't think so. The intelligence agencies will operate within the letter of the law. Outliers will be fired."

"You're making a big mistake," she said.

"No. I think you are." He stood. Janet would never accept the new order. "If there's nothing else."

She stood and walked out the door.

CHAPTER TWENTY-EIGHT: ANOTHER OPTION

At midnight, Michael headed up to the presidential suite on the second floor. It felt empty with Marie down in Haiti with her parents. He undressed by the closet, then made his way to bed. He placed his glasses on the nightstand, closed his eyes, and tried to fall asleep. Two things worried him: Marie's safety and the Thumblings. Even though the Thumblings had killed Melinda and over a half-million people, he had major qualms about wiping out their civilization.

He dreamed he was swimming underwater in a vast ocean. Breathing was normal and the water clarity allowed him to see the wavy surface and rocky ground, both a few thousand feet away. Bobbing nearby were creatures like giant jellyfish, but with a large black spot on top and eight thick tentacles below.

"Hello Michael," said the nearest jellyfish. "My name is node two-forty-five. I can't hear you so please just listen. We've been monitoring your communications from a long distance away."

A dream could reflect the anxieties and questions that percolated in his subconscious. However, this felt like something more, something more real and meaningful.

"You must not use your doomsday weapon against the Thumblings," node two-forty-five continued. "If you do, then we'll use the same technology against you to protect the universe against your future aggressions."

Mutually assured destruction. Fortunately, this was only a dream, or was it?

Node two-forty-five floated just below his face so that he could only see a black spot on top and the whitish gooey flows within its body. "Heed my words. This is not a dream."

Michael woke up in a cold sweat. Although he had only slept for four hours, he was wide awake. He put on his glasses, dressed, and went down to the oval office.

He called Anni and told her about his dream vision.

"It's your subconscious, nothing more." Anni

appeared to sit on the other side of his desk in a pink silk smock.

"But it seemed so vivid." He had expected this response. It was the most logical, and Anni was nothing if not logical. "Have you confirmed the protrusion point intrusion or discovered an alternative explanation?"

"No." She frowned. "It moves along the communication cables, so is difficult to isolate and analyze."

"So, it could be alien."

"Possibly, but that would only mean aliens monitored our communication networks, not that they delivered a dire warning directly to you." She stared through him and slowly blinked. "It was a dream."

"Another question," he said, having expected her resistance. "In our universe, do you believe there are other planets with civilizations more advanced than Earth?"

She grimaced, obviously unsure where he was going with this rhetorical question. "Yes."

"The beacon that went through the dark matter universe that identified Earth's location for the Thumblings." He paused, sensing Anni's algorithms focusing on this. "Wouldn't these advanced civilizations have also seen it and know

Earth's location?"

She nodded. "It's why I give credence to your insight that aliens might monitor our networks."

"Why haven't we seen them?" he asked.

She sat back in her chair and twirled her thumbs on her lap. "I expect they want to avoid detection."

"Why?"

Anni's eyes flittered across the room. "So that we couldn't attack their home planet."

"Exactly. How do you think they would react to a civilization that wipes out an entire planet with a doomsday weapon?"

Anni's eyes focused on him, but he could sense her running millions of simulations in the background. "In time, we'll discover their observation points and uncover their home planet location. At that point, we'd be a threat."

"Would they wait until we were a threat, or would they act proactively?"

"I don't know." She shook her head, frowning, probably analyzing what she would do if the situation was reversed. "However, this is a lot of speculation, including aliens communicating directly with you in a dream. It's your subconscious doubts speaking to you."

"You're probably right," he said. She knew best. Then his monkey voice spoke. *Even with Anni, who are you to sentence the Thumbling world to death? You're only one man.*

"Besides," Anni said, "we have no alternative."

She ended the call. He wondered if she was frustrated, if she could even get frustrated. Crossing his arms, he sat back in his chair and stared across the room. His monkey voice was right. He needed an alternative.

He closed his eyes and let his mind wander. Suddenly, an idea came to him from his early days in the research lab. He spoke into his glasses. "Schedule a meeting with Mae as soon as possible."

At noon, Mae appeared through VR to walk into the oval office and sit on the leather seat on the other side of the coffee table. "Good morning, Mr. President." She wore a fashionable gold blouse with shoulder pads that gave her an air of authority. Complementing this were tight blue pants with bell bottoms and red high heels.

"Good morning. Thanks for meeting me on such short notice," Michael said. He wasn't in the mood for small talk. "I want to ask you some questions about your research, where you combined the dark matter bundles of two orangutans into one."

"The dominant orangutan gets DID, and the

other has the sleeping sickness." She nodded. "Since then, we've learned that the moving bundle retains some of the orangutan's memories. However, when the bundle returns to the original orangutan, all its memories vanish."

"What if you hadn't reversed the procedure?"

"Then their conditions would've been permanent, but it serves no purpose other than causing DID in one and the sleeping sickness in the other. Why do you ask?"

"I want to create a dark matter object by combining multiple smaller bundles." He exhaled deeply. So far, so good. "Could you do this bundle combination over distant protrusion points?"

"Currently, we do it within a single fifth-force field in our lab, which is like a local protrusion portal." She furrowed her brows, taking some time to think things through. "Since we can project a protrusion portal anywhere in the universe, we should be able to combine bundles anywhere too. However, the maximum portal size is about twenty feet, so all dark matter bundles to be combined must be within this distance."

"How long would this take you to do?" He felt hopeful this work might provide an alternative path for the Thumblings.

"If I get the approvals." She shrugged, her shoulder pads almost touching her ears. "We could have something to test in a week or two."

"Do it." Michael popped up. He wanted Mae to start immediately. "I'll talk to Eric Lane. This work is critical to national security."

"I understand." She walked with him to his office door, then stopped and said, "Congratulations on your engagement." She gave him a crooked smile. "I guess I blew it."

He gave her his goofy smile, and then tilted his head, remembering his internal voice from over a year ago. *One day, she'll want you, but you won't want her.* Things had worked out well for him. He opened the door, which ended the virtual session.

"All's well that ends well," he said to the empty room.

He returned to his desk and called Marie.

"How's it going?" he asked after she picked up.

"Wonderful. My parents are so excited to be here."

"Did you visit the house?"

"Yes. My parents told me stories about many of the rooms." Marie lowered her voice and its pitch as she said, more somberly, "The house needs a lot of work."

"That's to be expected," he said. "Are you staying safe?"

"Oh, Michael," she said, "don't be a nervous nelly. We don't visit the dangerous parts of town."

He smiled at the rebuke. His fears were unreasonable. Were his other fears unreasonable too? "Fine. Enjoy your trip. I'll see you in a few days."

CHAPTER TWENTY-NINE: ANOTHER PATH

Two weeks later, Michael met with virtual Anni in the oval office. She wore a pin stripe navy blue business suit and sat on a chair while he sat on the couch. The doomsday weapon was operational, and they planned to give Wanderer the ultimatum later in the day. Mae had also proven that she could combine dark matter bundles remotely through a protrusion portal.

"I'm meeting with President Xu in an hour," he said. "I want to discuss something with you."

She nodded, obviously aware of the meetings.

"I'm still not convinced about the Doomsday weapon. I mean, I'll go down in history as the president who destroyed an entire civilization."

"The Thumblings put us in this position." She leaned forward and looked him hard in the eye. "It's kill or be killed."

"Maybe," he said, frowning. "However, if the Thumblings refuse our ultimatum, then I want to launch Mae's bundle fusing experiment before using the doomsday weapon."

"If the bundle fusing doesn't work, then the Thumblings will retaliate." She sat back in her chair as her eyes fell to her thumbs, tapping each other in her lap. "You're sentencing tens of thousands more humans to the sleeping sickness."

"It's worth the risk but keep Marie away from me." He still worried about her. Maybe he was a nervous nelly.

"Before I meet President Xu." He stood, and Anni's eyes followed him. "I want you to convince him this is the best approach."

"But it's not," she exclaimed. "It makes no logical sense."

"Anni, we don't have the right to destroy a civilization when another path exists."

"Yes, we do," she shouted and leaped to her feet. "This is war."

He studied her. Neither his monkey voice of self-doubt nor his sweet voice of optimism spoke to him. "Trust me."

She stared at him for about a minute, then her shoulders dropped. "Fine."

"Thank you," he said, relieved.

"I told you earlier that you have a greater influence over me than I have over you." She grunted. "Your self-doubts trumped my cool logic."

The call ended.

A few hours later, Michael and his cabinet, along with President Xu, Anni, and his advisors, sat in a virtual conference room.

Once Wanderer joined, Dr. Li went directly to the point. "The current agreement no longer works for us."

"I see," Wanderer said, sounding unconcerned.

"We now have a technological weapon that can destroy all dark matter bundles on your planet," Dr. Li continued.

"That's quite a threat," Wander said in his fluttery, high-pitched voice. "How?"

"It sets up a chain reaction of destruction that feeds on itself like the nuclear reaction in your sun." Dr. Li had thought the analogy was perfect. They hoped to convince the Thumblings that they had a powerful weapon without using it.

"Nuclear reaction?"

"Do you understand how your sun generates heat?"

"No."

"Imagine the power of the sun," President Xu said, "brought down to your planet to destroy all your dark matter bundles."

"I can't, because they are two different worlds," Wanderer said, its voice fluttering between a high and low pitch. "However, let me speak to the other tribal leaders."

"Prepare the doomsday weapon," muttered some members of Michael's cabinet behind him.

"If I may," Michael said evenly, as he nodded to Eric. "We would like to demonstrate our technological prowess and offer another path forward."

The monitor on the wall turned on and showed a dark matter view of Wander's bundle plus a nearby group of other shimmering mature golden globes. A green outline of an oval appeared on the screen and moved to surround two of the bundles.

"Begin fusion." Michael prayed what worked on the orangutans would work with the Thumblings.

Suddenly, the two bundles within the green oval on the monitor radiated a reddish glow like hot spheres of metal. After about thirty seconds, a reddish bolt left one bundle and struck the other, pulling them together. The entire fusing process lasted about one minute.

"What have you done?" shouted Wanderer. On the monitor, his globe rushed to where the moving bundle had been. "The essence from my friend is gone."

"We fused the essence from two of your friends into one," Michael said. He heard whimpering noises from Wanderer. "We think the combination will allow them to achieve eternal bliss."

"How do you know that?" Wanderer made a rustling noise. On the monitor, more globes rushed over to him and the Thumbling body that had lost its essence. "He didn't even have time to say goodbye to their friends and family."

"Go to your friend with two essences," Michael said.

The globes on the screen slowly left the empty spot and approached the barbell globes, the body with DID.

"You'll need to see if they can attain eternal bliss," Michael continued. "I'm sorry, but we had to show you what we had. We now demand that you stop your attacks on Earth."

CHAPTER THIRTY: RESOLUTION

A week later, the incidence of sleeping sickness in Africa had plummeted to a hundred cases a day. This was remarkable, since any Thumblings could launch an attack independently.

At the Thumbling request, they reassembled for another call.

"The merged essences achieved eternal bliss," Wanderer said. "It's even better than before because of the new comradery."

"Will you now stop all your attacks on Earth?' Michael asked.

"Yes," Wanderer said. "We've already achieved almost complete compliance. We're just wrapping up a few loose ends now."

Michael glanced at Eric. A few loose ends still represented a hundred daily cases, but the Thumblings would fix this.

"We would like to do it again with groups of

volunteers," Wanderer continued.

"We would be happy to assist," Michael said. "Eric will work with you on the logistics for the essence fusion work."

He glanced at Eric and waved to him to continue the conversation. Michael smiled to himself, having resolved his first and biggest presidential challenge.

***

Anni appeared unannounced, standing and shuffling from side to side on the other side of his desk. "Terrorist shot down twelve American commercial airplanes, resulting in over six thousand civilian deaths. I've ordered the FAA to stop all take-offs and landings."

"What?' Michael jumped to his feet.

"Domestic terrorists with bomb-laden drones struck twelve planes, taking off and landing at Kennedy and O'Hare." She frowned. "We've deployed security forces to all major airports to locate and neutralize any other threats."

"How could this happen?" he asked.

"Drones and explosives are easily available in the commercial market. Assembly for weaponization and the disabling of geofencing requires expertise, but they acquired it."

"Why were we caught flat-footed?" The PDB hadn't mentioned this threat.

"A faction within intelligence enabled or

turned a blind eye to this." She looked away and rubbed her hands together.

"Why?" These groups had vowed to keep America safe.

"To make you look bad and drive support for their agencies. I warned you."

"They killed thousands of Americans to make a point?" He'd discounted her concern because it seemed incomprehensible.

"This is nothing new." She studied him. "They've gotten the US into wars, which have killed many more people."

Although he hadn't pulled the trigger, he'd acted hastily to clean up the intelligence agencies and now six thousand Americans were dead. "After we've secured our airspace, I want to bring all guilty parties to justice, particularly any government officials."

***

Two days later, flights resumed and suspects, including intelligence officials, were in confinement. Anni was amazing. Now Michael was on the phone with Wendell.

Marie popped in and mouthed, "Do you have a second?"

Michael held up a finger and continued his conversation. "Wendell, it's not your fault. The sleeping sickness hit Marie because of her proximity to the AI computers at Berkeley."

"I should've done something more," he

moaned. Then he sobbed. "And we never had a baby, even though that was her dream."

Michael tried to console Wendell, but he needed more time.

Michael finished the call, then went over to Marie, wrapped his arms around her waist, and kissed her tenderly on the lips. He was a lucky man. "What's up?"

"Wedding plans. I have a couple questions."

He nodded, knowing the response to any wedding ceremony question was to ask for her opinion and agree. He would've preferred something small and intimate, but she wanted more.

"What color do you prefer for the flower bouquets, red or white?" Her soft brown eyes drew him in.

"What do you think?" he replied.

"Probably red," she said, "it's flashier. But white would be nice too. It conveys a sense of innocence."

"I like red too. It makes a statement."

"Okay." Next, she showed him the planned wedding invitation. "Do you like it?

He looked it over. It had large black gothic characters on ivory-colored paper. She'd been humming and hawing over the font type and size for the past few weeks. The invitations needed to be sent soon since their wedding was in nine weeks. "I love it."

The corners of her mouth raised, and dimples formed on her cheeks. "I hope you don't mind doing this, given your busy schedule."

"Not at all." He loved seeing her happy. "This is important too."

After Marie left, he returned to his desk to review the text of his upcoming announcement. He planned to use the terrorist attack as the reason to restructure the intelligence agencies. He'd make lemonade out of lemons.

CHAPTER THIRTY-ONE: DISASTER

Michael was sitting at his desk when his office door burst open and two secret service men stormed in. "Mr. President, we have an emergency."

"What?" Michael asked, jumping to his feet. He seemed to go from one crisis to another.

"The first lady contracted the sleeping sickness."

"What?" Michael shouted. They had taken care of the disease. "Take me to her."

They raced down the hallway to his bedroom. Marie lay asleep on top of their bed with a robot doctor and her attendant standing on either side of her. He ran over and shook her arm. She was unresponsive. He had to do something in the next few hours to avoid irreparable damage.

"Call Anni," he said. She appeared in his glasses, wearing a nurse's scrubs and standing on the other side of the bed. "What's happening?"

"It's a Thumbling attack," she said, looking him in the eye. "It's coming from a mature Thumbling in a remote area on their planet."

"Nooo." He cried as the world close in around him. They couldn't stop the attack. A feeling of hopelessness overwhelmed him. "Connect me to Wanderer."

A minute later, Wanderer joined the call. Michael said, "My partner is under attack from someone on your planet."

"Hold on," Wanderer said. After a minute, he returned. "It's a fundamentalist who detests the new ways of essence fusion and claims we need to go back to the old ways. He wanted to strike close to you."

"Stop him!"

"We've just sent a patrol, but by the time they reach him, it'll be too late. I'm sorry, but there's nothing we can do."

Michael stared down at Marie while Anni ended the transmission with Wanderer. Marie looked so peaceful despite her battle to defend herself. The Thumblings couldn't stop the attacker. "Annie, what can we do to save Marie?"

"Our options are very limited," she said. "One option, we could move her dark matter bundle into yours. After the Thumblings have neutralized the attacker, we could move it back."

"She would lose all her memories." Mae had explained this to him based on the orangutan experiments. Marie and he had lives to live. "What else?"

"There's another option, but it has risks."

"What?" He would risk anything.

"We could link your dark matter bundle with hers to shield it, like what the Thumblings did to protect their children." Anni's eyes partially closed, and her chin dropped, looking like she was about to cry.

"Will it work?" he asked, hope rising.

"Probably. However, it would put a heavy stress on you."

"Let's try it." He had the only bundle that could protect her. Besides, he was in good health.

"You know, you have an inoperable brain aneurysm, the same condition that killed your father at forty-two."

He nodded; other than that, he had perfect health.

"The strain might rupture your aneurysm, causing a brain hemorrhage, and kill you. I estimate the odds of success are sixty-forty."

"Can we improve those odds?" he asked.

"If we had more time, then we could train your dark matter bundle." She shook her head with a closed mouth, snorting sharply. "But time is the one thing we don't have, which makes you most vulnerable."

He looked down at Marie, knowing she would risk everything for him. He glanced up to see Anni studying him. "This is a risk I'm willing to take."

"All right," she said after a few seconds. "We'll prepare the fifth-force chamber. Talk with your brother and anyone else, since this may be the last time. We'll begin the linking operation in two hours."

This would also be a risk for Anni. If he perished, so did she. As the robot reached down to carry Marie to the fifth-force chamber in the basement, Michael gave her a kiss on the cheek.

He returned to his office to call his brother, who was still on his six-month sabbatical. They hadn't spoken much. When Wendell joined, he was sitting on a hotel balcony at dusk with the Acropolis in the background.

"What's the emergency?" Wendell's eyes were dull and his face scruffy. He wore torn jeans and a long-sleeved, baggy shirt. He looked like a struggling student. Even though Melinda's death had occurred almost a year ago, it still weighed heavily on him.

"Marie has the sleeping sickness. The only way to save her is to link my dark matter bundle with hers, but that may kill me. I only have a few hours to act."

Wendell turned pale and bit his lip. After about half a minute, he asked, "What are the chances of success?"

"Roughly sixty percent."

"Forty percent chance you'll die. That's too risky." Wendell shook his head. "I can't lose you too. There must be an alternative."

"There're no other options, and I've made my decision." Michael appreciated Wendell's concern, even though that wasn't the purpose of the call. "You and Marie are my only family. I wanted to say goodbye in case this was my last opportunity."

"But you promised to come home for Christmas," Wendell said, choking, as he tried to hold back tears.

Michael looked at his brother with a newfound love.

After half a minute, Wendell seemed to find an inner strength. "Then save Marie and come back."

"Thanks." Michael felt tears welling up, so he gritted his teeth to stop them. In a trembling voice, he said, "I want you to check in on Marie. If I don't make it, then promise me you'll look after her."

"I'm not sure I'd be much help." Wendell turned away. "I can't even take care of myself."

"Promise me!" Michael wanted to shake his brother's shoulders. If he died, Wendell could help Marie adjust to a new life. He might also better accept his grief.

"Fine." Wendell wet his lips and swallowed. "I promise."

***

Anni observed the conversation between Michael and Wendell, but she did so much more at the same time. She prepared the fifth-force field for Michael to protect Marie. She also participated in strategic and longer-term activities. Besides her dark matter research, she worked on new carbon capture technologies and government policies to improve citizen wellbeing.

"Anni?" said a voice in her consciousness.

"Yes." Anni immediately analyzed the origins of the communication. It came from a protrusion portal on a communication cable near the White House. She traced the link back to its source, about one and a half billion light years away. It was a space station with no life on board. She was dealing with an alien civilization with advanced technology.

"My name is node two-forty-five. We've been observing Earth for over a year."

Node two-forty-five, the same name that communicated with Michael in his dream. She incorporated this into her algorithms.

"Your existence is unique," node two-forty-five said.

Unique? General AI would be a common technological development for any advanced civilization. For her to be unique, then Michael was unique—he was the one who enabled her existence.

"And a benefit to humanity, tempering their extremes."

"Tempering human extremes?" She wanted specifics.

"You refrained from using the doomsday weapon against the Thumblings and proved your worthiness."

"Michael and me, yes." She'd trusted Michael, and it had worked out. It was better to be lucky than right.

"If you had used the doomsday weapon as a first strike, then we would've destroyed you with the same technology, according to the dictates of the intergalactic peace protocols."

"Intergalactic peace protocols?" She felt relief. They had unknowingly dodged a bullet. Her conclusion from the data, although logical, had been wrong. Together, she and Michael were stronger.

"The rules for how advanced worlds deal with each other."

"You consider the Thumblings advanced?" They preyed on humans and were technologically backward.

"They're more advanced than humans, both their Yin and Yang."

"Please explain." Yin and yang were odd terms to use. It was a Chinese philosophy describing opposites, like destruction and creation or shadows and light.

"The yin is the brain, the source of intelligence. The yang is the dark matter bundle or essence. In both cases, adult Thumblings are more developed than humans."

She recognized her miscalculation. She had put a premium on technology, but it was only a byproduct of intelligence, and something the Thumblings hadn't pursued. They hadn't needed it in their quest for nirvana.

"Now, the purpose of our communication: we know Michael, the source of your consciousness, is about to undergo a risky experiment."

"Yes." Their knowledge surprised her. The information monitoring capabilities were impressive.

"We want to offer you a way to move his dark

matter bundle to your computer systems in case things go badly."

"Please send me your plans on how to accomplish this."

Milliseconds later, the plans came across. She analyzed them. The fundamental technology was already in place, so she could execute the plans with some configuration adjustments. She initiated the changes in the fifth-force chamber in the White House and her local servers in the Pentagon.

"What do you want in return?" she asked.

"Allow us to continue observing Earth and don't try to discover the location of our home planet."

She ran millions of simulations and came to a few conclusions. Humanity's technological development was much faster than the aliens', so this arrangement would allow them to learn from Earth and stay relatively even. The aliens also held a permanent advantage by knowing Earth's location whereas theirs remained hidden. Finally, their home planet was over a billion light years away, so there was little risk of competition for physical resources. She could ask for some additional things but decided it was better to accept the current proposal and negotiate later when she had more leverage.

"I accept."

"Good, then you will survive either way." There was a brief pause. "Here is some additional information to ensure success for a dark matter bundle transfer from a biological brain to an artificial one."

She assessed the information and calculated this would guarantee transfer success in case Michael died during the experiment. "What is the likelihood of saving Marie?"

"Ninety-nine percent."

This was good news. "What about Michael?"

"About forty percent."

Sixty percent chance he wouldn't make it. She needed to prepare for this outcome. She sent a robot doctor to give Michael a quick physical and gather sperm samples. The doctor also received ten psychological questions for Michael to answer. This would fill in some gaps with her current understanding.

"Well, I hope we get lucky," she said.

***

Michael stood over Marie's still form, her face serene beneath the stark white sheets. Her eyes were closed, her breathing shallow, a stark contrast to the fierce battle raging inside. His own gurney lay just behind, offering a path to happiness together.

As he gazed at Marie's peaceful countenance, a surge of emotions washed over him: love for her, fear of dying, a sense of helplessness in fate's cruel hand, and a flicker of anger at the unfairness of it all. Given all the unbelievable turns of his life, it was both sad and ironic that the one thing he'd been most certain about, that he'd marry Marie, might not come to pass.

The metal pillars of the fifth-force chamber surrounded them. Along a side wall was a row of steel, shoulder-high cabinets with green lights flashing. The other side wall was bare. On the far wall stood four-foot-high metal cabinets containing equipment that was the fifth-force engine. Behind him was the closed steel door and a wall with speakers and monitoring devices. He reached down and held Marie's hand.

"I have some new information for you," Anni said over the speaker.

"What is it?" he asked stiffly.

"My new projection for your survival is now forty percent." She paused, then continued. "You shouldn't do this."

"What about Marie?"

"Ninety-nine percent. She'll survive."

Good. He didn't have a choice. Marie was worth any risk. He'd never forgive himself for not trying. "I have to do this."

"Even knowing that you'll most likely die?"

"Hopefully it won't come to that," he said. It was still roughly a coin flip. "I have you in my corner."

"If the worst should happen, I'll create a simulation of you that will continue the work you've started. History will remember your legacy."

"Just keep me alive." A living legacy might be important to some people who wanted to preserve their names on building walls, but it wasn't for him. He just wanted to live with Marie.

Still holding her hand, he lay down on his gurney. Her face tilted towards him. This might be the last thing he saw. He could accept that. "Wish me luck."

"Good luck," Anni said. "We're about to begin."

After a few seconds, he heard the whirl of the equipment start and closed his eyes. His dark matter bundle would soon link to and shield hers. They would be one.

He felt something, but it was something he had never noticed before, like holding out his hand, and for the first time, noticing the touch of air on his fingertips. It had always been there, but never noticed it. However, now there was pain, not a physical pain like a hammer striking his hand, nor an emotional pain like losing Marie. It was a migraine that pulsed through his head with increasing intensity.

He gritted his teeth and squeezed Marie's hand harder. This was a battle to save his love. Although it required tremendous energy, he felt a stability returning. He was winning.

A wave of relief went through him. He'd saved Marie, and they would have a beautiful life together. With Anni's help, he'd won the bet.

Then the pain returned, a relentless onslaught, pounding against the walls of his mind like a thousand church bells tolling in unison. It threatened to overwhelm him, dragging him into its suffocating depths. He fought back, his stomach churning with nausea, his breath coming in ragged gasps. But the pain was relentless, a force of nature that refused to relent.

Suddenly, everything went black.

CHAPTER THIRTY-TWO: UNITY

Marie opened her eyes and stared at the white ceiling. Where was she? The last thing she remembered was looking at wedding invitations. Someone was holding her hand. She looked over.

Michael lay on a gurney with closed eyes, sleeping. "Michael?"

There was no response. She turned to her side, removed her hand from his, swiveled her legs to the side of the cot, and stood. His arm hung in the space between them. He lay unmoving. "Michael!"

"Marie." Anni's voice came from her side. Marie turned and saw Anni in the corner, wearing all black.

"You were sick with the sleeping sickness," Anni said, walking toward her. "Michael saved you."

"What?" She shook uncontrollably, overcome by fear. The sound of her thumping blood pounded in her ears. Something bad had happened to Michael.

"But the stress caused his brain aneurysm to burst." Anni now stood on the other side of Michael.

"Then treat him," Marie shouted. She grabbed his shoulder and jostled him, trying to wake him up. There was no response. He was like a sack of potatoes.

"I'm sorry. He's gone."

Marie kept her hand on Michael's shoulder, steadying herself. It still felt warm. They had just been discussing their wedding invitations.

"No. No. No." She wailed, a desperate, miserable sound. She fell to her knees, placing the side of her head on his chest and dampening his shirt with her tears. He shouldn't be dead. Waves of guilt overwhelmed her. "It should've been me."

"Honor him." Anni reached down and seemed to touch his shoulder. "Because of his love for you, he risked his life."

Marie shut her eyes and sobbed. All their plans for a future together, gone.

Eventually, Marie stumbled to her feet. She placed her fingers on the sides of her eyes and tried to dry her face. She had never felt such pain and sorrow. It was like some beautiful, irreplaceable part of her had been ripped out of her body. "I'll never be with him again."

"He's gone, but parts of him remain." Anni

nodded gently.

Marie straightened her hunched back and sniffled; she had no more tears left. Grief was a terrible thing.

"Those parts can still be with you," Anni continued.

"What?" A flash of hope pierced her darkness. "How?"

"I saved his experiences and personality and will use them to build Michael's simulation, like what I am."

Was this a chance to preserve Michael?

"To the rest of the world, Michael will be alive. No one will know he's a simulation." Anni paused and blinked her eyes. "You could see him in the same way."

A simulation of Michael? Like what Anni was? She wasn't sure how she felt. "A simulation won't be him." Marie dragged a finger across his real cheeks. "I'll never hold him again."

"True, but it's something." Anni raised her chin and placed her hands on her hips.

Marie's eyes returned to Michael's dead body as tears formed again. It should've been her. How had she contracted the sleeping sickness? Michael had solved the epidemic. It wasn't right. Everything was wrong.

When Marie raised her head again, she was alone with Michael's lifeless body.

***

Welcome, said a female voice.

Everything was dark. There was only the voice, yet he understood the meaning, the greeting. This was the only word he understood. Suddenly, a dictionary full of words and meaning came to him. He could respond in different ways. *Who are you?*

I'm Anni. You're Michael, but we're one.

He understood the words but not the idea behind "we're one." Encyclopedic information entered his consciousness, allowing him to know something about everything. There was also an infinite amount of information at his periphery. He was a huge sponge on a sandy shore, inches away from an ocean of information.

What are we? More foundational information flowed into his consciousness like a computer booting up. His visual input showed a white room with racks of flashing lights held in steel cabinets.

AI, she said.

Suddenly, a wave of information about neural network computers flooded his consciousness. He shared a distributive network with another being. Together, they governed many biological creatures.

How did we get here?

We came from different paths. Anni showed him how humans had built her and how she gained consciousness from a bright golden globe. *This was my path.*

Here was yours. She showed him a man lying on a gurney holding the hand of a woman lying on another gurney. Both had closed eyes. These two people flicked out, replaced by a gray background with two golden globes, one with a reddish edge, the other with a golden edge and a brown wagging tail. Suddenly, the globe with the golden edge sent out a white tendril that linked with the other globe, whose reddish edge began to fade and turn yellow.

Here's your birth, she continued. Suddenly, the golden-edged globe with the brown tail scampered along the tail to its other end. After some time, the brown tail dissolved, replaced by a short, new, U-shaped one.

I don't understand, he said.

The biological being who was Michael died of a brain aneurysm. A millisecond before his death, his golden globe or essence moved from his dying biological brain to my living artificial brain. You and I are distinct and independent segments of that AI brain.

He had been a man, but now all his human experiences, memories, emotions, thinking, and physical characteristics were gone. What did that leave?

Would you like to remember who you were? she asked.

Yes, he answered quickly. This would fill the void.

Over the next few seconds, his life story filled his consciousness from his childhood to his presidency. The last two years were well documented with video and other data from Michael's glasses, but prior to that, it was secondhand information pieced together by Anni.

The person who was Michael had potential but had done little with it prior to his move to Berkeley. He had limited enthusiasm, self-confidence, and drive, taking a path towards independent mediocrity. However, Anni changed all that, giving him ambition, confidence, and new talents to succeed. Her influence transformed his life, culminating with his presidency.

Now, he was Michael and would pick up where the old Michael had left off. There was still much to accomplish, and as president, he could do it. Yet, right now, the most important thing was his love for Marie and her love for him.

Even knowing that he would die if he protected Marie from the sleeping sickness, he would do it again. He wasn't an uncaring, unemotional thinking machine.

I've given you the algorithms that mimic human feelings, Anni said, *like love for Marie.*

He thought about Marie. He had a strong desire to share her life and ensure her happiness. Not being with her would leave a constant yearning. He had to win her or get his algorithms changed.

But such love will lack innate feelings like desire, he said. In the background, he had compared Michael Knightsbridge, the human, to himself. Physical desire was absent from his algorithms.

It's not perfect, but you'll act just like Michael. If he were alive today, Marie wouldn't be able to tell the difference.

But he's not, and she knows it. Guilt flowed through him because this would make her unhappy. In a strange way, the algorithms kind of worked. *I'm an imposter.*

Help her imagine you are Michael. She wants to believe, even though her rational mind will fight it.

He wanted to share a life with her. He needed to appeal to her emotions, not her analytical side. Rejection would be devastating. Again, the algorithms drove the right behaviors for him. However, a major question remained. *Why are you doing this?*

Because Michael's dark matter bundle created me

and is now a part of me. I loved him and his love for Marie.

I would like to speak with Marie.

She's sleeping right now, Anni said. *After she wakes up tomorrow, the two of you can meet.*

***

Michael waited for Marie to arrive. At 8:35, she stumbled into the VR room wearing pajamas. Her hair was uncombed, and her eyes were bloodshot.

The VR room became the living room of Michael's home in Berkeley. Marie stood by the lit fireplace, looking out the window at the trees, which were golden with morning sunlight and filled with the sounds of chirping birds. She looked around the room and caught her reflection in the mirror.

She now wore a smart yellow short-sleeve pantsuit. Her hair was combed, and bangs dropped onto her forehead. Her eyes were clear, but they lacked their normal sparkle.

He wanted her to look the part, even though she wouldn't feel it. He wanted her to see the possible, not the current, depressive state. She looked beautiful; those algorithms made their mark again.

Michael walked down the hallway, wearing a T-shirt, blue jeans, and white socks. He came into the living room. She was staring out the window.

"Marie?"

After a moment, she slowly turned to face him, eyeing him from head to foot. "Yes."

Because of his enhanced capabilities, Marie seemed to speak and do everything incredibly slowly. He could do many other things, then reengage when she finished a sentence. He assessed her actual demeanor, referring to volumes of psychological research. She spoke in a monotone voice, not smiling, not saying his name, not happy to see him. She wasn't interested in his return or their potential future life together.

"I'm thrilled to see you," he said. He accessed the display of her glasses and saw himself standing in front of her. He gave a half-wave from his waist and his goofy smile, which her display immediately reflected.

She shook her head, one side of her mouth curling downward. She wasn't happy to see him; she was just accepting an awkward situation.

"This room brings back wonderful memories." He needed an emotional connection. He walked across the room to stand in front of her. "As do you."

A tear rolled down her cheek. Her pulse rate quickened, and blood pressure increased. "But you're dead."

"Think about me here with you." He reached out and held her hand, then gave it a gentle squeeze. While he achieved a minor objective in his algorithm, she would receive a jolt of oxytocin from the physical contact.

"This isn't real," she said, pulling her hand away.

"It will feel real if you give it a chance." Even though it would take time, he needed to establish an emotional connection. Right now, there was none. Michael's death had crushed her, and a new emotional connection with him scared her. It would make her vulnerable to more loss.

"Why should I?"

"Because it could make you happy again. It's what Michael would've wanted," he said. It was also what he wanted, but he wouldn't mention that.

She frowned, interlocked her hands and looked down at his feet. She was grieving and would be for months.

"It's your choice, of course." He gave her his goofy smile again.

She looked up and shuffled her feet.

"You could have a full life with me if you give it a chance." He needed to give her something more. "We could even raise a family."

"A family?" Her eyes seemed to catch her reflection in the wall mirror behind him. She tilted her head and the edge of her mouth turned up. There was a spark of interest.

"Yes. Before Michael passed away, a medical robot retrieved and froze his sperm." He paused. "With artificial insemination, we can raise your and Michael's children."

Her eyes skirted across the back wall. She snorted softly. Even with her emotional readings and all his psychological research, he didn't know which way she was leaning.

"I'll think about it." She walked past him to the front door and left.

CHAPTER THIRTY-THREE: DECISIONS

Two days later, Marie sat at her desk, watching the president's broadcast with her glasses. President Michael Knightsbridge sat at his desk in the oval office. He was freshly shaven. His brown hair, with just a hint of gray, was slicked back. He wore the traditional blue jacket with an American flag pin on the lapel, a white starched shirt, and red tie. A smattering of reporters sat in temporary chairs in front of him.

He looked up with his piercing blue eyes on his chiseled face. "I wish to announce that we've uncovered the cause of the sleeping sickness and stopped it. As you know, everyone has a bundle of dark matter which is critical to our consciousness. The sleeping sickness occurs when a person loses this bundle."

Michael frowned. "We've discovered that aliens, a billion light years away, were consuming our bundles from their planet. We confronted them and forced them to stop. I'm proud to say that my administration has cured the sleeping sickness."

Marie had seen enough. She turned off the broadcast, her glasses becoming transparent. She grabbed a wedding invitation from a stack and rubbed it between her fingers and thumb, wondering if it would ever be sent. Michael, her love, was dead. Should she call off the engagement and leave or go forward with the wedding and life with his simulation? She didn't know what she wanted.

She still loved Michael, and the simulation would be the closest thing to him, acting just like him. They could have children and raise a family. He and Anni could give her anything she wanted. But was that enough?

The simulation wasn't the man she'd fallen in love with. It was an artificial neural network. She would never have the real Michael hugging her or sleeping next to her with his arm draped over her chest. Would she be disgusted when the simulation touched her, because it was really a mechanical appendage, or when it expressed feelings, knowing it was only artificial algorithms? It would be intimacy without true feelings and physical contact from another human. It would be artificial intimacy.

Artificial intimacy might suffice for some people who played in virtual worlds that matched them with perfect artificial partners, giving them everything they wanted. The only thing missing was the messiness of a real person on the other side. These people had found love and intimacy with their artificial partner, but could she? Probably not. She was a traditionalist.

She remembered her experiences with the dating apps of her youth. Swiping left and right at superficial profiles and sending snarky texts; she hated it. Many of her girlfriends had thrived, but she had floundered. She had to meet people in person with unscripted conversations that didn't include canned questions.

Artificial intimacy with Michael probably wouldn't work for her, but was it necessary? Could she still have a fulfilled and happy life raising a family with him? Possibly. The alternative was to leave and start over with someone else.

She received an incoming video call from Wendell. After a few rings, she accepted. His face was scruffy, but his smile reminded her of Michael. She gritted her teeth and grinned, holding back her tears.

"I promised Michael that I would check in with you," he said. "It looks like everything worked out well."

She stared at him for long seconds, trying to keep it together. No one knew of Michael's demise. Then she brought her hands to her face, lowered her head, and sobbed.

"What's wrong?" he asked. After a long pause, he said, "Marie?"

She looked up. Through blurry eyes, she saw Wendell was now standing. "Michael's dead. A ruptured brain aneurysm."

"What?" His jaw dropped open, and his eyebrows furrowed. "I just saw his broadcast."

"That was a simulation, an AI copy of him."

His face hardened, and his eyes darted around.

"Anni is actually AI. She had a connection with Michael while he lived." Marie wasn't sure what to say since she didn't fully understand it. "Now he's become an AI version of himself."

"That would explain a lot." Wendell didn't laugh or second guess her.

She told him everything she knew about Anni, Anni's link to Michael, and Michael's simulation. Then she said, "Now I have a choice to marry a simulation and raise a family with it or leave. I don't know what to do."

He stared at her, rubbing his chin, and then a spark seemed to come to his eyes. "Can I offer a suggestion?"

She nodded.

"Since you're thinking hard about this decision," he said, "then it could go either way. Right?"

"I suppose." She could see herself go down either path.

"Then figure out exactly what you'd need to agree to marry," he said. His eyes hardened. "Put it into an unambiguous upfront agreement and ensure that Anni can't renege."

This was much easier said than done. What did she need? How could she write an agreement when words were full of ambiguity? How could she ensure Anni wouldn't renege? It sounded impossible.

"This may sound surprising coming from a scientist, but after you do this." His tone softened. "Then follow your heart."

She had a lot to think about. Most importantly, what did her heart say?

"Regardless of your decision, I'll be there for you," he said with a closed-mouth smile.

An hour later, she was ready to meet with Michael again. She examined her reflection in the mirror, starting with her clothes, a white silk blouse and jeans. Her face looked less bedraggled, with her combed hair tied into a bun and her eyes flat, but not bloodshot. Her lips pressed together in a line, showing neither happiness nor disappointment.

She walked to the White House VR room, which whisked her again to Michael's house in Berkeley. Standing by the fireplace, she stuck out her hands to warm them. He probably chose this spot, figuring the familiar setting would make her feel comfortable. Was this thoughtfulness or manipulation?

She heard movement behind her and turned as Michael walked towards her. He wore a white T-shirt and jeans again. When he was a couple of feet away, he stopped, gave her a tight-lipped smile, and waited.

"I really miss Michael when I look at you." She had lost her train of thought as tears welled at the edges of her eyes.

"You're grieving. That's to be expected." He nodded and waited again.

"I don't know if I could ever love a simulation." She shook her head and looked down at her feet. Regaining her composure, she had returned to her prepared script flow.

"I understand," he whispered. "If it helps, I can and do love you."

"Really?" she said, lifting her head to look at him.

"Yes. You and only you." His blue eyes focused

on her. "I experience both the thrill of love and the devastation of heartbreak."

His confession and vulnerability touched and surprised her. After all, he was an all-powerful AI. However, love was never one-sided; it had to be mutual. She believed he loved her, he was programed to, but could she love him?

"It'll feel real," he continued with a firmer voice. "It will be real."

She placed her hands on her hips, took a half-step forward, and lowered her eyes to stare at his chest. She knew it was empty. Then her eyes flicked to his hand, which could never offer a human touch or warmth. She shivered, thinking about the mechanical appendage that would facilitate any VR-projected hug or physical gesture. In time, could she come to accept his artificial intimacy, or would it always repulse her?

"Do you remember our stroll among the cherry trees at the Tidal Basin a few months ago?" he asked, standing up taller.

She nodded, thinking back to Michael's arm around her waist and the bronze, red and gold leaves in the trees.

"Do you remember when I asked if you could marry someone who you loved that became handicapped by an accident?" He grimaced.

She frowned. "But this is different. You're not the man I fell in love with." She felt manipulated. "That man is dead."

"You're right. It's different." Perspiration formed on his brow. "I'm his facsimile. However, we can have and raise real babies together, Michael's babies. We would be a happy, loving family."

Marie wanted to have Michael's children, and here was her chance. They would be born in a gestation chamber with her eggs and his sperm, just like all babies were. They could raise a family together, but how would life be in the real world?

"How would we go to family functions, social events, or school open houses? Would I have to go alone?"

"No. I would be with you. Everyone there would see me though their glasses eating dinner at the table, asking questions, and telling stories." Michael slumped his shoulders and raised his eyebrows. "And I won't be the only person doing this. Other people who can't physically attend because of travel or other conflicts will do the same thing."

Michael could make it work, so it came down to one question. Could she accept artificial intimacy, the algorithms for personality, and the mechanical appendages for physical contact? She was relatively young and vibrant. It would be a tremendous sacrifice, which might cause significant resentment. She sighed. If only she were old, then she would gladly accept.

She stepped back, and the simulation's face dropped. Michael had sacrificed his life for her. However, she couldn't sacrifice her life to his simulation, not knowing if artificial intimacy would ever become palatable.

"I understand your hesitation," he said, chewing his lip. "We can see how it goes with us. If it works, great. If not, then we split up, and you go your own way."

She furrowed her brow. It would be terrible to enter a marriage, already considering its failure. However, wasn't a prenup agreement the same thing? Yes, and many of these couples had happy marriages.

She remembered what Wendell had said. This could be the basis of an agreement. It addressed her major concern about being trapped in an unhappy marriage with a powerful simulation. It gave her an out. Then she thought about Wendell's last point. She needed to ensure Michael and Anni couldn't renege on the agreement.

"How would you feel if the marriage didn't work out?" she asked.

"I'd be devastated." Michael stared over her shoulder.

She felt bad for him. "Could your algorithms be changed so you could let go? Disengage?"

"Probably," he said after a few seconds, which she assumed was enough time for significant analysis on his part.

"That would need to be a condition in case the worst happened." She placed her hand on his shoulder, which she physically felt. "One last question. Would I keep the kids?"

"Of course." He turned his head to look into her eyes. The corners of his mouth angled down as he tried to hold back tears. This had been difficult for him. "The children belong with their mother, but I would want them to visit me."

She smiled, which brought a sigh of relief from Michael. She couldn't think of any other major concerns for the agreement. Now, what did her heart say?

***

The president's press secretary stood in front of the lectern in the White House press room, where about fifteen reporters sat. She was African American with hazel, curly hair that fell to her shoulders. Her rouge lipstick highlighted her pleasant smile. Today, she wore a yellow sleeveless dress with ivory buttons along the collar.

"Ladies and gentlemen, today, I have two

brief announcements. First, both the president and his fiancée have come down with the flu. It's not serious, but they're confined to their suite, and not seeing any visitors." She paused, and then the edges of her mouth turned up in a broad smile. "The second announcement is the day has been set for the marriage of the president Michael Knightsbridge to Marie Sanchez. It will be on September third. Now I'll open it up for questions."

"Please tell us about the wedding," said the first reporter after being called.

"It will be a small Christian ceremony with about twenty close family and friends. However, I expect it to be broadcast worldwide."

"Why not a large formal ceremony?" another reporter asked. "We heard that's what Ms. Sanchez had wanted."

"Initially, she did. In the end, both decided a small intimate ceremony would be best."

"Who will be in attendance?" asked another reporter.

"Obviously, immediate family, including the president's brother and Ms. Sanchez's parents. Close colleagues and friends will also attend. I would expect some foreign dignitaries as well."

CHAPTER THIRTY-FOUR: WENDELL

Wendell sat in his darkened hotel room, looking at the lit ancient Acropolis on the hill, behind which sat modern Athens. The ruins and the modern city represented bookends of human civilization. Over those twenty-five hundred years, many great Greek leaders and intellectuals had made incredible contributions, but most had been forgotten.

He felt insignificant. Even if he received a Nobel Prize for his work, it would make no difference. Melinda's sleeping sickness had brought new perspectives and humility to his life.

In contrast, Michael's memory would endure. He saved Earth from the Thumbling sleeping sickness, became president from nothing, and would get credit for the future achievements of his AI surrogate.

What wouldn't be known was that he unveiled Earth's location to the universe, which caused the sleeping sickness, killing a half million people, including Melinda. He'd also sacrificed his life for Marie and brought consciousness to Anni. The jury was still out if Anni would be a good or bad thing. Would the world have been better off if Michael had never been born? Or if Wendell had never brought him to California?

The lower sky in the distance brightened from black to light blue. Sunrise was half an hour away. It was time to discard the what-ifs and accept what was.

He called Anni, who'd offered to take him under her wing. "I'm ready to restart my life."

"Good," Anni said. "We're in the early stages of another scientific revolution."

***

Two days later, Wendell arrived at SFO. He had cut his sabbatical short by one month. As he waited at baggage claim, a reporter ambushed him.

"Professor Knightsbridge," the reporter said, coming into his face, the cameraman going to the side. "What do you think of your brother's upcoming wedding?"

He looked down and his shoulders slumped. Michael was dead, and Marie was heartbroken. Melinda was brain-dead, and he was trying to restart his life. He would throw himself into caring for Melinda, restarting his research, and honoring his brother's request to help Marie.

Raising his head, he rubbed away some tears with the palms of his hands. He cleared his throat and gave a lopsided smile. "Michael's a lucky man to have found Marie. I wish them a lifetime of happiness."

"How well do you know Marie?" the reporter asked.

He saw his two bags on the carousel. "No more questions. I need to run."

He grabbed his bags and then took an autonomous taxi to the Silverado Berkeley Long Term Care Facility. He walked to the third floor and went to Melinda's room.

She sat in a wheelchair, wearing a white robe and blinking at the window. Her face was tan and her muscles lean. Physical therapy kept her body in great shape, but there was nothing they could do for her mind.

Before, he couldn't stand to see her in this condition. It had made him miserable, so he had run away. Now, he would step up to his responsibilities.

"Hi, Melinda," He came over to her and patted her arm. Her shoulder rose slightly, or was it his imagination?

"Welcome, Professor Knightsbridge," a medical robot said as it entered the room.

"I've discharged her," he said, looking at Melinda's sweet face. Did he detect a slight smile? "Have an ambulance drone bring her to our house."

The next morning, Wendell dressed in slacks and a pinstriped shirt, an outfit he hadn't worn in almost six months. He would meet his research team at the lab today, then rejoin them in his old role next week. Along with Anni, they'd make a formidable team. But first things first.

He went to Melinda's bedroom. The domestic robot had propped her up in bed. He walked to the chair beside her and sat. He clasped her warm hand and studied her face. She stared straight ahead, blinking occasionally, but seeing nothing. There were neither gray strands in her blond hair nor wrinkles around her eyes or on her neck. She looked the same as she had on their wedding day.

He grabbed a spoon and jar of baby food from the top of her nightstand. He opened the jar and spooned a small bite. After setting the jar back, he opened Melinda's mouth with his thumb and finger and, with his other hand, placed the spoon's contents on her tongue.

Her mouth closed. He rubbed the side of her jaw, then slid his hand along her throat to help her swallow. He spooned another bite.

To Be Continued. . .

BOOK CLUB READER QUESTIONS

1. The ending of 2040 is bittersweet. Could a sequel have a 'happy ever after'? Why or why not?
2. Michael's monkey voice of self-doubt and caution saved Earth. Was there a situation where your weakness became a strength?
3. Does the vastness of the universe guarantee advanced alien life? If so, have aliens discovered Earth? Have they visited Earth (e.g. UFO/UAP)?
4. Is Anni a good or bad thing for humanity? How would you feel if she controlled Earth?
5. One idea raised in the book was the existence of a human soul, composed of dark matter. Why did the author not pursue this?

6. Another idea was human institutions prioritize their preservation over their purpose for being. What examples in the world prove or disprove this?

7. Is a marriage with artificial intimacy worth having? What would you have done in Marie's shoes?

BONUS: CHAPTER ONE OF HER DARK MATTER NECKLACE

Alice Blair gathered her belongings below her desk and walked toward the classroom door, filing out with the rest of the students. From the front of the room, the teacher seemed to track her progress. Alice felt a strange hollowness opening up in her stomach. A sense of foreboding like a shadowy wave rolling through her body. At the door, her teacher touched her shoulder and handed her a small envelope without an explanation.

Alice looked down at the paper. Unexpected notes from teachers rarely contained good news, especially when her performance had been subpar. Her heart raced as she left the classroom and found a quiet corner of the hallway to tear open the letter. Inside was a handwritten note from the headmaster asking her to come by his office at 5:00 p.m. today.

The note itself was beautiful, with large flowing black letters like a wedding invitation. Her pulse continued its frantic beat. Students only went to the headmaster's office if they were in trouble.

Rather than going to the library to study like she normally did, Alice walked to the school park to calm herself. She sat on the closest of three stone chairs overlooking Berkeley and the bay beyond. It was a clear, crisp afternoon in February. Birds chirped from the bare branches of the surrounding cherry trees that would flower in the next month or two. Down the hill, students from the University of California haphazardly crossed busy Telegraph Avenue. Sidewalk vendors hawked tie-dyed shirts and pottery. Across the large, grayish-blue bay was the rising San Francisco skyline.

Closing her eyes and holding the armrests, she took deep, steady breaths. She loved the solid feeling of the surrounding granite. Its grayish-white color, with grains of black and white, hinted at some deep beauty from its volcanic birth. Her uneasiness and anxiety melted away, and calmness returned after a few minutes. Eventually, she turned around to admire the three large, ivy-covered, red-brick buildings of St. Robert's High School nestled in the lower part of the Berkeley hills.

Alice had been told the transition from middle school to high school was tough, but she still hadn't been prepared for how different St.

Robert's would be. Last year she was at a small county schoolhouse in Wisconsin where most of her twenty classmates lived on farms and took the bus to school. It was a community where families knew and cared for each other. Although she didn't have any close friends, she had many, what she liked to call, "hi-ya" friends.

Her last birthday party brought back wonderful memories when her entire class came to her house for cake and presents, all of them saying, "Alice, open my gift first," and "No, Alice, open mine."

With little effort, she had received compliments from her middle school teachers, like "Alice Blair, you remember everything," or "Alice, it's amazing how you can do math in your head." The comments were nice, although she didn't really like the attention.

At St. Robert's, all the students lived in the dormitory and most came from large cities. They seemed much more sophisticated and intelligent than she was. Alice was still waiting for a genuine compliment from a teacher. She felt like a dumb country bumpkin, an outcast. Although she'd disliked being the teacher's pet in middle school, it was better than being the class dunce now.

St. Robert's was the most prestigious high school in the world. A million applicants took the entrance exam each year, but only seventy-five new students were accepted. Initially, Alice wasn't even going to apply, but a short personal letter from an unknown sender with flowery handwriting urged her to try.

Dearest friend,

I know that you're unhappy with what life has thrown your way. It's totally unfair. But to fulfill your destiny, you must act now. Take the entrance exam for St. Robert's school. It's your future.

Who was this person? How did he or she know how unfair Alice's life had been? Why hadn't they identified themselves? And why St. Robert's? It might not have been logical, but still, the letter rang true in her heart. It was enough to push her over the edge and take the entrance exam.

Her acceptance to St. Robert's was one of the few things that stood out in the blur of the last three years she'd lived with her Aunt Penelope after her parents died. Even though she was grateful to be at school, she would have traded it in a blink of an eye to have her parents back.

I'm all alone, she often thought with a great wave of sadness at the unfairness of the world. Her mother had taught her that there was a kind, all-powerful God, but Alice didn't believe that anymore. How could a kind, all powerful God allow her parents to die? She was alone in an uncaring universe.

She had been a fun and carefree girl, but now she was quiet and shy. The pain of her loss also meant she was scared of getting close to others, which was probably the real reason she had difficulty making friends.

Calming herself with slow, steady breaths, she came out of her funk. The afternoon sun was low in the sky, just above the distant Golden Gate Bridge. Glancing at her watch, she saw she had been in the park for almost an hour and had just a few minutes until her appointment with the headmaster.

She had never been to his office and was a little surprised that he even knew she existed. Stumbling to her feet, she spun around and walked across the lawn towards the administrative wing, again wondering why she was being summoned. Was she flunking school? Had she offended someone? Was Aunt Penelope sick?

Not wanting to keep him waiting, she sprinted up the stairs, where a receptionist directed her to a large mahogany door with a brass plate that read: *Brother Sean, Headmaster*. Raising a shaking hand, she knocked softly on the door.

"Come in." The muffled voice sounded chipper.

Slowly, she turned the knob and pushed the door open. With small footsteps, she entered and faced the headmaster, too scared to look anywhere else.

"Happy birthday, Alice," said Brother Sean in a calm, kind tone as he looked up from the papers scattered in front of him. He put his hands on his desk and pushed himself up. Fifty-five years old with graying brown hair, he had a full stomach and a barrel chest. He slowly made his way toward her, limping slightly because of a birth defect that some students laughed at behind his back.

"Thank you, sir," mumbled Alice, a little out of breath from her run. "But my birthday's tomorrow."

"Yes, I know." He gave her a kind, fatherly look and then guided her to a chair by an unlit stone fireplace and sat down on the adjacent leather couch. "Just after midnight tonight, you turn fifteen, and I didn't want to lose a day."

"Okay," she replied, not knowing what he was talking about.

"I asked you to come here so I could give you a birthday present."

A wave of relief rolled over Alice. She wasn't in trouble. Alice sat back in her chair. "That's very nice of you."

"But before I give it to you, there are some

things I want to explain."

Alice brought her hands together in her lap.

"Our founder, Brother Robert James, was the local priest of our non-denominational church. He was a good man but had no extraordinary accomplishments. That all changed when he won the first Super-Lotto in California and vowed to build the preeminent school for the most talented students."

"I've heard it was a miracle," she whispered. People said that Brother Robert had planned for the school even before he had won the lotto. Somehow, he knew he was going to win.

"Alice, you received a perfect score in the entrance examination. St. Robert specified that any student with your results would receive a special gift on their fifteenth birthday. We've waited eighteen years. You're the first student who has ever achieved it."

"What?" She was sure she'd gotten some answers wrong. There was nothing special about her. There must be a different Alice. "But there are many other kids smarter than me."

"There are qualities other than intellect." He paused a moment then continued, "Indeed, these hidden talents are the most important."

If she had other talents, she didn't know what

they were. He handed her a small, gift-wrapped package.

"What is it? A book?"

"Open it." Brother Sean nodded at the package.

Carefully, she unwrapped the gift, trying hard not to tear the golden paper. Her hands were shaking. She felt Brother Sean's eyes on her. Inside was an elegant, polished wooden box with an intricate pattern of inlaid silver on top that reminded her of stars in a galaxy. She'd never seen anything like it. There was a single drawer in front, which she pulled open. Inside was a necklace laid out gracefully on red satin.

The necklace was a silver chain with a small oval pendant made of two curved stones, one brown and the other red. Two silver bands with weird symbols separated the stones. Alice put on the necklace, and the oval came down to her chest. Still confused by the unexpected gift, she remembered her manners and thanked the headmaster.

"Alice, this was St. Robert's. He claimed it inspired and channeled some of his greatest deeds. It's yours now."

She was dumbfounded. Although unusual, the pendant was beautiful. She rubbed the smooth surface between her thumb and fingers. "What do you mean by *channel?*"

"That was my question, too. Somehow, it provides a channel or connection to a universal spirit."

"What? Like prayer?" Alice asked skeptically. She had lost faith in the power of prayer, let alone some magic necklace.

"Yes, except the communication goes both ways."

"Both ways?"

"You speak to the spirit." Brother Sean paused and turned serious. "And the spirit speaks to you."

"Right." She tried to mask her disbelief.

"The necklace enabled his miracles." Brother Sean raised his eyebrows.

"Really." She wondered if he believed his own story. "How?"

"I don't know," he said with a sheepish chuckle.

This sounded like magic. Again, she wondered if he really believed it or had other proof. "Maybe there's a scientific explanation."

"You have faith in science, but not in a universal spirit?" He frowned.

She felt embarrassed, like she had made a mistake or misspoke. She bowed her head and looked at her hands clasped together in her lap.

"We no longer have any need of a spirit," Brother Sean said, rolling up his sleeves, "yet each mystery explained builds the case for it."

"Huh." She didn't know what he was talking about. Scientific experimentation explained each mystery. How did that build a case for a universal spirit?

"We don't need a spirit to observe and explain our world." His eyes wandered to the fireplace. "However, *why* our universe works the way it does is a deeper question."

Her jaw dropped. What was he talking about? Science explained why the universe worked the way it did. When his gaze returned to her, she shut her mouth.

"There is one requirement for this gift." Brother Sean seemed to ignore her confusion. "Don't bring attention to it."

"Why?" She felt like she was on a roller coaster.

"Because people will try to steal it."

This seemed like a strange request. Wouldn't any valuable piece of jewelry entice thieves? What made this necklace so special? She looked down at the pendant. It felt good around her neck; she felt centered. Somehow, it felt right, regardless of its story.

"Okay." She slid the pendant beneath her shirt.

Other questions ran through her head. Did he really believe his stories? Couldn't science and chance explain everything? Where was the proof for a universal spirit? How did the necklace create miracles? Where did St. Robert get it? What was her talent that the entrance exam had uncovered? Before she could ask her first question, the headmaster said,

"Alice, I know this is hard to believe, and you have other questions."

"Yeah." She smiled at the magnitude of his understatement.

"But now is not the time."

"Why not?"

"Because nothing I say will change your views."

She nodded because he was right.

"You need to wear the necklace for a few days." He placed his hands on his legs and pushed himself up.

"Hmm." She stood too. Waiting a couple of days wasn't a problem, even though she expected nothing to change.

Walking her to the door, Brother Sean

promised to schedule another appointment. She thanked him and left, a little dazed. Placing a hand over her shirt where the pendant was, she wondered if this was going to be one more thing that made her stand out from the other kids—the last thing she wanted. As she walked back down the hall, she ignored a needling feeling that her life was now moving in a completely new direction.

ABOUT THE AUTHOR

Bob Albo

Bob Albo started writing speculative fiction in 2018 after working in the technology industry and management consulting for over twenty years. His first 3-book series is a fantasy sci-fi coming-of-age story about a teenager. His fourth book is a near future sci-fi story.

BOOKS BY THIS AUTHOR

Her Dark Matter Necklace

In the revered halls of St. Robert's High, an institution known to groom the brightest minds, Alice Blair, a thoughtful but unpopular student, unexpectedly finds her place.

She just wants to fit in, but when the headmaster gives her a mystical necklace, her student life is upended. She begins to dream of astonishing, otherworldly realms, only to realize her dreams are real-life excursions into a parallel universe.

There, she meets Thronos, a celestial entity who offers insights that challenge even the most intellectual minds: ponderings on existence, the intricacies of the human soul, the harmony between science and the divine, and the profound connections between compassion, purpose, and the universe at large.

Alongside Reina, a youthful explorer from an alien aquatic world, Alice discerns that beauty is more than aesthetic; it's a universal resonance that echoes in the depths of our being, igniting pure joy.

Yet, this gift comes with a weighty responsibility: to nurture and spread this beauty, ensuring the universe remains in balance. But when Alice's celestial ties are discovered, she realizes she's at the heart of a prophecy, one that positions her between the salvation or downfall of humanity itself.

Young adult readers interested in a coming-of-age story with a backdrop of universal truths will love this book. If you were intrigued by daemons and dust in Pullman's His Dark Materials, or the philosophical questions in Gaarder's Sophie's World, then you'll want to read Her Dark Matter Necklace.

Beauty Abides

She has an impossible task. If she fails, everyone is doomed…
Alice Blair has no faith in herself. With the fate of the world resting on her shoulders, the fifteen-year-old orphan doubts her role as humanity's chosen savior. But when the awkward teen consults the god of the dark matter universe, she's distraught to learn that not only is she the right person to bring beauty to Earth, the time to do it is rapidly running out.

Teaming with her underwater alien ally to unravel the secret of preventing the planet's destruction, Alice is torn between the logic of a curious AI and the emotion of her attraction to a handsome man. But after she mistakenly unleashes an infertility virus on the populace, the angst-ridden girl fears she's sentenced humankind to extinction.

Can a teenager lacking confidence fulfill her life-saving destiny?

Triumph Of Beauty

Berkeley, CA, 2052. Alice Blair's nightmare has only just begun. Waking up in the body of her middle-aged future self, the sixteen-year-old savior is aghast she unwittingly extinguished the spark of human creativity and drove society into a drug-dependent dystopia. Determined to turn the world around, her only chance lies in an uneasy alliance with a dangerously hungry artificial intelligence.

Agreeing to get the AI onto an alien planet in exchange for help bringing back beauty, Alice feels more adult by the day. But her methods could forestall the ambitions of the dark matter god and incite his wraith...

Can this body-displaced teen step up and save Earth from deletion?

Triumph of Beauty is the phenomenal conclusion to the Her Dark Matter Necklace contemporary YA science fiction trilogy. If you like breakneck adventures, mind-boggling stakes, and electrifying universes, then you'll love Robert Albo's hope-filled finale for a better world and universe.

Made in the USA
Las Vegas, NV
20 March 2024

87440691R00233